Business As Usual

a novel

by

Wendell Shannon

Go Daddy Productions, Inc.

Baltimore * Maryland
Printed in U.S.A.

Business As Usual: a novel / Wendell Shannon

ISBN 0-9753938-1-2

GDP, Inc. website address:
www.go-daddyproductions.com

Photos by Robbin Colson,
Exposing U Photography (MD)

Cover Designs by Tonya Blackstone of
Slammin Graphix

ACKNOWLEDGEMENTS

To my Dad: *Peace escaped us while you were here, but it is my sincere hope that you rest in it now.*
R.I.P. *Tarik "**Lil Todd**" Walker, Tyrone "**Ty**" Rogers, Tavon Jacobs, Antoine "**J.J.**" Lucky, Marcus "**Zay**" Alston, **Frank Nitty**, Kenny "**Tupac**" Morris, Michael "**Mike**" Smith, Homegirl Trina, Darryl "**Lil' Lucky**" Williams, Constance "**Connie**" Smith, Denise "**Cock-eyed Neicy**" Chase, Julia Brown, Boo Brown, Rhonda Spence & Doletha Bembow-Dillard, Tony Kessler, Melvin, Bell, & Amy Ford, Lucretia "**Crisha**", Dana & Eric Bryant, Crystal "**Mommy**" McKinney, **lil Bernard**, Michael Blount, Michael Waters, Bobby & Henry Prince, Elliot "**L.T.**" Scott, Gary Coleman, Kin King & Eric Carroll, "**Baldie**" & Marcus "**M.D.**" Felder, Reginald "**Reds**" Spencer, Angel Madison, Tonya Henry, Richard "**Ritchie Rich**" Gaines, **lil Bear**, Kennard & Jeffrey Alston, Anthony "**BirdsEye**" Gordon, Anthony "**Chinese Anthony**" Robinson, "**Boo-man**" Strickland, Terry "**Smokey**" Davis, Derrick "**Bo**" Anderson, Charles "**Boo Boo**" Anderson, Jr., Beldin Dillard, Ricky Lane, Alfred Blue, Anthony "**Hammer**" Vandiver, **Lil Edward (Poplar Grove Street)**, **Gut**, **Fat Tank**, **Alfie**, **Face**, Tracy Austin, Michael Street, Ricky Nelson, Michael Blount, Valentino "**Tino**", Keutrone "**Trony**" Barnes, Big Shane & lil' Shane Morrell, Anthony "**Antmoe**" Modica, Craig Crowder, Willie "**Pop**" Hubbard, Harry "**Fat Harry**" Johnson, Antoine "**Poopie**" Ellis, **W. S. Scott** and all others too many to name.*

To my Wife: the beautiful woman from Portland, Jamaica who has surrounded me with "my life is totally in your hands" and took my dreams to another level. You taught me that not only did I have a gift as a writer…I was also worth your two shoulders that I stand on. A season, a reason and a lifetime couldn't be more pertinent on both today and the day we met.

To my Mom: I know you miss your husband of 52 years. We all do, but you'll continue to find comfort in the family you produced. We love you, Margaret!

To my Sister: Carolyn, you invested in me when all I had were creative ideas. I know you didn't really understand it all then, but you simply wrote the checks. We're putting our "everything" in! Heav'n knows what's coming out!

To my Neice: Damara Knox: You put a lot of miles on your car and showed a lot of love for your uncle's dreams. I'm so proud to have you and Rosailyn not only by my side but also having my back, too! (smile)

To the Shannon grandchildren this time: Jermaine (Smurf), Labria, Jerbreal, Derrick, lil' Derrick, Derricka, Teardra, Donte, Futali (Tish), Ronisha, lil' Jimmy, Addriene, Kamila, Kayla, Shandora, Shantierra, Angelo, Deshon, Omari, Jabari, Capria, Barbriana, Staciana, Corey, Jordan, Shacorya, Shamera, Ray-Ray, Kiah, DeAndre, Danairae, Kiray, Syair, Cassandra, Quanequa, Desmond, Lazuwaun, Damara, Kweli, Dea'Montae, Taurean, Donte, Dannyelle, lil' Kevin, Tierra, Trayvon, Megan, Diamond, Dorian, Tremayne, lil' Tremayne aka lil' Dink, Jamaal, Ladana, Janae, DaNaeja, Tayla, Lakierra, Wendell, Shakeem, and Christopher. **Aunt Brenda...these are all of your children.**

To my big brother Raymond Walker—it's only a matter of time before Barbara and your Baltimore family are able to take you in our arms and walk with you through life. **We Love You Big Brotha!**

To my Cherry Hill Family: Aunt Anna, Cuz'n Kenny, Romey-Rome, Dana, Johnnie, Tara, Arde, Cordae, Raymond, Corey & Tameka Walker.

To my Best Man: **Greg Washington**—it's about to happen around the world, but I don't know if the world is ready for us yet? **One Love Between Two.** I missed you in Jamaica!

Dennis Wise: The release of our project, **The Wolf Trap**, will soon let the world know of your many talents. I'm wishing us luck by giving it all I have! U R the first! Other releases will follow—just say the word!

To those who have shown me the way: *Kevin "Blackface" Glasscho, Joe Taylor, Tracey Toney, Alvetta Stith, Jackie & Shaunetta, Kenneth Coley & Debbie Taggart, & Shelly Jenifer. A special shout-out to Terschia and "Unity in Words" book club in Annapolis.*

Tonya Blackstone: You are the graphic truth! Thanks for your skills on both projects. *Kanika McKerson*: We've got it going on! And soon the whole world will know what we've been working on. It's about to go down!!! Special thanks to *Robbin Colson* of *Exposing U Photography,* Baltimore, Maryland for his professional expertise. **Much love to my front cover crew:** My beautiful granddaughter Janae K. Johnson, Damara Knox, Dwayne Alexander, Darius Brown, and Mark Watford.

Flashback

In the final chapters of For the Love of Fast Money, conflict loomed in Baltimore City. Tavon and Juvenile were two partners who pledged their loyalty to one another through thick and thin. Life on the streets guarantees conflict and they were ready. But life never prepared them for war against each another.

With Fast Money desperate to gain his reputation back, no measure was too extreme as he tried to manipulate both partners from the middle.

Trapped in a dangerous liaison with Precious, Tavon and Juvenile's relationship would be permanently threatened when Fast Money discovered the double cross.

To keep Juvenile's secret from Tavon, he wanted cocaine and money. After receiving payment, Fast Money broke his word.

From Tavon, Fast Money thought he'd receive the same reward for his information, but was trapped. After informing Tavon of the sexual liaison his partner, Juvenile, was having with his woman, Precious, Fast Money was kidnapped by the FBI to face charges of interstate drug trafficking and conspiracy.

Now Tavon played the hunter after placing a big money contract on Juvenile's life. It was now do or die, killed or be killed.

To save himself, Juvenile had to become a fox with several holes to hide in. But Baltimore was too small. Friends like Butter and Precious played their part in trapping the fox.

At the same time, Tavon found himself trapped. The hunter was hunted down. Faced with numerous violations after a high speed chase, Tavon was forced to choose whether to surrender or run from the police. Before the police took action, he had been warned.

Precious was trapped between her two young hustlers. From the moment she was caught with her boyfriend's partner, her life would never be the same.

And Jameel, of all people, was forced to carry out a confusing request and now is caught in the mix.

Welcome back to Baltimore City…

Chapter 1

JAMEEL

"Every time it's a tragedy
I'm the first one to help."

Jay-Z, Blueprint 2
The Blueprint Album

I was trying to get myself together—still not believing all that had happened! It had been more than two hours since Mr. Freedman left. I keep telling myself this wasn't true. I don't want to believe anything else, but the more I look through these papers in front of me, the more it is becoming real. And all that money Mr. Freedman had in that briefcase.

'Ummh, Uummh, Uummh,' I kept saying to myself. All this is too much for me to handle, especially all of a sudden. That's why I told that lawyer to hold onto it.

I didn't know what to do with myself, so I nervously paced the floor. God knows I don't know what I'm doing—whether I'm coming or going. I've never been so nervous in my life. It was too early in the morning, first of all. And that was the first time I'd seen that much money in this house. I couldn't take what he was saying or the money. He kept saying it was left for me as the primary beneficiary and I had to make some arrangements. Now I was seeing it with my own eyes that my name is on everything.

I started feeling like the house was closing in on me. I had to sit down, catch my breath, and face one fact. Today was going to be the longest day of my life.

I couldn't stay seated, so I eased myself up from the loveseat. My feet were feeling a little wobbly because my body felt like I weighed three hundred pounds. My heart was beating so fast I could feel it. Suddenly, I felt cold. I should be calling 911 the strange way I was feeling, but I took my chances to walk over by the window at the front of the room. I pulled the blinds and opened the window so I could get some fresh air.

It's so hard to accept that my life had just become a movie. I was looking and living my worst nightmare. Deep inside was a hurt I couldn't explain. The uncontrollable emotions roaring deep in my chest showed no signs of letting up. The tears started streaming down my face. My body began to tremble as I stood by this lonely window holding myself.

All of sudden I felt light--like I was flying. I fell to my knees crying and had no other choice, but to pray because I was losing my mind.

'You know Lord, I don't know why you chose me for something like this, but I've always trusted you. And I'm not about to start doubting you now. That's why I'm asking you to help me because I never wanted any of them dying on those ugly, bloody streets. In the name of Jesus. You know my heart. Every time it's a tragedy for any family in my reach, I'm the first one to help. But this time I need your help—because this is too much for me. I seek your face in everything I do. I trust you God and I live for you, so keep me in your glory and give me the strength I need to face this great loss in our lives. In Jesus name I pray, God. Amen.'

I nervously went into the kitchen. I was still in shock and didn't know where the energy came from to pour another cup of coffee--my 4th since I got up. Just then I realized that it had been an hour or more since I called my mother. I didn't call her when the lawyer was here because I was too nervous. She would've known. When I did work up the nerve, I called and told her I'd *be right over to drop Tiffany off because of an emergency. One thing I have to do is be strong, so others can understand, but the funny thing about it is I don't even understand all of what's going on myself. As much as I tried to get myself together before waking Tiffany up, it seems like there was a stronger force weighing down on me. I stood near the stove in deep thought.*

"RRRRRing! RRRRRing!"

The sound of the phone interrupted my silence.

'Ouch! Ouch!' I screamed. 'Why did Tiffany leave her dolls lying on the floor?' I hopped on one leg over to the phone trying to ease the sharp pain at the bottom of my foot and barely caught it before it went to voicemail. "Hello?"

"Baby, are you okay? I thought you said you had something important to do and was dropping Tiffany off right away?" she asked, all in one breath.

"I'm fine Ma," I answered, sounding stuffy and out of breath. "I just stepped on one of Tiffany's dolls and hurt my foot. That's why I dropped the phone–that's all; I'll be there shortly."

"Okay, but if you need any help let me know because you don't sound too good. I don't know what it is that is so urgent, but something made you upset. I sensed it when you called earlier."

"Ma," I said, trying to interrupt her before she started on her tangent.

"Baby, you ain't never been scared to talk to me 'bout nothing 'cause I'm your mother."

"Ma, I'm gonna be okay. I told you I had some news to deliver and it wasn't good!" I screamed, losing control because the pain was welling up inside of me again. "Momma, please. I'll tell you everything later."

"Baby, is something wrong with Juvenile? Because you know I heard--"

"Ma, I have to go! I have to get Tiffany ready," I said, talking over her voice, hoping she would get the message before I break down again.

"Alright Jameel, but if—"

"Bye Ma," I said and hung up the phone. *I got off the phone and just stood in the middle of the kitchen in a daze, but still aware of the throbbing pain under the bottom of my foot. I felt like I was neither coming nor going until a small voice broke through the silence.*

"Mommy," Tiffany called out to me. *She was on her way down the stairs dragging her favorite teddy bear.*

"Yes, Baby?" I asked, trying to sound my best. *I know I sounded stuffy, so I quickly wiped my tears.*

"Are you okay? I heard you down here and it sounded like you were crying," she said, sounding concerned.

'Everybody is okay baby," I said lying. *I hate to lie to Tiffany, but I just couldn't tell her all that has happened because I'm still trying to process it myself.*

"Is daddy okay? Who was here with you early this morning?"

"Baby, no more questions right now, okay?"

"Mommy, are you crying?" she asked, still pressing for more information.

"As a matter a fact, I fell and hurt myself because you left your dolls on the floor. I stepped on it trying to get to the phone and hurt the bottom of my foot real bad."

"I'm sorry, Mommy. I forgot to put it in the toy chest last night before I went to bed," she said, looking extremely concerned that I had hurt myself.

"That's okay baby. Just make sure you pack your things away before going to bed at nights and don't leave anything lying around on the floor."

"Okay I will, Mommy."

"Now listen, I'm going to have to drop you off at Grandma's for a couple hours this morning," I said, trying not to sound upset.

"Now?"

"Yes, now, Tiffany," I answered. "I have to go take care of some business really quick and then I'll be right back to get you."

4

"What should I wear?" she asked, making her way back up the steps.

"Just put on anything. It doesn't matter," I answered, making my way up the steps behind her.

I changed real fast before rushing back downstairs. I picked up my keys from in the kitchen tray and headed for my car. I'm glad the ride to my mother's house wasn't very far so Tiffany didn't get a chance to ask any more questions.

Quickly pulling up in the front of my mother's house, I could see her living room light on. Her reflection was rocking in the window. I know she's fuming right now because she has no clue what is happening, but she'll get over it. I left the engine on so she would know I wasn't stopping.

By the time we got half way up the walkway she was already out on the front steps.

"Come on baby, you can go right back to sleep," she said, reaching out for Tiffany and taking her little bag.

"Thanks Grandma," Tiffany answered, sounding like she could fall back to sleep in a short time.

"Thanks for doing this for me Ma. I'll talk to you when I get back--I promise," I said before hugging her and walking away. "Call me if you need me," I said, getting inside my car.

I needed help to gain some kind of calm because my stomach was still upset and I was visibly shaking trying to drive. It's no way I could show up at this woman's doorstep this early in the morning in my state, so I fumbled with the radio. Donnie McClurkin was playing.

'Lord you're looking out for me this morning,' I said as I listened to Donnie sing, 'I'll Trust you Lord."

I couldn't hold back the tears...

...will you let go?

I trust you Lord.

And stand on my word?

I trust you Lord.

Against all odds will you believe what I've said?

I trust you Lord.

5

When it seems impossible, will you believe every promise that I
made...
I trust you Lord...

As the words of the song moved through me, I could feel
a chill running through my body. I turned the volume up as high
as it could go and sang even louder. Despite the tears tearing my
soul apart, I kept driving the winding road on Baltimore Street.
As I turned right at the corner onto Franklintown Road and
crossed Hollins Street, I saw the lights from two parked police
cars flashing. My heart dropped because I was trying to get here
first. I know these cops don't really care for people in this city--
because they think we are all criminals and that's just how they
treat us.

Pulling up behind the second car, I saw three policemen
standing in front of the house. One cop was on the top step
banging on the door. I took a deep breath, got out of my car, and
walked towards the house.

"Good morning," I said to the officers, walking to the
front steps.

All three of them returned my greeting as if it was
rehearsed, "Good morning, Mam."

"Do you by any chance know the occupants of this
house?" the tallest white cop asked.

"Yes. I do," I answered, "and I was hoping to break the
news to her because she's not well."

"That's what we're here for, Mam."

"Actually, I can take care of telling his mother without
you being here to make matter worse."

"Good, maybe she'll respond to you because we've been
out here for a while knocking and it sounded like she answered
and is inside. But we haven't seen her yet."

*The two officers in front of the house stepped aside as I
made my way to steps and her front door.*

"BANG! BANG! BANG!" The stress of banging on the door brought more pain to my light head. "Ms. Kamila. It's me Jameel. Can you open up the door? I need to talk to you."

I turned around and used the back of my foot. She was inside this house and I needed to talk to her. Kicking the bottom of her door, she was definitely going to hear me this time. "BOOM! BOOM! BOOM! BOOM! Ms. Kamila! It's Jameel-- open the door."

Chapter 2

P-NUT

"Please! Not Jay!"

Jay-Z, "Takeover"
The Blueprint

I was in my bedroom still enjoying my high when I heard some hard knocks on my front door. I knew it couldn't be Tavon because if he forgot his keys he would have called first. He rushed out of here with those guns talking about he was going to straighten something out with Juvenile and I haven't heard from him since, so I know he would call first. I tried to get an idea from him when he might be coming back, but he seemed so pre-occupied.

That was good, too. He was leaving my presence, at least for a little while. The only time I can get my high on is when he's not around so timing is everything. While walking through the house last night after he left, I noticed that the safe in the closet was still open. He was certainly in a hurry this time because he hardly ever forgets to lock that safe. That's why I've been enjoying myself. He rushed out of here like a bat outta hell leaving me what he hates for me to have and he didn't even know it. I got me enough dope out of that safe to stay high for a week. I also took some money. I'll put that up for a rainy day. He gets so much of this stuff he won't even know it's gone. I better lock it back though, because if that's my 'get high' partner, Sticky Fingers, he's always sneaking over the house looking for something he didn't even put down.

If I let Sticky Fingers in we may get to talking. My man speaks real fast when he talks about what he stole. I halfway listen to him when he tells me how he took another spark plug and smashed through another car window. He goes through all of that to steal handicap stickers so we can get high. Listening to him he sometimes distracts me, but not this morning.

I'm nice already, but not nice enough to forget about Tavon's shit. I can't forget that my son's safe is open. He'll try to use the bathroom and sniff around the house. That would be the end of whatever Tavon had in sight.

"BANG! BANG! BANG!"

"Dammit! I'm coming!" I yelled as I tried to close the heavy safe door. This shit had better be important! Nobody should be up this early in the morning banging on somebody's door.

I got myself together to answer the door, I thought about how much my son hates seeing me like this—especially when it's his stuff. Every now and then he lightens up and gives me what I need. That keeps me from chasing outside of my house. The one thing he doesn't do is stick around and talk to me when he knows I'm getting my fix.

When putting me on punishment and hiding his dope somewhere else, I do what I have to do to get it. My first resort is simple. He knows I'll swipe my Independence Card for people spending cash on cold food down Lexington Market in a minute. Days like that don't come that often, but when they do...my high money is only a swipe away.

Just like his father, he can't stand seeing me go through withdrawal pains. If he doesn't give me the money I need, I know where he keeps another money stash in the basement. Between those two strategies, that's how I get money from him to buy bottles of methadone from some of my friends on the bottle-meth program.

I really love my child in a way no one understands. He was born to take his father's place in my life. How can a mother not love a child with a good heart? That's why I exaggerate my withdrawal pains sometimes. I know it ain't right, but I do it just to get some much-needed special attention. One good thing about me faking my sickness is him not knowing the difference, but that's another story...

It was no use looking for any good clothes in this mess of a house. Besides, under my own roof that my son pays for each month, I was comfortable in my underwear and bra. Never mind my Social Service money. He takes care of his mother like he is supposed to. I quickly put on a pair of dirty sweatpants before looking into my mirror and grabbing my son's dingy, white T-shirt. I passed by my little table outside my bedroom doorway and quickly grabbed my warm bottle of Heineken. I took a quick drink to wet my mouth and freshen my early morning breath.

Looking into my living room mirror after staggering down my squeaky steps, I caught a glimpse of my hair and really didn't care that it was all over my head. My high had me where I wanted to be. Nothing else matters.

I kicked those smelly old clothes at the bottom of the steps so I could get to the door. This house is a mess. When Tavon gets back I'll have to get some quarters from him and go to the laundry mat. I took the last gulp of my warm beer and threw the bottle on the couch. 'I'll put it in the trash later, much later,' I thought to myself.

"BOOM! BOOOM! BOOM! BOOM!" The knocks on the door started again. Only this time it was sounding even more impatient than the time before.

"Who the hell is it?" I shouted.

"Ms. Kamila. It's Jameel. Open the door," she answered, on the other side of the door.

"Oh, it's you. I'm coming."

Pulling the locks on the door, I had a quick thought. 'Why would Jameel be here this early in the morning? I hope Tavon and Juvenile didn't send her with that intervention bullshit again. I couldn't give a damn about that makeup-to-breakup shit right now. Friends go through that—and this child has to understand that.'

"Jameel, is my son's Godchild okay?" I asked, opening the door to see her standing there with a nervous smile. Taking another step toward the screen door, I could see the police officer standing behind her and two more walking closer to the door. "I ain't got nothin' in here!"

"We are not here looking for anything," the freckled face, red head cop said. He tried stepping ahead of Jameel and said, "Mam, we have some information we need to give to you…"

"Ms. Kamila, can we come in?" Jameel asked, sounding quite agitated and then looking at the cop in frustration.

"Alright but let me get myself together," I answered. *I looked and tried to figure out what this was all about, but I couldn't just yet. I turned away from the door leaving it open so they could come inside.*

I used my foot again to kick through the mountain of dirty clothes piled on the floor. As I made my way to the steps, I thought to myself: 'Every time they come it means trouble. Whatever the reason, they better make this shit quick because I hate dealing with them.'

Without looking back, I ran up the steps, so I could hide my syringe, straight shooter and other paraphernalia I had out in my bathroom. While quickly hiding my stuff, I could still hear them talking downstairs while I cleaned up.

"Is she okay?" the young black officer asked in a loud voice to Jameel. "She looks kind of … you know?"

"She's fine, Sir. She's probably just a bit out of it because she just woke up. It's still early for some people."

"Does she live by herself?" another cop asked Jameel.

"For the most part, yes."

I could hear their questions, but not knowing what they were here for had me concerned. 'Dem boyz in blue ain't nothing but trouble. Let me hurry up and get back down stairs so they can stop questioning Jameel. I have to get these people out of my house.'

I made it back to where Jameel was sitting on my front room couch. The others in uniform were standing near the front door. I cleared my voice and spoke, "Uhm, Ummm. Now, what's going on, y'all?"

"Mam, I'm Detective Jeffers and my partner Detective Carson and Officer Dixon," the other police man said. "Sorry for coming here this time of the morning and the news we bring, but we have reason to believe that your son Anthony Truston—"

"What y'all trying to say my son did this time? Do y'all have a search warrant?" I asked putting on my best what's-going-on-now grimace on my face. *I was getting more and more annoyed by the minute because these officers were really blowing my high.*

"Mam, as my partner explained we're not ..." Officer Dixon tried to explain.

"Ms. Kamila. Did Tavon call you last night?" Jameel asked, interrupting the policeman's speech. *She looked at him with an evil eye while taking my hand into hers.*

Whatever was happening it didn't feel good right about now. This dope was quickly becoming a sickness in my stomach. "No, I haven't heard from him baby. Why you ask—what's going on Jameel?"

Detective Jeffers said, "Well, there was a shooting and Tavon just happened to be in the wrong place..."

"Please, not J!" I screamed. "J! Oh, my God! I know my son ain't shoot no Juvenile! Jameel tell me that ain't happen!"

"No, Ms. Kamila. That's not what happened. It wasn't Juvenile that was shot. I know you're gonna find this hard to believe, but it was Tavon. That's why we're here. I'm so sorry!"

"NO! NO! NOT MY SON! NOT MY SON! JAMEEL HE'S THE ONLY ONE I GOT!" I screamed, using my hand to beat the couch in frustration. "MY BABY WOULD NEVER HARM A SOUL! WHO WOULD WANT TO DO THIS TO HIM?" I screamed, falling back on my couch in disbelief.

With absolutely no look or sound of sympathy, Detective Jeffers asked, "Mam, we need you to come with us to the Coroner's office so we can get a positive identification on his body?"

"Come on Ms. Kamila. Let me help you? We have to go with them to get this taken care of," Jameel said to me. "I know how shocking all of this is and hard it may be holding yourself together. That's why I'm here. But we have to go because you're the only one that can do this."

I heard her. I know I heard what she just said, but she's not talking to me. *"OH GOD! NOT MY BABY! OH GOD! NOT MY BABY!" My entire body was shaking. I tried to hold myself together, but soon loss control.*

* * * * * * *

JAMEEL

I knew this was going to happen. I could tell Ms .P-Nut had been drinking. Knowing her habits, it was more than alcohol. Lord only knows. I grabbed her because her entire body started going into convulsions. I tried to hold her up but her spasms were more than I could handle.

They were just standing there looking at me trying to do their job. "Call for the ambulance, don't just stand there, do something!"

"Unit 7. Unit 7. We need an *ambo* at 57 South Franklintown Road. Copy?" Detective Jeffers said, making the call on his radio.

"Dispatch copy Unit 7. That's 57 South Franklintown Road. Copy?"

"10-4."

"Medical is on the way Unit 7. Stand by."

It took medics about seven minutes to come. Hearing her moans get more and more faint scared me. Paramedics strapped her on to the stretcher and rushed her outside.

Quickly drifting into a daze, sad thoughts surfaced forcing me to speak out loud, "This can't be happening again."

"Mam would you like to ride in the ambulance?" a calm voice asked.

"No! I have to drive. Which hospital are you going to?" I asked, trying not to panic.

"We're rushing her down to University," he said and asked, "Are you sure you'll be able to drive?"

"I'll be right behind you," I answered. *I sat inside my car just thinking about the shock that P-Nut is going through. In a stare, I watched the ambulance start its siren and race down the street.*

I heard a loud knock on my driver's side window. "Knock. Knock. Knock. Mam, do you think…"

"Ooooh! Oh, my God…you scared me!" I screamed in fear. "I didn't know you were still here Officer Dickens."

"I'm sorry Mam. I didn't mean to startle you, but we were wondering if it was possible for you to come and identify the body since we are under some time constraints."

"You know Officer Dickens, it's because of people like you why so many people in this city dislike the police and very rarely cooperate with them. I have no idea what is wrong with that woman. For all I know, she could be fighting for her life! I need to be there with her--and you are talking about some time constraints!"

"Mam, I know how you feel and it doesn't have to be today. And I'm sorry if I sound a little pushy," he said, trying to pacify me, "but could you please take my card and give me a call me as soon as Ms. Marsh is able to identify the body?"

I took his card and threw it on the passenger side. As he moved away from the car, I got myself together and drove off in a hurry. I made my way down Baltimore Street, across Martin Luther King Boulevard, and down to the hospital. So many thoughts ran through my mind. And I couldn't help but think how hardened our society had become. I found a spot on Greene Street and pulled in. I had no time to do anything rushing inside. Briefly, I tried calming down and regaining my composure. Then I thought about calling my mother to see about Tiffany, but that had to wait because I really wasn't in the mood for more questions.

Chapter 3

JAMEEL

*"Was born in the belly.
That's the way the streets breed you."*
Jay-Z, *"Hola' Hovito"*
The Blueprint

Hospitals are not my favorite places in the world, but they serve their purpose. I don't think anyone likes being in one. One good thing they have going for them is that most of the people are helpful. Just being in this spooky place makes me nervous.

I rushed up to the information desk as soon as I got through the revolving door. "My family was just rushed in here emergency," I said, in a panic. "Could you please tell me how to get to the emergency room?"

"Sure. First of all you're gonna need this," he said, giving me a hospital badge. "Now sign this sheet for me?"

I grabbed the pen he extended my way and scribbled my name. "Okay. That's done."

"After you clip on that badge just go straight down this hallway and hang a right. Take the elevator at the next opening. It'll be straight in front of you. You can't miss it."

"Thanks," I said, without looking back. *I ran straight down the long hallway like he said and made a right turn.*

'I hope nothing bad has happened to her,' I thought to myself. *Just like he said, I couldn't miss the entrance doorway to the emergency room. It was right in front of me. Every nurse I*

15

could see was busy taking vital signs and talking to patients. I walked over to the reception area to find out where I could find her.

I stood in front of a glass window excited and out of breath. "Excuse me?" I asked, still breathing fast. "Where would I find someone rushed here by ambulance a few minutes ago?"

"Calm down, Mam--and catch your breath. If you give me her name I should be able to tell you," she replied.

"I don't think you'd have her name because I didn't tell the paramedics before they left and it doesn't seem as if she was conscious enough to tell them either. I can tell you the type of clothes she had on and where the ambulance came from, if that would help."

"Okay, let's see if we can work with that," she answered, a bit hesitant.

"The ambulance came from 57 South Franklintown Road. She was wearing a white T-shirt with sweatpants..." *Before I could finish my sentence, a nurse, who must've overheard my conversation with the receptionist, came up through the hallway.*

"Excuse me? Are you her daughter, Mam?" she asked, using her authority to butt in.

"No, I'm not, but I was there when..."

She didn't wait for me to get finished before using her power. "Mam, we can only give out information to immediate family members. I'm sorry, but is there any immediate family member you can contact?" she asked, sounding a bit pushy.

"Actually, there is none," I answered, knowing I sounded a bit annoyed myself. "I was just with the police at her house relaying the news of the death of her son, her only child, when her body started going through convulsions. She passed out right in front of us. But to answer your question, I have never heard her talk about anyone else except her son."

"I'm sorry, come on back with me," she said, as she turned and walked away. "By law," she continued, "we are not supposed to give out any information about any of our patients to anyone without their written consent."

"I understand that, but I'm all she has right now."

"Well, I had to make sure because it's my job—and that's the law. I didn't mean to be short or offensive—and I hope I wasn't."

She walked me toward the emergency area. Everything seemed so big entering the hallway filled with professionals running around in white coats and colorful scrubs. Their voices seemed loud and clear. I could hear various conversations between staff and patient and amongst the staff themselves. "I understand and you sure were not, in the least bit, impolite. And thanks for your help. She needs somebody at her bedside."

"Doctors are still working on her, but she's in that room straight ahead of you. Stay out here until I go inside and check on their progress with her."

After about twenty minutes of waiting, watching several hospital technicians go in and out responding to Ms. Kamila's emergency, I was finally able to go inside.

"Doctors had to give her a sedative to calm her down and get her regulated. She's stable now. You can go on in and I'll be right there to get some information from you," she said pointing.

Pushing through the door and walking into the room, machines were everywhere. She was hooked up to all kinds of devices. She had an IV in her arms. Two bags of fluid hung just overhead: one had a clear liquid; and the other was filled with a thick, milky substance. There was an oxygen mask covering her nose and mouth and a heart monitor making sounds. Stepping closer to her bedside, not wanting to disturb her but make sure she was okay, I touched her forehead.

"She'll be fine," the nurse said, startling me. *I didn't hear her enter the room.* "She went into shock and the drugs in her system didn't help. She's sleeping now but she'll be just fine."

"I've been praying for relief. All I know is God answers prayers," I said to her, feeling relieved. "Thank you, Nurse. That's good news."

"Now let's see what information you can give me about her. Let's start with her name?"

I gave the little information I knew and they were able to pull her up in their system. Apparently, she had been there before on more than one occasion. Minutes after the nurse left, the doctor came to explain what happened. Basically, she was okay. She should be out by tomorrow. He just wanted to keep her overnight for observation, especially because she was a drug user. I sat there a little while longer after the doctor left just trying to make sense of it all.

I hadn't heard from Dorian since he called me and saying he needed help because somebody tried to kill him. He was in an uproar and I had no idea things were this serious. I only hope he wasn't involved in this.

I was able to leave when the attending physician gave me her final prognosis. I stopped by the Nurse's Station to leave my contact information in case of another emergency. After taking my numbers, she gave me a piece of paper with the unit she would be transferred to shortly.

As I walked out of the hospital, I felt relieved that she was gonna be okay. I still couldn't get the image of her just lying there looking lifeless out of my head. I also realized how challenging this task—the one I didn't even volunteer for--was going to be. She was so dependent on Tavon. Come to think of it, I don't know what my own mother would do, God forbid, if something should happen to me. My two brothers live right there in the house but they are no real help. But that's another story...

I was about to get in the car when I felt a sharp pain in my stomach followed by a loud growl. I looked at my watch and realized that it was way past lunch time and I hadn't even eaten breakfast. The events of the morning had me feeling drained; all I wanted to do was go back to bed. I was sitting in my car contemplating my next move when my cell phone rang. It had to be Mama.

"Hi Ma, I was just about to call you."

"Hi Baby. I was just making sure you were okay since I hadn't heard from you," she said, not sounding too please that I hadn't called back all morning.

"I'm fine Ma, but this has been an eventful morning, to say the least."

"So where you at now?" she asked.

"I'm sitting in my car, trying to get myself together, in front of University Hospital."

"University! What are you doing at University? Is Dorian hurt? What's wrong with Dorian?" she asked, her voice getting louder and louder.

Feeling a bit annoyed, I asked, "Ma--can you lower your voice before Tiffany hears you?"

"She's outside playing Jameel, and I wouldn't talk like that in front of her anyway. I'm not stupid!"

"Okay, Ma. I'm sorry, but it's not Dorian. He called me and asked me to do something for him but I have not heard from him since. I hope he's okay."

"Then who else could have you out of your bed so early at the hospital—because your brothers are in here."

"It's Tavon, Ma."

"Is he okay?"

"No, there was a police shootout and he got killed," I said, breaking into tears.

"He did what! He got killed!" she repeated.

"Yeah, Ma!" I screamed into the cell phone. *My tears ran uncontrollably.*

"Tiffany's godfather?"

"Yes."

"Lord, have mercy. What is this world coming to! People can't even walk on the streets of Baltimore safe anymore without…"

"Ma," I said, interrupting her. "Tavon was no angel, so don't even bring the Lord into this. He lived the same reckless life your two sons and Dorian live right to this day—and I hate it!"

"You're right, but that's not the whole story. You know that poor boy never had a good example to follow. He was born in the belly while his mother and father lived the drug life—and that's the way the streets raised him. I've seen it time and time again, Jameel, so it's not all his fault."

"Ma, I tell you all the time not to talk about people like that. But anyway, I had to go tell Ms. Kamila the news. When I got there the police was standing on her porch. It took a while for her to open the door. When she did, Ma, I could tell she was high. The place looked and smelled terrible. Then, as I told her what happened, she fell out and her body started going into convulsions. The doctor said she went into shock. They're saying she should be fine. They're keeping her overnight for observation. I imagine her drug addiction doesn't help any. I'll go get her tomorrow and carry her to identify the body."

"I told you that boy ain't have much of a chance in life—more like a snowball chance in hell with a drug addict for a mother and his father is always gonna be in prison. The way he was going, it was either prison or the grave. It 's a damn shame and was just a matter of time."

"People make their own choices, Ma. Tavon was grown and he made his own choice," I answered, getting sick on the stomach again. "He knew wrong from right."

"Jameel, how did you get in the middle of this anyway?"

"That's a good question. Tavon gave my name to his lawyer as the person to contact if anything should go wrong with him. So his lawyer showed up this morning with all kind of papers and instructions on funeral arrangement and how everything should be divided. He even had a briefcase full of cash, Ma. Plus, the lawyer said he had some more money in a holding account that the law firm would be taking care of for him, too."

"What's this you're telling me?"

"So you see, Ma. He could do things differently if he wanted to. He even left money for his mother and Tiffany."

"He did!" she said.

I could hear the excitement in her voice when she heard about the money. "But Ma, you know I..."

She jumped in before I could get another word out.

"I think that was very nice of him," she said, "he always did love his god-daughter and you can always put up that money for Tiffany until it's time to go to college and you--you could use a new car before that car leaves you stranded once again. Of course, you can't forget your motha."

"Ma, I don't believe you're saying that," I said, driving away from the hospital. "You know what? I'm gone because all this money stuff is getting me sick to my stomach. I'll be there to get Tiffany as soon as I can."

I never liked the fact that Mama didn't have a problem taking that money from her sons and from Dorian. She probably took money from Tavon, too.

"So why do you always have to get so mad when I talk about..."

I didn't allow her to finish her sentence. "Ma you know me better than that! I don't even take money from Dorian for Tiffany, although sometimes I really need it."

"Alright, but I tell you all the time. Sometimes you have to swallow your pride to better yourself in this world."

"That's it Ma, bye! I'm getting off the phone because what you're saying isn't right."

Chapter 4

PRECIOUS

"I lead a life
You can write a book on."
Jay-Z, "Money Cash Hoes"
Vol 2...Hard Knock Life
(feat. DMX)

I hadn't seen or heard from Tavon for two nights straight. And that's not like him. I tried calling his cell and Outlaw's phone, but both keep ringing without an answer. I don't know why I've been just lying around the house. You know something must be wrong with me if I don't even feel like getting up to go shopping. I guess it's good to keep yourself hidden--let people miss seeing you sometimes. I went to bed early last night and couldn't sleep throughout the morning.

I know Tavon is convinced that Juvenile is the only one to blamed for all of this mess. That's why I've been putting this pussy all over him. For Tavon, I even went as far as setting Juvenile up so my man could get his ass.

My man ain't no fool, though. He ain't gonna walk away from all those vehicles he got parked outside and not to mention me.

The more I think about it, I'm really gettin' tired of living like a prisoner in my own house. Shidddd, I'm hardly getting any money and I have to tell him everywhere I go. Maybe it's time for me to be around some real men for a change. I'm tired of dealing with them little young mama's boys.

"Ring! Ring!" *The loud rings caught me off guard. I jumped up from the bed to grab the phone.* Ring! Ring! *I figured this to be Tavon so I had to put on a show.*

"Hey you," I said, speaking in one of my more seductive tones.

"This is a collect call from the Pretrial Detention Center..." *I sat there feeling so disappointed, really not wanting to hear any gossip now, but I guess taking the call was in my interest. I sure was hoping it would be Tavon, though.*

"Oh my God, gurl! How you holding up?" Pretty asked quickly as soon as the call came through.

"How I'm holding up? I'm fine Pretty. Why are you asking that?" *I found it strange that she would say something like that. I'm the one usually checking on how strong she's being in jail. Now she's checking on me?*

"You haven't heard?" she asked.

"Heard what? Pretty, you acting mighty strange--what's all this about?"

"Precious, Tavon got shot," she said, "From what I'm hearing, he's dead!"

"Pretty you know you shouldn't play like that!" I said, speaking in a serious tone.

"Precious you know I wouldn't joke like that! I'm serious! I thought you heard--him and Outlaw and somebody else was in some high speed chase with the police. Tavon kept on going and they shot him, but Outlaw got caught and he's locked up over here on the other side of the jail."

Listening to Pretty on the other end shook me up. My hands started to tremble. I wanted to speak, but my mouth starting getting dry and my heart felt like it was racing over its speed limit. Something went wrong with what we set up. I couldn't think or even believe what she was saying was true.

"Precious, you there? Are you okay?" she asked, sounding concerned.

"I am, but I just can't believe this shit! This shit ain't making sense," I said, as the tears started rolling down my face. *I* couldn't believe what I was hearing. "Where'd you hear this shit?"

"It was all over the news!"

Pretty stayed on the line with me and listened to the few words I could get out between the pain. She tried to do her part.

"My time is up now Precious, but I'll try calling you the next time we make phone calls," I heard her say.

I was so out of it I couldn't even respond. Stiffly, I laid there with the receiver on my chest looking up into the ceiling trying to make sense of it all. This wasn't supposed to happen. He was supposed to take care of Juvenile. Then I would have him all to myself, without any restrictions on me.

The annoying noise from the receiver made me realize that the phone was off the hook. 'This wasn't supposed to happen this way' I said, beating my pillow and burying my face. I couldn't bare the thought that all of this happened because of me. This was the life I chose. And flipping back through all of these years of doing it this way, I've lead a life somebody could write a street novel on.

I kept calling Tavon's cell phone, but there was no answer. I went downstairs and poured me a half a glass of Remy. I came back upstairs. I sat on the bed long enough to gulp every bit of it down before picking up the phone again. I tried calling Tavon's cell phone again and any other number I had on him.

I put on some clothes to drive through West Baltimore. The phone rang. After about four rings I checked the caller ID and saw it said 'UNIV of Maryland.' I quickly grabbed the phone to see who was calling from the hospital.

"Hello," I said, trying to shake off the shock.

"Precious, you hear 'bout Tavon?" a sickly voice asked, on the other end of the phone.

"Yeah, I just heard. Who is this?' I answered, trying not to get choked up once again with tears.

"Bitch don't be asking who dis is!" the angry voice screamed, sounding mean and nasty. "You know who it is and I know you had something to do with my son getting killed and if it's the last thing I do I'm gonna get your ass!"

"You betta get your facts straight before you accuse me of anything? I'm the one who loves Tavon. Who the hell you think you are--calling here talking to me like that P-Nut?"

"Bitch! Don't be calling me no P-Nut! Trust me--I'm not your friend! I am Ms. Kamila to you. And I know you did it 'cause every man that come in your path either got killed or goes straight to jail."

"It's not because of me!"

"Yes it is, bitch! You're worse than a black spider – you witch! And you are gonna pay for this! Trust me!"

"I don't have to listen to—"

I didn't even finish my sentence before I heard the dial tone in my ears. I couldn't tell you if it's shock or just my survival instincts setting in, but after that phone call from that crazy-ass mother of his…I decided to secure whatever it is in this house to make it mine. Not to mention, the vehicles parked up in front of this house. Good thing is that they're all in my name.

I know Juvenile might wanna come and take stuff--and not to mention P-Nut. I could still try to get with Juvenile, but after this…I'm not so sure he'd even see me. I looked at every possible place I could think of in this house, but only found the three grand he had on his side of the night table. I knew there was much more than that, but I couldn't get myself together to think this through.

25

Chapter 5

JAMEEL

"When she got the news
Her boy body could be viewed
Down at the city morgue
Opened the drawer saw him nude."
Jay-Z, *"Meet the Parents"*
The Blueprint 2

I was glad Tiffany wanted to spend the night at her grandmother's. That gave me the time and space I needed to get my mind straight and take out whatever papers I need to go through. After a full night with no sleep, I decided to go back to the hospital. It was about 11:30 in the morning when I got there. Before leaving the car I grabbed that police's business card.

I took a slow walk from the parking area to the front door. I saw the same guard at the front desk who directed me to the ward yesterday.

"How are you today," I asked before passing him the piece of paper the nurse gave me the day before.

"Fine. I guess everything was okay yesterday?"

"Yes. Thank God. I'm trying to find her room now."

"Here's another badge. You're gonna need this one to enter that floor. The elevator is to the right."

"Thanks again."

"Have a nice day," he said, as I left the counter.

"You too," I answered, turning around, acknowledging him for the last time.

I got off the elevator on the 7th floor which opened directly into the main nursing area. "Good Morning. Could you please tell me where I can find Kamila Marsh?"

"Sure sweetie," she said pointing, "she's right down the hallway on the left hand side. She's in room 703."

"Thank you," I told her, walking towards the hallway she directed me to.

"Miss, Excuse me? Excuse me," someone said.

I turned around. I saw the same nurse I just spoke with trying to get my attention.

"Are you her daughter?" she asked.

"No, I answered. Right now, I'm kinda in charge of her care. Why did you ask?"

"She's been up since this morning raising hell about the death of her son. She called some girl on the telephone and cussed her out. We didn't even know she was awake until we heard loud talking coming from her room. She was cursing somebody named Precious. Do you know who that is?"

"Yes. I sure have heard of her."

"The doctor is in there with her now, trying to calm her down."

As I got closer to her room I could hear her talking to the doctors. 'Good morning everyone,' I said, as I entered the room, walking next to her bedside. Ms. Kamila how you doing this morning?

"Hi, Jameel," she said hugging me and crying. "I'm about ready to get this over with. I got a few people I wanna deal with, too. So I'm ready to get outta here."

"Okay, Ms. Marsh. You have company now. And she's gonna make sure you get home safely," the doctor said, trying not to upset her as he left the room. "I'll bring in your discharge papers in a minute."

I pulled the card from my pocketbook. Looking at it, I told her, "I have to call the officer who gave me his card and let him know we're ready. He can tell us where to go."

I stepped out of the room to make the phone call. "Detective Carson speaking," he said on the other end, "How can I help you?"

"Yes, this is Jameel. I'm here at the hospital with Ms. Kamila Marsh. You told me to call you when she was discharged."

"I appreciate that and thanks for your call."

"Where am I taking her?"

"You don't have to take her anywhere. We'll be right over to pick you up at the front of the hospital."

"She should be discharged in a few minutes."

"Got it. I'll be right there."

"Detective Carson and his partner are on their way to pick us up, Ms. Kamila."

"So why you can't take me?" she asked, sounding very annoyed. "Are you going with me?"

"They prefer to take you there personally. Besides, I really don't know where to go. So we'll just go with them."

Not really thrilled about having to go, she said, "Alright, but make sure you're there because I don't like police."

After signing her discharge packet, we were escorted downstairs. Standing outside the front door, we saw the detectives pull up about ten minutes later.

"Good afternoon ladies," both policemen said. They got out of both sides of the unmarked police car. "Ms. Marsh, are you feeling okay now? We apologize for having to deliver the bad news."

"I feel fine officer," she replied, sounding like she didn't want to continue the conversation.

Detective Carson seated her in the back of the car. He asked, "Ms. Marsh, can you remember the clothes your son had on when you saw him last?"

"I don't remember. I think he had on a black hooded sweat top."

"Do you know of any incidents he was involved in or anybody he was having problems with at the time?" he asked, shutting the door and quickly got in the front seat.

"No. I don't know my son's business. I don't get involved in his and he stays out of mine. Tavon doesn't have any enemies out here on these streets—only friends who love him," she snapped.

"Ms. Marsh, we know how emotional this can be for you, but we're gonna have to ask these questions to get to the bottom of what really happened out there."

"I still can't believe all this shit, so I just wanna get all this over with."

"We'll be there in a minute. Let us know if you need anything."

"Jameel," Ms. Kamila leaned over and whispered. "This is making me sick to my stomach. Now my insides are jumping like a bouncing ball."

"You gonna do just fine. I've been praying for you." *I took her frail hand and squeezed it lightly just to reassure her that she would be fine. As we got out of the car on Penn Street, she stopped after taking only a few steps.*

"Officers, I gotta stop! I can't do this—it's too quick!" she said, holding onto my hand as tight as she could.

"Okay, there's no rush," Detective Carson said, walking over to help me hold her. "We'll wait for you."

"Can I beg one a y'all for a cigarette and some matches? I really need one," she asked, visibly shaking. "Look at how I'm shaking! Dis shit is really starting to scare me y'all. I ain't never been through nothing like this before. I'm telling y'all, you got the wrong family. This won't be Tavon."

"Sorry, Ms. Marsh, but neither one of us smoke cigarettes."

"Alright. I'm ready then. Let's just get dis' shit over with. Y'all gonna have to apologize for this mistaken identity. And I don't know whether any apology will make me feel like forgiving y'all for taking me through this hell!"

Without a care in the world, the other detective said, "We understand, but we're still going to ask you to follow us, Ms. Marsh."

This was routine, definitely routine for these officers. Hearing them speak sounded like a recording. They both walked us to the front desk where we took turns signing a log book. We walked down the hallway to this big open room. You could hear all of our footsteps in the empty hallway. Walking, getting closer to our destination, took us to the very end of the hallway.

"This shit is getting spookier," Ms. Kamila whispered. "It feels like I'm living a real nightmare."

The smell of the entire building caught my nerves off guard. As soon as we entered the front door those strange chemicals and human odors caused my stomach to flip.

"Inside here sure smells strange,'" I said to her. *I was just making sure she's still with me every step of the way. I could feel her trembling.* "Ms. Kamila this is new for me too, but the good thing is we have each other to do this – right?"

"That's true Jameel. If it wasn't for you, I don't know what I would be doing now."

I braced myself as we walked into this cool room. It was set up like a crypt in a scary movie. This large wall had these larger than life cabinet drawers on them. Each drawer had tags on the front with a number and a date. A man dressed in a white coat addressed us as soon as we walked in the room. As he spoke, Ms. Kamila grabbed my hand for support.

"Good Morning. I'm Dr. Edwards."

"I'm detective Detective Jeffers and this is my partner Detective Carson. We have the mother of Tavon Anthony Truston here. We're trying to establish identification, Dr. Edwards."

The doctor turned directly towards Ms. Kamila as he spoke. "Thank you for coming. We'll try to make this as quick and comfortable as possible."

Her grip on my hand started to tighten as the doctor moved away.

"You know what Jameel," she whispered again, "the sooner we get this over with, the better-- because this is not my son. After we finish they'll be calling somebody else's mother to identify her son."

I didn't respond to her remarks verbally. I just rubbed her hand. Most of her frail body was resting on my right side.

"Can I have your name, please, mam?" the doctor asked.

"P-Nut."

"I'm sorry, but I need your birth name for the state record, please?"

"Kamila Marsh," she answered weakly.

"And your son's full name?"

"Anthony Tavon Truston, but this can't be my son because I'd just seen him and he was gonna go see his friend Juvenile. It can't be!" she screamed.

"I understand that, Ms. Marsh. Come with me, please?" he asked, while checking another log book with names and numbers.

He pulled out a long drawer with a body covered up in a white sheet with bloodstains in a few spots.

"Ms. Marsh, do you need some time to get yourself together before we do this?" Detective Jeffers asked. *He seemed to be the more compassionate of the two.*

"Jameel, you got your phone on 'cause I know Tavon's gonna call you. And I want to make sure you can hear it ring when he calls."

"It's on, Ms. Kamila. I just checked it a few minutes ago. He hasn't called. I'm sorry."

"Are you ready?" the doctor asked, ready to go through his normal process.

"Yes, you can go ahead."

As the doctor uncovered the body she quickly turned away and buried her head in my chest just like a child would in a mother's arms. Lifted her head up, she finally looked.

31

"Oh, my God—Noooo!" she screamed, as her body collapsed in my arms.

"It's gonna be okay, Ms. Kamila," I said, reminding her that she wasn't alone in this.

"WHO DID DIS' TO MY BABY! GOD, PLEASE? Who did dis'shit to my fuckin' son! Look at how they killed my boy!

"Jameel, help me, please? Help me--let me see my baby?"

I helped her to stand directly over him. She let go of my hand and wrapped herself around his lifeless body.

"My baby ain't never hurt nobody!" she screamed hysterically. "Tavon, baby, if Precious did this to you her ass won't live to see tomorrow!"

"Mam, please, calm down," Detective Jeffers said in a low tone.

Before he could say another word I snapped. "With all due respect, sir. This is her only child and this is the only way she knows how to deal with her pain. I think you need to step back and grant her that much!"

"I never meant to sound harsh. I was just trying to help."

"Why don't you just help by staying out of it for now," I said without a second thought. *I grabbed a piece paper that was laying on the desk and started to fan her as she lay over Tavon's body.*

"What happened to my baby!" she screamed, moving away from the drawer.

"Ms. Marsh, your son was involved in a police shooting after a high speed chase. We have reason to believe he was involved in a separate incident, but we haven't fully investigated the matter yet," Detective Carson explained.

"My son would never hurt anybody, so why did y'all shoot him? Why!!!"

"Mam, all I can tell you is police arrived at the scene of a regular 911 call to search several suspects. On or about that time they heard a wild commotion and several gunshots not far from Greenmount Ave and 21st Street. While responding to this incident, several cars attempted to speed away from the scene."

"How y'all gonna shoot somebody and they don't even have a gun? My son ain't have no gun! Oh my God—they killed my son Jameel!" she said, looking at me in disbelief.

Pulling out his note pad, Detective Jeffers said, "I understand what you're saying, Mam. But we have witnesses saying he tried to run from the police. Did you ever see your son riding in or possessing a blue Grand Marquis?"

We walked her a few feet away from Tavon's body. She sat on the couch sniffling and looking into the floor as she vigorously shook both legs, refusing to answer any more questions.

"Do we have to do this now?" I asked.

"Mam, we have to do what we have to do, regardless," Detective Jeffers replied.

"No, he ain't have a car like that!"

"Reports show that responding officers followed the Grand Marquis closely, at a high rate of speed. After having an accident, your son tried to run from the passenger side of the vehicle," Detective Jeffers made clear before continuing, "Although he was not the driver, he was commanded by Police Sergeant Dozier to stay in his vehicle before his squad was forced to shoot."

"By the way, Ms Marsh. Do you know a friend or associate of your son named Vernon Carey?'

"No, I don't!" she snapped, jumping to her feet and walking back to her son's stiff body.

"Why y'all asking all of these stupid ass questions, anyway! Just tell me why did this have to happen to my son? Look at him," she said, pointing to the hole he had on the side of his face. "Y'all killed my only baby boy!"

"Ms. Marsh, I know you're upset, but I still have to ask you a few more questions. Do you know or have you ever heard the nickname Outlaw?"

"Why?"

"Have you Ms. Marsh? This is important to this investigation to find out whether your son's rights were violated leading up to this tragic incident?"

"Yeah, I heard of him, but I don't know him."

"Do you---"

"Just tell me what happened to my son because I ain't trying to talk about nobody named no Outlaw? Fuck an Outlaw! If you wanna tell me something—tell me what hospital he was rushed to or how he died. Tell me that! Tell me something that will bring my goddamn son back!"

"Ms. Marsh, your son, the deceased, was a passenger in the suspect's vehicle. After trying to charge officers with what they all suspected was a weapon, your son was shot several times before being rushed to John Hopkins Hospital Trauma Unit. He was pronounced dead upon arrival. There was nothing the hospital staff could do for him because of the wounds he sustained."

"That's it!" she screamed.

"Mam, I do apologize for this but--"

"Apologize? My fuckin' son is gone and that's all you can do—apologize! Y'all shot my son so bad that he died and all you wanna do is apologize. Well, guess what? You can go straight to hell!"

"I guarantee you, Ms. Marsh, that there will be a full investigation into this police-involved matter and we will find out the truth."

"Well, if you don't then I will. I will find whoever touched a hair on this boy's head. My son ain't never hurt nobody, so why would this happen to him?"

"We'll investigate and find out why."

"Come on Jameel. I'm ready to go."

"Please sign right here Ms. Marsh before you leave," the doctor instructed, as he came hurrying back into the room with a paper attached to a brown clipboard.

We took a slow walk back without the help of the police.

Chapter 6

OUTLAW

*"Can't be too safe
'cause [snitchers] are two-faced.
And they show the other side
when they catch a new case."*

*Jay-Z, "A Week Ago"
Vol. 2...Hard Knock Life
(featuring Too Short)*

"Good Morning. I am Agent Dillon and this is Agent Oslowsky. For the record, is it correct that you asked Baltimore City Police to contact us at the Federal Bureau of Investigation immediately after your arrest because you had information you believe should be brought to our attention?"

"Yes, Sir."

"For the record, we have come to the Baltimore City Detention Center today to interview you with no promises of a lenient sentence in this *help-yourself room*, although we may have the power to speak on your behalf to the courts concerning your cooperation and subsequent testimony. Do you understand?"

"Yes, Sir."

"We always offer help to people who provide substantial assistance to the federal government by testifying and gaining a conviction. Do you understand?"

"Uhmm-hu," I mumbled. *I wanted him to hurry up so I can say what I gotta say.*

"Sir, for the record, you have to reply yes or no."

"Yes, Sir."

"Thank you. Just the same, we will have to judge from the information you share whether that's possible. It is not guaranteed. You understand that?"

"Yes."

"And based on the information you provide we will have to decide whether to place you in our Witness Protection Program. This program offers physical protection from any danger you may face as a potential federal witness in a case which may be a threat to your life or that of your family. Do you understand?

"Yes, Sir. I understand clearly."

"Are you under the influence of any medications, alcohol, or drugs that may impair your judgment? This means any mind-altering drugs prescribed by a doctor that would not allow you to make competent and fair-minded decisions?"

"No, Sir—and I know about my rights contacting a lawyer and my right to remain silent and not tell the federal government anything. I also know that what I'm about to tell you can be used against me, too, but I called y'all to come here today because I wanted to tell all that I know so I can get off."

"One more question. Has anyone forced you, or used coercion to compel you to share this information during this session?"

"No. I'm doing this to help myself. That's why I called."

"Alright, Mr. Carey, sign here. This is just saying you understand your rights and to acknowledge that we haven't made any promises to you in exchange for what you are about to tell us."

Without reading, I just signed the paper. It was too much to ready anyway. I wanted to get this over with.

"State your name for the record?"

"On the streets they call me Outlaw, but my name is Vernon Carey."

"For the record, we need your mother's full name?"

"Mrs. Catherine Carey."

"And your father's full name, sir?"

"Monroe Everett Carey."

"For the record, have you ever contacted us before?"

"No, I haven't contacted the feds, but I have called Baltimore City Police several times."

"So you have contacted the Baltimore City Police Department?"

"Yes, I have. I called the police when I was hustling before I got with Fast Money and then Tavon. I used to be out there hustling all day making no money because other people's stuff was better than mine, so I called on them.

"When the police took them off the block, I would go out there trying to find their stuff. Then I came back out on the block. I did that a bunch of times. But that was then. I ain't hustling no more, so."

"And why did you call us this time?"

"I ain't trying to sound soft or nothing because I go hard in the streets, but I wanted y'all to come and get me. I knew if I helped you, you would help me."

"What information do you have?"

"It's a lot of stuff I want to talk about. A little while ago, Fast Money was locked up on federal charges. His real name is Craig Carter. I know him and have dealt with him selling drugs for a long time."

"Hold on let me get all this down," Agent Dillon said, scribbling in his note pad.

"Me and Fast Money first met when he was getting drugs from Rock—who is a well-known dealer on the Westside. Fast Money had me selling drugs for him in West Baltimore. That's back when he was giving those Platinum parties for major dealers in Baltimore and D.C. I still got pictures of the parties if you need it because it's a lot of known hustlers on them.

"But, anyway, I had a crew and we sold large amounts of cocaine and sometimes heroin on consignment. We sold whatever Fast Money got from his connect. He used to collect from me and Alize, dat's my girl, everyday. Making him thousand of dollars a day was nothing! Alize, controlled things, really. She took care of business with him more than I did. That's before Alize and I had our son. Fast Money always complained that I was too slow for him. He wanted money and was always in a hurry to go back to his New York connect. I was always messing shit up."

"Would Alize be willing to testify to these facts?"

"I don't think so."

"Not even to help you out in your situation with Baltimore City's State's Attorney's Office? The more proof and witnesses you can provide—along with those photos--the better off you will be. This is all with *our* help, of course."

"No. She wouldn't talk to the police when our apartment was invaded and the stick-up boys robbed her at gunpoint. I was willing to go to the police back then, but she refused to cooperate. She has always listened to Fast Money when he said over and over again that what goes on in the streets…stays in the street."

"Did you report who the actual robbers where to authorities?"

"I heard it was two brothers who did the stick up— Flubber and Fruity. But I don't know that for sure. That's what we heard on the streets, though. I found out their real names and where they live at."

"Okay. You can continue," the other agent said. *He showed little concern for what I was revealing.*

"Another thing I want to discuss is the jewelry store heist where the store owner was killed and innocent bystander was hit. They took almost a half of million dollars worth of platinum jewelry. Well, the guy Rock, the one Fast Money was working for at the time, bought close to a hundred thousand dollars worth for about twenty-five thousand and some ounces of raw cocaine. That's what we were selling at the time."

"How do you know Rock and what's his real name?"

"I know him through Fast Money. Fast Money is the person Alize gave the money to. He also showed 'em to me after Rock got 'em, but the guys who committed the robbery ended up getting locked up with some of the jewelry a few weeks later.

"Some people were saying that Rock was an informer because of all the charges he beat. Most times the street rumors are true about those telling. He's still out there selling weed. I'm quite sure if he was picked up that he'd be providing information, too."

"Does Fast Money or Rock still have any of the jewelry to your knowledge?"

"I think so because Fast Money was still wearing them at his Platinum parties even after things went bad for him with his connect in New York. And if you can't get anything from them, my girl Alize has a piece of that jewelry she wears. Fast Money gave her that piece. You know I didn't like that he was giving my girl jewelry back then. I would have gone to the police about everything, but at the time I was getting high. So, I just left it alone. I knew Fast Money wasn't fuckin' my girl, but I was jealous because she was under his spell. This is the first time I've said something. I always held it inside."

"Do you know more about this New York drug connection that Fast Money was involved in?"

"Yeah—I mean yes. I just know he was gettin' kilos of high grade cocaine and sometimes dope. He did tell me one time—and this ain't no lie--that Big Toney introduced him to a guy named Raul or something. I'd be willing to testify to that. Big Toney had the guy Raul in Baltimore. He was at one of Fast Money's parties before. My girl has the picture."

"Were Big Toney and Fast Money partners?"

"No. They didn't have a partnership, but they were both working for Raul in New York. It had something to do with a police station or a New York Police Officer. They took turns going to get it, bringing kilos back. They both helped each other that way. Fast Money was the one who had the gurl, Pretty, carrying stuff—sometimes ten, fifteen, twenty bricks. She was helping to make arrangements at them fancy hotels. Y'all raided her house and got all that money and drugs from outta there. She's over here waiting for a bail or something. Now she'll probably be willing to testify, too. If she's not telling already, then, it's just a matter of time."

"What were you selling?"

"Tavon had just bought a lot of dope from New York. Juvenile was his lieutenant. He was the one I was working with. He put different stamps on the bags. We were selling D.O.A. on Franlintown Road. This wasn't far from Tavon's mother house. We would switch up sometimes and sell *Suicide* and *Lethal Weapon* and *Poison*."

"Anything else?"

"He was buying stuff from a guy named Jose before he beat him for close to a hundred thousand dollars. That's not the only thing, though. Fast Money and Tavon once told me how they were able to get all kinds of guns from Virginia at some terminal or dock—straight off of cargo ships—with the help of one of their F.B.I. friends. They were getting the large shipment of guns from some Doctor or somebody like that in Virginia. Plus, they were getting those big guns from an agent name Carl. All you have to do is search around and you'll find out who I'm talking about. He's one of your own."

"Why do you suspect him of being, as you said, one of our own?"

"That's all Tavon talked about. Carl was the only one of them who made it out of the hood with a career. I do know this, though. Carl, the F.B.I. guy, was the one who supplied them with fake identification so they could shoot at this range out in Anne Arundel County. I met them once or twice to give him money and Carl was there.

"Another thing—'cause I don't want to forget. Tavon, the guy I was with that got shot by the police, was working for Fast Money, too. That's before he branched out. I started working for Tavon like everybody else. He was taking care of my girl and my son for me. Juvenile was Tavon's partner, but started messing with his gurl. I was with Tavon because Juvenile had violated the code. Tavon had too many people pressuring him to do something."

"Did you have any weapons? Or at any time did you discharge a firearm?"

"No, I ain't do nothing. Tavon was the one who set everything up—not me! Tavon's girlfriend's name is Precious. She probably has all his money and the drugs he just bought at her house. That's where he was staying. Plus, he got the guns from his mother house up Westside. Dat's where he keeps his guns and drugs most times."

"Do you know his mother's real name?"

"All I know is that they call her P-Nut. And his father is Dollar Bill. Y'all got him already in the feds."

"Do you know where we can locate his girlfriend Precious?"

"I sure do. Give me something so I can write the address down. If y'all go inside her house, she'll definitely have something there."

"Where's your friend by the name of Juvenile?"

"He was the one Tavon shot. I just happened to be in the right place at the wrong time. I didn't have anything to do with what happened!"

"Anything else?"

"Yeah. I'm trying to tell you everything I know because I ain't trying to stay in no jail. I got a newborn son and gurl out there that needs me.

"Plus, if you need a gun, I can send you to my girl's home address to get two. I just want out of this—no matter what!"

"Well, Mr. Carey. We have all the information you provided. We'll be in contact. Until then, I want you to read these notes that I took. After reading each page, I want you to initial each acknowledging that you agree. Sign and date the last page."

After signing, they gathered the papers ready to leave. I asked, "Man, alright. Are y'all going to get me out?"

"Don't call us—we'll call you," Agent Dillon said.

I listened to them laugh while waiting for the guard to open the security door.

"Tom. They don't get it, do they?"

"Get what, partner?"

"We don't have to do detective work anymore because rats like him make our work easy."

Chapter 7

PRECIOUS

"Spread Love to all my dead thugs.
I pour out a little Louis to a head above."
                                    Jay-Z, *"Lucifer"*
                                    The Black Album

A couple of days had passed by since I found out what happened. I'm still in shock because my whole life changed with one death and there's nothing I could do. I tried shutting down and not answer any phones, but life wouldn't allow it. It was too late for gossip now. My young hustler was gone.

Andre, one of Tavon's friends who was a federal agent, stopped over the house. And if it wasn't for his persistent banging on the front door, he wouldn't have got inside either. He told me, from information he gathered, that they were having another memorial service today in a different part of town and thought I should be there. I'd already missed one. One was already held in West Baltimore on Franklintown Road.

I know I wasn't expected. I probably wasn't welcomed, but I showed up anyway. I pulled up in Tavon's gold Mercedes, the last one he bought--or should I say the one I bought because it's in my name. Come to think of it, even the BMW he bought for Juvenile is in my name, so when all this shit blows over I'll have that one, too. That's not important right now anyway. What people were saying about me was.

The rumors about why he died were getting out of hand, especially when my name comes up. This seems to be what everybody is talking about. They're even saying all of this happened over me. Nobody is blaming anything on Juvenile. He was the one who started this fire, with a little help from me of course. Besides, a girl has gotta do what she has to do to get those unmet desires satisfied. Now that weak ass Juvenile is too scared to show his face and put the fire out.

I sat in my car and watched the people interact while I took a couple shots of Hennessy. A quick thought ran through my mind. If it's one thing I'm not, it's stupid. With all of these cars in my name, I don't have to deal with his crazy ass mother. Now everything is mine. I still wish I would've found more money. I know it's in there and I looked everywhere, but I can't find it.

I'm gonna miss him because he made me one of the stars in this game. He was another hustler making sure I was living proof that crime does pay.

A good smelling fast food aroma filled the air—even over the strong alcohol smell in my nose. I watched several cars lining up in front of the memorial site. Familiar and not so familiar faces gathered at the corner of Greenmount Ave and Preston Street. Just like me, many people came out to see what was going on.

Young adult males were outnumbered. Daps and the sounds of skin slapping hard against two human hands was heard randomly in the crowd. More women were exchanging more handshakes than men.

Passing cars paid their respects each time a horn sounded. This was a sign of hood respect to those living and dead. This was the street, the space where dried red bloodstains made us remember his life; and the place where white chalk marks identified his death. For one person, life in the fast lane had ended and today's gathering helped to remember a common tragedy that happens far too often.

I usually travel with Pretty in situations like this and really miss her not being here. She's had my back for years. The only time she crossed me was with my ex-husband Dollar Bill and we worked that out a long time ago.

I had to get my nerve up, so I took another shot of Hennessy. I looked around again, since I was alone, to make sure it was safe before I got out. This was a little tough for me to handle because I could feel the suspicious stares. I don't know how many phone calls and voice mails I received cursing me out. I don't know if I can be another no-good-bitch *and still be alive. You would think I pulled the trigger.*

I put the cap on my bottle because several marked police cars were circling the block. Suddenly, I heard the sound of tires screeching and looked up to see two undercover policemen jumping out of an unmarked Ford Explorer with tinted windows. They had blue Auto Task Force t-shirts on and vests under them. Both officers threw a man who was sitting on his car against the wall for a search. Then they forced him to kneel on both knees and put his hands behind his head. One officer was holding him at bay while the other was searching around for anything he could find. He was picking up soda cans, potato chip bags and aluminum foil wrappers from Yellow Bowl Restaurant trying to find anybody's stash.

All this action forced regular activity on the strip to stop, only for a minute, since they had no other choice but to give those crazy police respect.

"Keep your hands on you head. Now stand up real slow—and don't make any sudden moves," he said, standing behind him closely.

"What did I do, Officer?" the man said, obeying the officer's commands.

Patting him down in a quick body search, the officer said, "Shut your ass up. I'll ask the questions."

"I ain't got nothing on me—and I ain't do nothin'."

"Keep your ass still," he said, slamming him against the wall. "I don't care who shit it is. If my partner finds anything, your black ass is going to jail."

It was clear that they didn't find anything. It's like they wanted him to get out of line so they could lock him up, but he never said another word. Eventually, they let him go.

Damn. I can't imagine going through that with the police. Worse than that, I can't see how all these guys risk their lives everyday. Oh, well. That was their business. Today, mine was paying my respects to my man.

I had my hair in a wrap and my jewelry could be seen probably from across the street. I had to make my presence known. I was styling one of those Christian Lacroix dresses with a sharp pair of Zanotti designer sandals to match. This was the first time I'd worn this outfit Fast Money bought for me in Hollywood at one of those small boutiques. I remember that trip with him like it was just yesterday...

I got out feeling a buzz. Looking around, all I could see were sad faces on hand to celebrate the life of a hustler. This candlelight vigil was one of the ends of the game. Tavon was gone. It didn't matter whether he was dead or locked away. It all meant the same to me. The replacement process has to start all over again.

People were standing around in scattered bunches waiting for things to begin. A woman with a small box was passing out candles to the crowd. She extended the box my way, so I took one.

Not far from where I stood, some of Tavon's friends were gathering in a separate group. His crews from different parts of the city represented at his street memorial. Some barely waved to me while others were looking at me like I was a ghost. One heavy set guy dressed in black had just come from across the street at the bar carrying two cases of beer. A big bottle of Louis was being carried by another guy who was dressed in all black as well and was literally shining with diamonds. 'Hmmm? I wonder who that is?'

The whole crew took turns pulling bottles from two Heineken cases sitting on the steps next to them. Crew members dressed in black with Tavon's picture showing on their t-shirts took turns spreading love: As each one of them spoke, they were pouring out some Louis in his memory and passing the bottle around.

I could hear them talking about the good times they shared with my man. They even shared some words about some other dead thugs. A couple of them told Tavon to hold them down because they would be following behind him.

People were still gathered in small crowds talking about what happened.

"I was out here when it happened," this older man said, pointing not far from where we were standing. "I was standing right there 'cause the young boy PayDay had just served me a pill of dope when they crashed the car right there. The police jumped out right behind his car and started screaming on the bullhorn. I thought they were trying to get my old black ass, so I swallowed the dope real quick and ran the other way! I wasn't trying to spend no time over *The Bookings!*"

"Oh, yeah," the younger guy said in response. "I wasn't out here, but my girl was. She saw what happened with her own eyes. Plus, she almost got hit by the car the guys were driving. She said they crashed because they were going too fast trying to bend the corner."

"Well, I was. And I saw the shit with my own eyes," the older man said, demonstrating with his hands how the police held his gun. "The police only gave him two short warnings before they started shooting. BAM! BAM! BAM! Dat' shit scared the shit outta me!"

"My girl said he died right there near the pole," the younger guy said pointing behind me. "She said you could tell he was dead, but they stilled dragged his body in the middle of the street."

"Yeah," the older man chimed in, "he was out and we all could see it! They were still asking him questions. You could see the boy was dead. All he needed was a fucking ambulance."

"No shit?" the young boy commented. *He stood in disbelief while shaking his head.* "My cousin Rabbit said the dude was getting money, too. But he had a high-maintenance freak riding him and his partner and that's what started this whole thing."

A younger girl standing there listening to all of this conversation broke out into song: "*I ain't saying she no gold digger, but she ain't messing with no broke-broke. Get down, girl—go head—get down...*"

Why did I know that would eventually come up? I was a bit surprised by this comment or the little girl's song, but knew that I had to endure much more in the coming weeks and months as long as I stayed in Baltimore.

"It was right there where she's standing," the older man said, pointing to the blood stains close to me. As they both looked at me, he said, "His head was right here where this red spot of dried blood is before they dragged him."

I had no idea I was standing so close to the spot where he was shot. Looking down on the ground, the bloodstains were right under my feet. I felt myself getting sick from all the descriptions I was hearing about how he got killed.

I heard a commotion behind me and turned around to see what was happening, I saw a lady pointing towards me and a younger woman coming at me in full force.

"There's that bitch right there!" some older voice screamed in the crowd.

"Get her ass—'cause she's the reason why this happened to Tavon!" another voice screamed, feeling a wild fist landing against the side of my head.

The force knocked me backward. I staggered a bit, but luckily maintained a standing position. When I turned completely around I noticed it was Tavon's mother, P-Nut, screaming at the top of her voice. She was cheering on this wild acting woman whose fists kept connecting with my face. I felt another punch in my stomach. This time I couldn't keep standing. I fell protecting myself, trying to keep down the alcohol that was anxious to come up. Everything shook when I crashed hard against the ground. Looking up, trying to figure out who this was, the only thing about her looking familiar was Tavon's face on her black shirt.

48

"Now beat! dat'! bitch! Ass! Alize—and I mean make her cruddy ass pay for all that shit she caused!" P-Nut screamed. "I told you! You ain't gett'n away with none of this!"

It seemed like the crowd was shifting and moving out of the way. It was just the two of us. I could hear voices in the background shouting at me. With no signs of help, I fought back trying to get her off of me.

"Get the hell off of me!" I screamed, trying to free myself.

"Snatch all dat' *bitch* jewelry off her neck, dat's Tavon's Money," P-Nut screamed.

I could feel the burn from her scratches to my face. I knew I had to find a way to get this crazy woman off me. She was tearing my clothes and snatching my jewelry like it belonged to her. Tavon had already bruised my damn face. Now she was trying to destroy it.

"Help me somebody! Get dis' crazy bitch offa' me!" I screamed. *I was crying out for some help, but everybody just stood there.*

"Cry some more, bitch—cause ain't nobody gonna help your dirty ass!"

"Hell no! Bitch, you better get your dirty ass off a me! Help me somebody, please!" I screamed. *Defensively, I tried to push her upwards. I could feel my nails tearing backwards.*

After throwing another punch that thankfully missed, she screamed, "You think you a cute Ho--hah, Bitch?"

"Who the fuck are you! You better get your ass *offa'* me. Why are you doing this?" *I yelled.*

"You got Tavon killed and my son's father locked up. All this shit is because of you," she screamed before spitting in my face.

"Beat her ass Alize—and I mean: Beat! Her! Ass! She's the one who took my son away from here!" P-Nut screamed before kicking me in the side.

"Somebody help me, please? Ms. P-Nut, I can't fight this gurl--she's crazy! Somebody--please, help!"

Before I knew it, I was feeling her fist crashing harder into my face again. This girl was too wild for me to handle. I didn't come down here expecting to fight. I knew I wasn't welcome, but never did I expect something like this.

I could hear a man's voice screaming in the crowd. "Police, y'all. Here comes 5-O!"

The heavy blows stopped, but my ears were still ringing. I could hear police walkie-talkies close to my head.

"Alright! Break it up!" one officer screamed.

"Joe, you get her and I'll take this one," the other officer said to his partner.

Someone had finally come to my rescue.

"Dat's right. She assaulted me officer," the young girl said angrily to the officer who was grabbing her. "I was just standing there and she walked up and hit me. Officer, I want to press charges against her ass!"

I finally got my bearings and was ready to respond. All of a sudden, I felt strong hands snatching me off the ground. My head felt like it weighed a ton. And I was tasting blood in my mouth instead of the drinks I had earlier.

"Officers, that's not true," I screamed in disbelief. "I was just standing here and she came from behind and started hitting me. She should be charged with attempted murder because she was trying to kill me down there!"

"Mam, have you been drinking?"

"Yeah, my man was just killed—so, hell yeah, I had a goddamn drink!"

I could hear the handcuffs snap. I felt a sense of joy because they were actually locking that crazy woman up. Justice had run its course, finally.

"Thank you, officer, for saving my life," I told him.

"I'm sorry, mam, but you're also under arrest for disorderly conduct and disturbing the peace. We're taking you in, too."

"For what officers? She attacked me! I was just..."

"Save it for the commissioner over Central Booking," he said, cutting my explanation short.

"Unit 366 to dispatch. I need a female officer on the scene, Greenmount and Preston. We have two female suspects in custody."

"Alize. You'll be out in no time baby," P-Nut boasted, walking away with the crowd. "That's right, Precious! You thought you got away with killing my son, but this shit ain't over yet. That was just the beginning—you snake!"

Being slammed against the car didn't bother me as much as the cuffs. That cold steel was stopping my blood from circulating. Still, I don't care! I'm just glad the police came when they did because this crazy gurl would have killed me.

Chapter 8

P-NUT

"This can't be LIFE...
It's gotta be more."
                              Jay-Z, *"This can't be life"*
                              The Dynasty Album

    This has been the longest week of my life. Only six days had passed since my whole world turned upside down but it seems like forever. I shouldn't be on my way to the front row of the church burying my son. The way I was living each day, I just knew my son would be burying me.

    I still can't believe it! First of all, the cops murdered my son. Now I'm hearing the other person who helped to kill my son was supposed to be his best friend. Juvenile was like another son to me—him and Tavon grew up in the streets together. To make it worse, it was all over dat' bitch of a woman he had because she was creeping off with Juvenile. That's why I had Outlaw's girl, Alize, beat her like she stole somethin'. I hope she won't try to show up here today. If she does, what this funeral won't be is nice!

    I'm losing my son. So, every time I get a chance she's losing something, too. She's not getting away with this! Neither will Juvenile for that matter. Can somebody please tell me why I'm thinking about all this stuff on my way to church? I think the Lord will understand though because he knows it ain't an easy thing burying your only child.

I tried not to use anything this week because it really hit me when Jameel told me Tavon's wish was for me to get clean. And to make it worse, he doesn't want her to give me any cash until I get my act together. I tried not to get high, but couldn't hold out. It wasn't like I was trying to get high for the hell of it. I just needed something to make me relax. But as soon as I get out of here, in memory of my son, I'm gonna tell Jameel to find me a place. I'm going straight into rehab.

I know my son left me a whole lot and I'm gonna get mine. I tried to go around Jameel's authority when I called the lawyer directly, but that didn't work. He said everything had to work through Jameel.

I knew my son was popular. From the turnout, it seemed like a lot of people loved him, too. It was nowhere to park when we pulled up in the limousines. All of these fancy cars were double-parked. Some cars parked in the space reserved for family.

Walking into the church, my mind played tricks on me. It was if I was being punished the way my body trembled. I never knew there was any other pain that felt as bad as withdrawal pains. This shit ain't easy, I'm telling you.

Young people attending the wake stood just outside the chapel entrance. Most of them were young and wore blue bandanas tied around their heads. Their T-shirts had my baby's picture on the front. One shirt said, "Tavon, hold me down because I'm right behind you."

When the family processional walked into the sanctuary of the church people started crying and screaming. That made me weaker at the knees. I had no strength to hold myself up. Jameel was right by my side whispering a sweet gospel tune in my ear as we walked toward my son's lifeless body.

I was just standing there, still not believing my eyes, looking down at my baby boy in this casket, when a sea of painful tears broke free of my control. I couldn't stop crying. With wet tears on my hand after wiping my face, I was able to fix his tie and straighten out his clothes. My son needed me to support him all the way to the end. His father did, too. And I treated him just like I did when he was my growing child.

So many thoughts keep racing through my head— leading up to this day...

When Leroy called me a few days ago in tears about his son I was speechless. It's a damn shame that the federal government denied his father permission to come to the funeral. Granting him a furlough to come to view his son's body was out of the question. I tried to comfort his father, but I was in pain myself, and had a hard time keeping it together. My body was shaking, and my nose wouldn't stop running down in my mouth. I had nobody to lean on because the only person I could trust with my life was dead. I couldn't take it any more and finally dropped the phone. I was going through this all by myself.

* * * * * * * *

The floral arrangements Jameel and I chose sat at the base of the pulpit. Tavon always liked flowers and she really got it right. I didn't know it was enough to surround his white casket. On the right side of him, there was a bleeding heart with my name on it. Jameel took me to the florist to get that one especially. Just looking around I couldn't have done any better myself. And when this is all over, I'm gonna have to thank Jameel and Charmaine.

My only request was having a photo of Tavon, his father and me be placed inside his casket. That's the one photo reminding me of days gone by. If I could turn back the hands of time and do it all over again...I probably would. I just wouldn't start using. Soon, that's gonna change.

"Ms. Kamila," the soft voice said, lightly tapping me on my shoulder. "Are you okay?"

Although stepping into my thoughts gently, the interruption still caught me off guard. "Jameel, I'll be alright, baby," I told her. "I just didn't know so many people loved my son like they do."

"We all did. That's why so many of us are here. And we love you, too," she said, embracing me as she's done since this happened.

"We thank God for all those who have come to the House of the Lord for this funeral service. We'd like to give a special thanks to Charmaine at Brownstone's funeral home for all these beautiful arrangement. We invite God in our midst and send out a special prayer for the family--as this is the ending of the waking hour," the minister said.

I'm sitting here not really believing I'm at my son's funeral service. Even now, the preacher is talking, but my mind is coming and going. What I can't do is get things off my mind. Like now, I can't stop thinking about that early morning knock on my door with this news.

The young minister continued, "We ask the family, if they would like to come around again—and then those who wish to greet the family with compassion may do so after that time."

"Would you like to go back up Ms. Kamila?" Jameel asked.

I tried to get up by myself, but I couldn't even make it half way. "Help me, please?" *I had to see my baby one last time—for my husband who couldn't be here and the memories of saying a final goodbye. Jameel put her arms around me and helped me up.*

"Oh, God! Why did this have to happen to my son!" I cried out, as the pain ripped through my body. "He was a good boy and ain't bother nobody!"

With no more tears to cry, I sat back down in deep sorrow. The pain had me existing in weakness and all I could think was how it's a damn shame that my son's life had to end like this. My conscience keeps chasing and I can't lie any longer. I have to accept responsibility for him being involved in the hustle. That's the hardest part. I raised him to fail and throw his life away. Failure was the only thing possible in that life because there are no successful drug dealers. I knew that, but I had no idea it would be his death. And maybe I'm not in so much mourning for him as I am for myself in guilt. Just look at me. I don't know when I'm gonna be able to look in a mirror again. I can't stand how I feel much less what I would see.

"Ms. Marsh, God bless you. And if there's anything I can do, you be sure to let me know," this woman said to me in a calming voice, fanning me, bringing fresher air to my pain. *Her daughter was standing right by her side in tears looking down on me.*

I looked up to see some of Tavon's workers standing over the casket.

"Oh, God!" I screamed. *I started wondering if Tavon knew some of the stuff I was doing behind his back to get high. I guess the worse part of it is trying to suck his workers off so I could get money when he wouldn't give me any. When he did give me money, I was supposed to get food and pay bills—I know—but there were more important things to do, like denying my body food so I could feed my brain a hit of that crack.*

My son always wanted me to clean myself up. And all I wanted in sobriety *was to abuse the word to get money for my next blast. I'd beg him to send me away, but first I needed to get my last one. He'd give it to me and I'd disappear for days.*

As I leaned forward, trying to ease some of my mental pain, my horseshoe pendant dangled on my necklace. 'That was the only thing I had left to remind me of Tavon,' I thought to myself. I had pawned everything else. He gave me this horseshoe for good luck. But I took him through so many changes with this thing. Just looking at it, you can see it was very expensive. I would pawn it either at the pawnshop or to some of his competition on the block when he cut me off. Some way he'd find out—like he had somebody always watching me. He'd get it back. This time I got it back on my own using the money in the safe, but he'll never know it.

"Ms. Marsh, you remember me, I'm Agent Cousins, but you remember me as Tavon's friend Andre? We all went to school together and was just together some time ago," the familiar face said, embracing me and talking softly in my ear.

56

"Tavon is definitely going to be missed. Here's one of my cards—and if there's anything I can do for you, just let me know.

"Ms. Marsh, there were other people involved in what happened to your son before city police intervened. And I promise, as a federal agent, I'm going to help find all of those with information about this case. If you have any information, please, call me at this number," he said, shaking my hand before moving on.

I didn't have the energy to respond. I wanted tell him how heartless and cold those police have been, but now wasn't a good time for my complaints. Besides, he was right, it wasn't those who were involved with him in the streets that were to blame. It was them—the police who killed him. I held his card tightly in my hands with all the energy I had left. All this was coming to an end too soon.

I noticed two guys almost dressed alike walked slowly pass me to look at my son in his casket. They were the last to see him before the family was called for a final viewing. I recognized them right away because they look like twins. I always get them mixed up. They were Jameel's brothers. Flubber and Fruity both knew my son and I very well. They both hugged me, Jameel, and Jameel's little daughter Tiffany.

"That concludes the wake," the young minister said, as Jameel's brothers moved away. "Bear with us as we prepare for the home-going service of Anthony, most of us know him as Tavon Truston. Thank you," he said, rubbing his hands together nervously in his white gloves.

After briefly bowing his head and keeping his hands in a prayer position, he began pointing at Jameel inviting her to come forward.

As the other caretaker started covering my son's body in his casket, I could hear screams coming from every corner of the church. It was all too emotional for me. Every time I think I've got myself together with the tears, I fall apart again.

As soon as Jameel stood, someone came and sat beside me. The sounds of screams shot through me and I could no longer control myself. The last thing I remembered was trying to get up. My faint body couldn't take anymore. When I came back to, I found myself wailing in Jameel's mother's arms as they tried to lift me from the floor.

"No God! Why my son?! He was supposed to bury me!! Tavon, I'm soooo sorry, baby!"

"Ms. Marsh are you okay?" Jameel asked, as her voice finally cracked in pain.

"Why did it have to happen to my baby! Jameel—why?"

"Ms. Marsh, God won't put anything on you that you cannot bear," she said, holding me. *Her tears fell on my face.* "We're going to give Tavon a real funeral service," she told me. "I have to get up and start the service. Remember, I'll just be up on the choir loft. If you need me just give me a sign. Momma is gonna stay right here beside you."

The preacher introduced her to the crowd as she turned away from me and walked to the podium.

"I pray my strength as I sing this song to my brother, Tavon Anthony Truston," Jameel said. "*God* ensures us life— and *He* ensures life more abundantly. But we know we have to continue condemning the devil because he constantly *kills*, *steals* and *destroys* our people. This body lying here is only Tavon's shell. This is not him. We all have him inside our hearts. We can no longer sit quiet and allow this to happen to our black men. I ask that all the believers continue to pray for his mother and family and ask that *God* heals our land. And to change this, we have to take action. Praying for change on our knees is fine. But we also have to get up with ambition to influence change or this is going to happen again and again."

"Amen!" a voice shouted from behind.

"Precious Lord.
Take my hand.
Lead me home let me stand.
I am tired, I am weak, I am worn..."

Jameel sang my son a heartbreaking version of Precious Lord. I'm not spiritual at all, but it brought me and everyone else to our feet. After she finished her solo, Jameel introduced my son's goddaughter. Tiffany was right beside her ready to read a poem she wrote to my son.

"My mommy and I thanked Jesus in a prayer for my godfather. That's why I asked mommy to help me write him this poem called My Godfather."

"My Godfather I love—
so funny and true.
You loved me ever since I was a baby.
Now I'm sending you home. I miss you already.
Mommy is always crying and I don't really understand why.
But I told Mommy and Daddy,
Jesus took you home.
Heaven is a peaceful place. It is filled with love and everything nice.
I hope you accepted Jesus.
My Sunday school teacher showed us, "He is the key to everlasting life."

Love, Your Goddaughter
Tiffany

The shouts of "Amen" *and* "thank you Jesus" *seemed like they were never gonna stop after little Tiffany's words and Jameel's song. It took some time for the crowd to calm before the Pastor took the floor. He came to the pulpit with his message from God. All I could think of was how fast this all was happening.*

"We thank *God* for all those family members and friends of Tavon Anthony Truston who came out for his last rites," the young minister said. "Tavon was a neighborhood kid. We all are guilty of standing by—watching him in silence—as he grew up in the footsteps of those who came before him. I don't mean to speak any evil against anyone who this may affect, but this is a tragedy. God knows it is! Having Tavon lie in a state of rest at his young age could be nothing but a tragedy. I know there was a time in my ministry that I would sugar coat *The Word* just to give comfort to those who are living, but I have grown. I have grown to understand *God's* word when he tells us *He* is not a man that will tell a lie. Being *His* disciple, neither can I. *God* promises us all in *His* word that we should have life—and we should enjoy life more abundantly. But each time we turn on the news we hear of another tragedy the devil has provoked.

"We hear in one night how two or three or four people were gunned down on these wicked streets of Baltimore City. I don't know about you, but I get tired of turning on the news— fearing what I may hear next. Somebody help me because this can't be life. It's gotta be more that being alive has to offer us.

"See, I'm tired of the devil trying to shame God's word. At times, the devil seems to get the best of us in a bad situation. I know he sometimes gets to me, but I have to rebuke that devil and stand on *God's* promise.

"See, there are issues as a Minister and Disciple of *God* I have to stay away from," the Pastor screamed. "I've asked Tavon's mother whether he was saved. We're mere man and woman. Tavon's mother nor I can say whether he was really saved because he could've confessed his sacrifice for *God* to come into his life in his final hour. It is not for us to judge. *God* will open the books and judge our young son and determine whether he is worthy for the kingdom of promise or not.

"Too often are we having these funeral services for soldiers of the wrong army. I'm careful in my ministry because I don't say too often that those outside of a church are going home to be with *The Master*. That's not my call. Only those belonging to a church family, our church family, can I say 'home-going service.' Those who are worthy of the promise of John 3:16 understand what I'm saying. 'What are you saying Pastor?' I'm saying for *God* so loved the world that *He* gave His only begotten son. I'm saying this child was born through *God's* handy work. His life was of *God*, but his death is not the work of *God*. A planted tree was cut down in the prime of his life. You see, Tavon was supposed to be caught up in the spirit to meet *Him* in the air when he comes.

"We must know that service is important to being saved and eternal life. We can't be doing the devil's work and claim to be of *God*. We can't tear things up selling drugs and then think that service can be converted to mean something else at funerals. Tavon had his chance to serve. And as I said, it is *God* who opens the books to make that judgment. Hopefully, and only God knows, Tavon was able to confess before he was killed by a police bullet. Let the church say Amen?"

"Amen, Pastor!"

"I prayed and asked for guidance in what I was going to say to Tavon's family and friends—all of you gathered here today. I had no personal message I wanted to relay besides one of sadness. It's sad when we moan for another mother because she has lost her child at a very young age. It's sad when we have a mother bury her child long before his rightful time to depart this earth. It's sad that we keep doing the devil's work and allow people to blame it on God why this happened. We should see our male children caught up in the spirit and not caught up in conspiracy or shot down in the streets. The church can no longer be silent and play along with all that's going on.

"We have all the answers. There's no question whose work this is. The devil has tricked another one of our young black males into service. The devil knows the condemnation they all face if they get caught serving him. He was cast down first and he wants others to follow. For all those who know the streets, the devil needs a rap-buddy. He needs a codefendant to help violate *God's* law and blame things on. That's why the devil tried to tempt *Jesus*. He told *Christ* that he could have it all if he

61

would bow down and worship him. For that split second the devil expected *Christ* to fall down on his knees and worship him. To do that, to praise the enemy, *Christ* would have been forced to curse *God*. His service to the enemy would have been a disservice to his mission for us to follow and his life upon this earth. But a thought comes to mind about what we see all the time riding through the streets. How many times, congregation, do we see young boys on their knees in the service of the enemy? What's the first thing police do when they ride down on these corners?

"The bible said the devil came to steal, kill, and destroy, not *God*, church. There are people here under the sound of my voice who don't know *God* in the pardon of their sins. Now is the time to accept him into your life."

The message was harsh but it was certainly the truth. I just hope some of them young people heed this message today, I know, I'm gonna set my life straight. As I surveyed the church one last time, I saw that evil woman, Precious, sitting in the last row. I could feel anger starting to take over from my sadness. 'She got some nerve,' I thought to myself. 'How could she show up here knowing full well how Tavon died?'

I turned away and looking straight ahead of me. I was trying not to act on my first instincts and cause a scene at my son's funeral. Looking back to the front of the church, I saw Jameel trying to make eye contact with me. As soon as she realized I was looking for her, she put both of her hands together in a praying position. That was my sign. I guess she sensed that I was about to burst.

Those thoughts had me zoned out. When I realized it, the preacher had finished his message and was giving the benediction. My son's body was going home to his Maker.

After everything was said and done at the church, we followed the processional to Lansdowne Cemetery. We gathered while the minister said a few words. That was it. A few words marked the end of my baby boy's life.

Chapter 9

JAMEEL

This can't be LOVE...
It's gotta be more."

Jay-Z, "This can't be life"
The Dynasty

Pastor gave a powerful message. The devil is certainly busy working on people he knows will shine God's light. Three young people were saved at the alter call at the end of Tavon's funeral service. A church family like ours can never thank God enough for sending more and more followers to the truth.

After a short burial, Tiffany, Momma and I followed the funeral car to Ms. Kamila's house. She and Tavon had no family beside each other. It's really sad because all the others are either locked up or dead. What friends she did make through the years in the streets were by her side to offer what little support they could at a small repast.

If there was ever a time I used the word hate it was related to these senseless killings and the funerals that follow. He was a good friend and godfather and showed a great heart to those he knew. Still, I know that isn't enough to get him into heaven. All this sad excitement keeps me thinking about Dorian.

'When will the killings stop?' That's all I keep asking myself in silence because Dorian just showed up at my house the other night acting very strange and needing some place to stay. Right now he is in my basement, windows covered, and has my cellar door barricaded. He's paranoid--living in fear, thinking

the same thing is going to happen to him. He knew I wouldn't offer him a place to stay until I gave him a piece of my confused mind. He made me promise not to tell, but all that was going on between them had me feeling like somebody else was going to die...

In my silence, I couldn't stop thinking about what brought us together. I think it's crazy what happened between two friends. They let the power of the streets trick them out of their power of love. The real sad reality left for all of those living is how everybody around us becomes one in pain when somebody is murdered. Living like this can't be love. We say a lot more than we actually do because most of us go right back to the life we blamed for causing each tragedy in the first place. And it has got to be more that life has to offer.

What was good, I thought, was having Tavon's wish come true when Ms. Kamila came to me crying during the funeral...

"Jameel, I need a program," she said between her tears. "I need to get some help because I can't keep living like this no more! God knows I can't live like a dope fiend all my life!"

"Don't worry, you can get all the help you want," I assured her. "An associate minister from the church runs a treatment center called Tuerk House up on Ashburton Street. Placement at that center is fast and I'll make sure I get you in there—right away," I said as Tiffany used some Kleenex to wipe her tears.

"I promised God, if he keeps me strong and carries me through this storm in my life, my soul is *His* for the taking. I'm promising to get my life together by getting off those drugs. I've been messing up my life and my body for the last three decades, Jameel, and it's time for a change."

In the News
Baltimore City

Over the weekend authorities reported a fatal house fire in West Baltimore. Wayne Fossett, a long-time heroin addict, was under the influence when he lit a candle in attempts of burning a heroin filled spoon. A small flame is needed to warm the chemical substance turning it from powder to liquid before injection. Fossett admitting to leaving the candle burning in the basement area.

The property was without gas and electric and has been for some time now, according to family interviews. His grandchildren were injured in the fire. Ebony, 5, and Latasha, 7, were both pronounced dead at University Hospital's Shock Trauma Unit from first degree burns and smoke inhalation. Investigation into this tragic fire is continuing.

Chapter 10

JUVENILE

"Putting it down hard for my dawgz
that's locked in the thang
When you hit the bricks...
Money Ain't a Thang."
    Jay-Z, *"Money Ain't A Thang"*
    Vol. 2... Hard Knock Life
    (f/ Jermaine Dupree)

I've been trying to avoid her, but I knew she would have to say what's on her mind before I would get some rest. She told me she was taking the day off to talk to me without Tiffany being in the house. Almost half the day had already passed because I was pretending to be too busy or sleeping every time she came downstairs.

"Dorian, you can't keep living like this! You're acting like a wild animal and all this stuff is scaring me and Tiffany," Jameel said to me, sitting down beside me on the bed in the basement.

"Jameel, I know but I just need some time," I said still pretending.

"And I don't have a problem with that, but why are you acting so paranoid? Is something else still going on?"

"Jameel, I told you my life was in danger! That's why I couldn't go to the funeral."

"And I believed you when you told me. That's why I was trying to get in touch with Tavon, but he wasn't returning my calls. So there was nothing I could do, Dorian. God knows I'm just glad that you're alright! I was so scared that something happened to you because I hadn't heard from you and then that lawyer came knocking on my door so early in the morning!"

"They tried to kill me! Everybody can't survive, but I did, Jameel—I did! And it's a reason why I'm still here to talk about it! I just need you to let me stay until I can get myself together. I'm scared of what may happen if I stay out on the streets because I know they'll be looking for me."

"I would never leave you out there to die, but Dorian I hope you understand why I'm going to help you. Living that life is a curse because we lost Tavon and so many others who should still be here—alive."

"I think about that even when I don't want to. I saw my own life flash in front of me. And all everybody talks about is 'How J get up out that?'"

"I hope you know how much we pray for you. One day you'll realize why you are still here. That's my wish before I die and leave this earth. I'd give my life so you could live yours. I hope you get yourself together and give yourself a chance."

"I can't justify genocide Jameel and I know you wanna understand what we go through out there, but the killing ain't gonna stop with Tavon. It's a lot more people that's gonna die before it's all over with. That's how it goes," I said, feeling like I was about to get a bit emotional.

"That's not how it has to end Dorian. That shouldn't be the end to anybody's story. The killing has to stop!"

"Jameel, that's why I'm here!" I said in anger, "I need your help. I'm tired of hustling. That's over for me—especially since all this crazy stuff is happening. Now, I'm so scared that I can't sleep. And when I do I can't wake up to a dry pillow."

"Dorian, don't think for one minute that I'm trying to raise our daughter by myself."

"I think about that all the time, too."

"That's why I refuse to let that happen to our daughter. She's going to have you in her life—and so am I. So you better get your act together and do it timely," Jameel said, sounding a bit stern, "because we need you in our lives."

"That's why I came to you."

"With all that being said, I'm gonna leave now, run some errands, and pick up Tiffany from school. Today I'm gonna check on Ms. Kamila to make sure she's okay because I need to pay her rent," she said, walking up the basement steps.

"Okay, but don't tell nobody I'm staying here," I answered, walking up the steps behind her. "And make sure you lock the doors real good."

I wasn't too pleased that she was doing all this for someone who tried to kill me. I know she's not looking at it like that and I'm not going to stop her from doing things her way. As soon as she left, I checked the door locks. I peeped out of the back window to make sure nobody was out there before getting something to eat out of the refrigerator. A few minutes later, I went upstairs to get a hot shower.

I've been through a lot of changes since Tavon's death. All that keeps running through my mind is that this can't be us. I couldn't even go to his funeral.

Come to think of it, that may have been a good thing. Hustlers draw other hustlers out, especially for a funeral service. It becomes a fashion statement—the who's who of the game shows up in record numbers. Of course, unseen pictures are snapped there. Photographic notes were being written across mental notepads because of the presence of special agents. Reports related to their investigation were probably due right away. Undercover cops taking photos fit in like neighborhood friends. That's why it probably worked out for the best because the feds and homicide covered that funeral like journalists did the O.J. Simpson murder trial. They were on it! That was then, though. Today is a new day...

But I can't help but think about everything. Having him as a partner was everything to me. I've seen better when he was here. Nobody could ever convince me that something would happen like this to him and me. All of a sudden everything fell apart and now he's gone--forever--and our money went with him. He held on to the cash and I can't get to it. I had Precious check the safe at her house. She said nothing was there. My back was against the wall and I had no other choices.

Even though I don't trust her greedy ass, I have that to deal with. I still have some money, but Tavon kept the bulk of it since we've been hustling on a bigger scale. That's how much I trusted him. That's why I know it's gotta be more somewhere.

After that hot shower, I went down the basement to stretch out on top of the bed with a fresh set of pajamas Jameel bought me. The first thing I grabbed in the room was my controller. I had time to get in a good game of NFL Street. That's how I relax and get all this crazy shit off my mind.

I suddenly changed my mind about playing my video game and walked back upstairs real quick to get me a soda. I peeped out of the window just to make sure everything around the house was okay. I keep my eyes on these eleven and twelve year-old kids running a crack spot across the alley. They run back and forth, up and down the alley all night. A quick thought of days gone by down on Franklintown Road ran through my mind before I went back down the basement.

I flipped through the channels to find something to watch. I surfed through HBO movies and found one of my all-time classics playing. I always had the dream of becoming a black Scarface in our neighborhood. I fluffed the pillows and put them at the headboard and got comfortable. I drifted a minute thinking of what Scarface would do if he was in my situation.

Other out-of-control thoughts were speeding through my mind like shooting stars. And it keeps playing over and over again because other people were involved—I know--and they have to be dealt with, but I can't deal with that by myself—not right now. For my own safety, I have to recover—by getting my mind right--and get on with my life with my family.

It wasn't my fault what happened to him. I might've been wrong about the girl thing, but he tried to kill me. Tavon shot me in the chest at point blank range. Still, everybody blames me for his death. He tried to run from the police after jumping out a getaway car, not me! I ain't have nothing to do with that.

My buddy Ty was lucky sitting high up in his Navigator truck, but I was even luckier for having that vest on. I thought I'd died and gone to ghetto heaven when I felt Butter dragging me in that house. Those shots blinded my eyes, knocked the wind out of my chest and replaced it with fire. I could sense things around me but the impact knocked me into another world. That weed had me gone! By the time police got there, Butter had me in the house snatching my vest off so I could breathe.

Hiding has me out of the game, for the most part. Yet, the streets stay on my mind. I was worried about what everybody was thinking about this whole situation. And I knew some of our homeboys, those who loved Tavon much more than they liked me, would be trying to get me. Truth is, I have that shit to deal with when it comes my way. I had to get even with everybody, but first I had to deal with Butter.

My plan is to stay away from everybody until things fall completely in place. And I will--until Trigger comes home. He's the only one who understands what's going on. He is my right hand man and when he hit the bricks I'll have everything he needs. Between us, money ain't a thing.

Trigger got Jameel's number from the message I gave his sister and called me the same night. He made it clear what he wanted. He vowed to get to those who helped Tavon try to kill me as bad as I did. He keep on telling me to be patient because he only got a few days left and once he came home we could deal with it together. He believed Butter knew more than what she's admitting. He also called me upset a few times after that conversation because he'd been hearing different stories. The streets were talking and all everybody kept confirming Dead-eye's involvement. Trigger knew Dead-eye could be dealt with, but Big Toney and Outlaw were locked up.

In the meantime, I had a plan for Fruity and Flubber. It was no secret how close I was with Tiffany's two uncles. Flubber and Fruity were wild and had reputations for slinging their guns in the faces of serious hustlers. They both had principle and I had plans...

Chapter 11

TRIGGER

"I'm so confrontational
They should've never let me go on probation, Yo.
I'm a hustler accept that—
No correctional facility can correct that."

Jay-Z, "Nymp "
VOL. 3...Life and Times of S.Carter

    I'm counting down my days in this hell hole. This shit ain't no joke. But any day now I'll be coming up outta dis joint. That's right, they would love to keep me here for the shit I've done, but there is something in the system called mandatory parole...and there's nothing these fake police can do about it. Ready or not, Baltimore, here I come!

    I'm mad as shit, though, with all that's been going on between my two homeboys on the street. Tavon knew he was wrong for making that trick Precious come between him and Juvenile. What da' fuck was he thinking? We never ever let any one break us down or come between us, especially a freak. Was pussy the reason why he violated loyalty amongst us brothers? I've been carrying both of them on my back in this joint for all these years and now he's done some stupid shit like that! I know what it is, though. Ain't none of them ever been to prison, so they have no idea how to stand strong and remain that way.

    Me, I've been in and out of juvenile joints from as long as I can remember. And I always hold my own. As a matter a fact, I set these punk ass guards straight from the first day I came up in this system.

It's not enough that they strip you of everything that defines you as a person when you first come in the system, but these punks force you to strip naked in a room with a bunch of other grown-ass men. I don't know 'bout you but that's some embarrassing shit and I don't roll like that. I wasn't having it when that police told me to turn around, squat and split my ass cheeks. That was it for me. I looked at him as if he was crazy and he could tell from my facial expression that I wasn't about to play that game. He told me to step aside and as I started to move, he called himself grabbing me and trying to turn me around. I grabbed that big muthafucka and slammed his ass to the floor. His fat ass was on the ground calling the code, sounding like a little pussy. It took six of them to hold me down and put me in shackles. They beat my ass like I stole something, but I got my point across.

That act got me sent straight to Supermax. They call it the Maryland Correctional Adjustment Center. They adjust you alright. Thirteen months of 23 hour-a- day lock down. That's a lot of time for a man to spend with himself. I had so much time that for a while I kept going over and over the incident in my mind that landed me here.

I'd shot another dealer over a street beef and got caught right there on the spot. It was a crazy move but if I didn't do that all three of us would be gone. Judge Renaldo told me he was going to send me away for a long time and I should make use of the programs the system provided for people like me with such a "troubled history." He hoped I would return to society a "changed man, ready to contribute positively to the community". That old man must've bumped his head 'cause no correctional facility can change me. I'm a hustler and society had to accept that. Everybody would think prison broke me if I changed my life. Besides, surviving prison is supposed to be a stripe for a hood-soldier, and a badge of honor that brought you respect when you returned to the street—or at least it used to.

Everybody keeps telling me how rough it is in the streets now. It may be rough for a lot of other people, but I'm going home to a homeboy that has my back. For what we have done for each other, it's like I owe him my life.

Ever since Juvenile told me he thought that whole thing was planned out by Tavon and others to kill him, I've been plotting. My mind is controlled with thoughts of revenge like a blood-hungry predator. Nobody can try to hurt my homey and get away with it. Tavon should be lucky his soft ass got killed or he would've been the first one I'd go after. I always told Juvenile that Tavon was soft in business because he trusted anybody coming his way. That's why I really preferred to deal with Juvenile. He was the opposite.

I'm glad I was able to get back in contact with him because for a while I kept calling and couldn't catch him at home. I was hearing all sorts of rumors. Revenge is all I wanna talk about now. I wanna hurt the dudes that turned their backs on me. I wanna hurt the friends, the ones I grew up with, who crossed me with wounds and intended on leaving me for dead.

I'd heard enough when he said he saw the death angel. He couldn't get over looking death in the eye and still being alive to tell about it. I can definitely relate to death because I got stabbed up pretty bad one time. Every time I look at those marks on my body I get mad as shit. Since I can't get to Apple or the cowards that stabbed me up, I'll be taking my frustrations out on those fools who tried to kill Juvenile. I realize how confrontational I am, but the system shouldn't let me out on parole and probation.

I'm just glad to get my chance to get outta here! All those years I watched the reasons why they call prison a revolving door. You would see guys going home looking real fresh after being incarcerated for years. With no job training, no preparation to make a better life, they push them through these maximum security prison doors. Higher education is gone because the government phased out Pell Grants to prisoners here in Maryland and across the country.

There's no hope in this prison system where they claim they focus on rehabilitation. Former governors took that away— even though the system was working. I remember when the incident happened in the camp system with one person serving a Life sentence. This crazy system took its frustration out on all the rest of them. They sent all Lifers back in the maximum security setting because of the actions of one. One damned fool caused disruption to the entire system while so many others had been on work release without any trouble for five and six years.

It wasn't like we could call somebody in Congress to complain. If it would've made a difference I would have been one of many fighting for their rights. Besides, if I was a parole commissioner...the first group of people I would give a chance to would be the Lifers who already got a whole bunch a time in. Some have served over thirty years and are lost in the system with nowhere to turn. Those are the old-heads who are always trying to guide young kids like me in the right direction. If I really look at it, I'm not the one who deserves parole. They do, but what can I do? I didn't create the system, but I'll send them some money when I hit the bricks.

I told Juvenile what I needed upon arrival. Along with a tight limousine ride, my homecoming had to include some of those freaks from around the way, money, and a new 9mm Heckler & Koch fresh out of the box. I had a plan. Them old heads keep telling me not to get involved in those ongoing beefs on the streets, but they don't understand that you have to protect your homeboy at any cost. They were saying how too many dudes come right back to prison because they walk into somebody else's conspiracy—and end up getting charged just like everybody else. I wasn't worried about any judge throwing the book at me! All I know was my homeboy needed me and had been by my side for all those years. How could I say no?

If the purpose of prison was to change a person, did it change me? I came into this joint not worrying if I lived or died and I'm leaving with the same thoughts. Now I don't care whether I live through this street or die trying. You be the judge.

Chapter 12

JAMEEL

"Spread rumors--
Would you defend me tooth or nail
They try to frame me--
Would you be there until the truth avails?"
Jay-Z, *"(Always Be My) Sunshine"*
In My Lifetime

We were all lying around in my room watching television and enjoying a lazy Saturday evening after dinner. Spending our weekends and some evenings together as a family has certainly been something to look forward to. Tonight I felt like using this opportunity to talk to Juvenile about getting a job.

"Baby, I heard that the Maryland Cup Company is hiring. And you know Momma knows the man hiring at the hospital. I talked to her about getting in touch with the man at the hospital last night," I said, with no response from Dorian.

"Daddy, this is the part I like in the video," Tiffany said, interrupting the awkward silence I created.

"I see it baby—you like when Sponge Bob starts dancing, huh?" he asked, tickling her having fun. *Tiffany was giggling and jumping all over her father. She's the one who really enjoys the time we've been spending together in this house.*

"If it's better, I can drive you down to the cup company on Monday—since that's my early day at the Post Office?"

"I have some other things to check on first," he said, speaking in a stern tone. "Did Fruity call for me while I was out, Jameel?"

"What do you want with them' two?" I asked, not being able to hide my disapproval.

"Tiffany, Daddy needs you to go downstairs for a while so I can talk to Mommy. Cut the movie off, baby. And I'll finish watching it with you another time, okay?" Dorian said, sounding angry.

"But Daddy I wanted you to finish watching the movie with me," Tiffany protested.

"I know baby girl, but we can do it another time," he said, trying to soften his voice. "Go ahead in your room for now."

After shutting the door behind her he said, "Now, to answer your question, I was waiting for a phone call—dat's what, Jameel. Now, don't be assumin' nothin'! You can't keep acting like my babysitter."

"I'm not assuming anything, Dorian."

"Well, I know what I'm doing. I know you want the best for me, but some things I just have to do on my own!" Dorian said, flipping back to that same borderline angry tone.

"Baby, if that's what you think I'm doing--then I apologize. I just want you all the way out of what they are into. Losing Tavon was more than I can handle and I know what my brothers are into. I can't stand people always looking at me like they do. I know they're staring because of Tavon, but that wasn't your fault."

"Do we have to talk about that again?"

"No, but—"

"No but nothing! Just leave that alone while I try to figure my way through all of this. What matters now is how we're putting our family back together. And we have been doing fine since I've been here! The streets are spreading rumors and trying to frame me, Jameel--and that ain't cool with me. I know you'll be there for me, but no questions for now about what's in the past. Okay?"

"Now Dorian, I didn't mean to get you upset, but I have to express how I feel. And I'll be right by your side—tooth and nail—as long as you're right. That's why I'm saying something."

"Just do what I ask, Jameel," he said, opening the door and walking down the steps.

"Dorian, I'm not finished talking."

"But I am!"

I let him go. He has to experience some things before we finally get it all together. The one thing I have to accept is he still has friends, like my brothers, who may be still out there. That doesn't mean that he is. He's in the house most of the time, anyway.

I walked downstairs to my desk just outside the kitchen door and started getting my books together to do some more reading. Despite what was happening between us, I still had to finish up my assignment.

I heard Tiffany go downstairs with her father. Shortly after, all I heard were giggles. I guess they both were playing a X-box game. For a moment, I felt a bit slighted that Dorian preferred to play games rather than talk, but it was good seeing Tiffany happy. Everything in time, I guess.

I took what I needed and went to my room to get some work done. I flopped across the bed to read and found myself nodding off to sleep when the phone rang.

I picked it up and heard a voice recording, the same one I hear when my brothers get in trouble and need bail money. 'I don't need this now,' I thought to myself.

"Collect call from "Trigger" at the Maryland House of Correction. Do not use three-way or call waiting or you will be disconnected. To accept this call, dial zero now."

I pressed zero and waited. "Thank you," the automatic recording said before I heard a human voice.

"Who dis?" he asked.

"This is Jameel and who are you?" I asked, not amused that someone is calling my house being rude.

"Dis' Trigger--put Juvenile on da' phone!"

"Trigger, let me just set the record straight. You don't call this house and ask 'who dis?' You acknowledge the person who accepted your call with a polite 'hello' and then ask for who you want, okay?"

"Oh, my bad--Jameel. I was in a rush because they just told me I'll be going home Monday and I want him to pick me up!"

"I understand and congratulations, but you have to do better on the phone, Trigger," I said, "Now let me get Dorian on the phone for you."

I walked to the steps and yelled, "Dorian. Trigger is on the phone!"

I could hear him running up the steps like he was a little puppy being summoned for a treat. I handed him the phone and slowly walked back into my room.

Dorian shouted, "Yo! What they say?! Monday! No doubt! What time you want me to pick you up?" he asked, still standing on the steps.

It's been a while since I've seen him so genuinely happy. I know he enjoys the time we spend together but you can see that there is always something on his mind and rightfully so. I'm sure it's not easy being accused of something you didn't do.

"I'll be there earlier than that! I wouldn't miss this to save my life—and you know that! I'm just glad you're coming home, man!" he said, hanging up the phone. With a great big smile he walked into my room and said, "Here's the phone, Jameel."

I was sitting at the foot of my bed when he came up behind me and kissed me lightly on the back of my neck. I jumped in surprise because it not only tickled, but also was totally unexpected.

"Dorian stop," I told him playfully. "You know how ticklish I am."

"I know but I couldn't resist," he replied.

"Right!" I said, turning to face him.

"Baby I'm gonna run out for a minute and I'll be right back. I have some things to take care of. I can't believe Trigger is finally coming home!"

"Okay. But what are you going to do about tomorrow?" I asked.

"I'll be there. I already told Tiffany I'll be there. You know I won't disappoint my baby girl. It's at 11 o'clock, right?"

"Yep," I answered, still a bit puzzled.

"Tiffany," Dorian screamed downstairs, "It's time for you to go to bed now, let's pack up the games. Daddy has to go out for a minute."

"Come on sweetie. You know you have a big day ahead of you tomorrow so you need lots of rest."

"O—kay," she answered. *She wasn't enthused at all about leaving those games behind. She's getting as bad as her father.*

After Tiffany and I did our nightly devotion, I went to my room for a little 'me' time. I fell flat across the bed looking up into the ceiling just recapping the day's events. I felt like a love struck little girl as I relived Dorian's light kiss on the back of my neck. It reminded me of old times before he got so caught up in that street stuff. I've been telling him how proud I was now that he's trying to change his life. He's going to do whatever it takes to put back our family together...and I'd do anything to help.

******

There's no better day of the week for Tiffany and me than Sunday. This Sunday is a lot more special. It had taken more than two months of rehearsals and program practice to get Children's Day right.

We made it to the church with time to spare. All the children were dressed in African garbs ready for the day. They did an excellent job ushering, handing out programs and escorting people to their seats. Church took a little longer to begin but that's understandable. When I heard those two notes from Brother Andre, I knew the march inside the sanctuary was about to begin.

I turned around to see my baby leading the way down the isle. There she was with her left hand behind her. Her right hand was swinging. Their swinging arms made the march look like a strut, a casual slide with a soulful step in between.

As they made their way down the isle, I noticed she glanced over to her left and suddenly flashed a big smile – almost like she was surprised. When she got closer to me I could see she was trying to tell me something without anyone noticing, but I couldn't understand. When she got directly in front of me the message was clear. She was saying, "Daddy". I quickly turned all the way around to see Dorian sitting a few rows behind me with that big silly grin on his face.

I couldn't believe Dorian made it! He was barely up when we left this morning. He wanted us to go ahead so I thought he wasn't coming, although he mentioned something about us driving separate cars.

He moved beside me after the march was done. As he settled in beside me, I thought about the card in my pocketbook that I purchased for him. I intended on giving it to him tonight, but hopefully he can go out with us for brunch. I can give it to him so he knows how I really feel...

I Love Me...

I simply love me some you...
there's no other way I can explain it
and
I know I keep on saying it...
but we have a love that's very special to me,
a love that's one-of-a-kind.
It's special because of the dreams we share.
And the end result is our satisfying love
affair...
Really, it is everything in our relationship
I admire about us two...
And it's all because
"I Love me Some You!"

©GDP, 05

Chapter 13

TRIGGER

"Chasing this cheddar
To the end of the road...
Because the end I'm told
Is nearer than we know."

"Jay-Z,"
The Blueprint 2

It's funny, no matter how big and bad we are, after all the years we spend in prison, how silent and reflective we get when it's time to go home. I spent almost my entire day just laying in this bed--not wanting to do anything or go anywhere because this is the time when anything could happen. Although they can't hold me another day pass tomorrow, I ain't taking no chances. Tired of looking out the window, I turned over and looked toward the end of the dorm. Brotha E was walking towards me with a big grin on his face.

"Are you ready for the party?" he asked, still grinning like he won a million dollars.

He came over to my bedside and sat on my bunk. We've been doing it this way for years. He's one of the few brothers I trust with my story and have talked with him about stuff that's happening in the news.

"As long as the party is right here," I said, "because I ain't moving from here until I need to go to the bathroom or until it's time for me to get the hell outta here."

"We doing it right here, my brotha," he said, reaching under his bed for the hospital pan full of Ramen noodles.

"Damn right!" I told him. *He's been a friend to me when nobody else had my back. Besides, the party was more for them than me. Tomorrow Juvenile is having something special for me, anyway.*

"I know you ain't gonna miss dis' place, are you Trigger?" he asked, smashing each pack of noodles on the floor.

"How in the hell could I miss a dormitory with a hundred and four other men!"

"Did you look at this rat hole, Trigger—I mean really look at it?" he asked, now tearing the seasoning packs from the noodles with his teeth.

"All I can do tonight is look because I'm not moving my ass off this bunk!" I emphasized, banging both hands on the mattress, marking my territory for the next 24 hours or less.

"Look at how they got us set up in here?"

I could feel his last sermon coming on. 'Brotha E is about to preach,' I thought to myself before looking away. "What you talking about, Brotha E?"

"Look around," he said pointing. "It's four long rows of bunks—one beside the other in this chicken coop. For all these years we've been locked up, we've been forced to live beside hundreds of other men who have different scents, hygiene problems and issues. Look at Food Stamp over there," he said, pointing towards the oldest man in the dorm. "For the life of me, after serving thirty-nine years, I can't figure out why the state would have somebody that old still locked up. Are you listening to me Trigger?" he asked, getting up taking other ingredients out of his locker.

"I'm listening, even though my mind is running in a thousand different directions."

"Man, I'm definitely gonna miss your crazy ass when you're gone."

"That's what I was just thinking about! But I'ma getatchu!"

"I know that, but what you gonna do, Trigger?"

"Whatever I do--I ain't coming back. The system can kiss my ass because I'm holding court in the streets," I shouted, banging my hand on the locker emphasizing each word. "Ain't-no-coming-back-for-me!"

"Open them cans of tuna," he said, looking around for the police first before handing me what he was taking out of his locker.

I opened the cans and bent the lids so we could have something to slice the ingredients with. One sharp lid would become our makeshift knife.

"Brotha E, check this out. This system caged me like a wild animal and made me even worse. One adjustment hearing after the other, stabbing and fight after fight—whether I started it or not, and staying on lockup, too! Man, all that shit did was make me wilder and more frustrated since I've been here. This system don't wanna help nobody. Punishment is all they want...so I'm gonna show them what real punishment is now that I'm returning to the block. I know what I am gonna do, though."

"What's that?"

"I'm suing the people uptown! The City and State of Maryland is gonna feel my pain and suffering. Everybody is going to pay Brotha E, everybody!"

"Well, all I want you to do for me when you get uptown is send me some money down here and pictures of those fine uptown women. I'm tired of those books. Don't forget, even if you have to pay somebody, I want some fresh pictures."

"You got that?"

"But on a more serious note," he said, lowering his voice and speaking in a more confidential tone. "I wish I knew where my son was living--and his mother. I'd ask you to take some letters and pictures over there to him, but I don't know where to find them. You know how long it's been since I've seen my son?"

"How long, Brotha E?"

"It's been nine years now. I don't know if they're still in Maryland or not. Hand me that mayonnaise and honey," he said, speaking from the pain of being locked away for so long.

"Damn! That long, Brotha E?"

"Yep. That long," he said, "Now give me the cans of fish so I can drain them."

Trying to sound happy, Brotha E shouted across the dorm playfully. "Ayy, John-John! What you got there son, what you got?"

John-John walked over to us and untied his sweat pants. Out of the crotch of his pants he pulled all the ingredients we needed to make plain fish taste spicier: onions, green peppers, cut up celery, bread and boiled eggs. All this was provided courtesy of the kitchen. Even though the bread was smashed, it was good enough for us to eat. Eating sandwiches smuggled under somebody's underarm and tasting a piece of chicken hidden in the crotch of somebody's work pants all taste the same. Back here, behind these walls, it's about survival.

"When we gonna be ready to eat?" John-John asked, waving for Mike and Allen to come over to the buffet.

"Trigger, take one of these tuna can lids and cut those peppers up. I'll mix this stuff together," he said, before giving another command. "Oh, I gotta get the party mix. And John-

John--stop talking so much and grab that six pack of Pepsi from my locker. We'll be ready to eat in about ten minutes!"

I ate with them, talking about everything you could think of, until it was time for the late night count. It was all small talk because I didn't know myself what life had in store for me. A lot had gone on in these last few months uptown that we had to straighten out.

* * * * * * * *

Midnight signaled the day of my release. I watched each and every move in the dorm throughout the night because I wouldn't sleep at all. I listened to snores and grunts and sleep talk. Five in the morning signaled a wake up call for breakfast.

Brotha E was moving around with his toothbrush still in his mouth while straightening his bed. He asked, "Trigger, take this last walk with us, homey?"

"Hell, naw. The one I took with y'all the other day was the grand finale! I'm getting me a shower and sitting my ass right here until they come get me!"

"You want us to bring you something back just to hold you?"

"I'm not eating another piece of state food," I said laughing. 'Thanks anyway, Brotha E, but I'm cool."

They knew what I was going through. I wanted to walk down with them. But when you're as close to going home anything can go wrong. A simple fight or somebody's revenge could cause a setback. That's why I'm keeping my ass still!

I took a quick shower before sitting all my clothes on Brotha E's bed. The rest of the guys had just come back from breakfast. All kind of thoughts were running through my mind. I had a hard time believing this time had finally come. Thinking about everything caused me to lose control of my nervous stomach. Running to the bathroom over and over again became normal. Anxiety had taken control of my body and it wouldn't be long now before I'm called.

After everybody settled in it was time for the eight o' clock count. I just sat there still thinking of how this would be my last count at the Maryland House of Correction. Right after the count, I was called down to Center hall to get processed out. I walked through the hallways remembering everything that happened to me. It's funny. Usually when I'm called down here it would be for a couple of things: to put me back on lockup, to take me through the urine test or for some investigation. I never thought the day would come that I'd be going home—finally walking outta here like these police do everyday.

"Hit the gate, Center hall. You got one bad-ass mandatory release hitting the streets," the officer said, screaming through the grill. He looked over to me and asked, "Juan, you're gonna make them pay, aren't you?"

"Damn right, Rose! I'll make you pay if I see you!" I said, meaning every threatening word. "You put me on lockup too many times. I gotta make you pay!"

"Not if I see you first. I'm shooting somebody like you on site—anywhere I see you. I'll ask your corpse questions later!"

"Oh, yeah!"

"I'm glad they're getting your crazy ass outta here," he said, searching my body for contraband. "Trouble will die down in here and all *hell* will break loose uptown."

"Don't you think this is the wrong fuck'n day to talk shit to a soldier?"

"I don't know about that, but I do know one thing. You'll be surrounded by white chalk and rushed to the hospital flat-lined in a week. That's how long I'll give you. That may be too much. The streets have changed, but you haven't!"

"Juan Bolden?" another officer asked as we walked through the metal gates.

"Yeah?"

"Let me see your ID?" she asked, impatiently stretching her hand toward me.

I handed her my dog tag. I looked to my left to see other polices taking lunch down in the Officer's dining room.

"Ayy! Bolden," another officer yelled. "Man, don't be takin' this Cutt shit uptown. If you go outta here with that Trigger image shit you're in trouble. You ain't gonna make it out there too long. One thing is guaranteed: Those young kids will let every 911 operator know about you the same day you hit the streets. You better do the right thing and get a job."

"Fuck you!" I shouted back at him. *He was one of the officers that beat me up on lock up. He had a nerve to be giving me advice.* "I ain't never coming back! And you don't know shit about my life! You couldn't walk in my shoes if DOC paid your dumb ass! Keep turning keys and kicking ass in teams until somebody like me catch you slippin' on the other side of this wall! Then we'll see how you do one-on-one. Now write a ticket about that, bitch—and I'll sign it before I leave!"

"We'll be reading about you in the newspaper. Just get the hell outta here!"

"You heard what I said, Big Black. You treat people like shit," I said, remembering how bad he treated the prison population. "Always remember…what goes around comes back around. Remember that!"

"I'll tell you what! I'll give you six months before you or somebody you know will reach the end of the road!" he screamed before pulling and waving a nine-to-five wad of money from his pocket. "All because you wanna chase this chedda!"

"The same shit goes for you in here chasing every paycheck! The end of the road is nearer than we all know. That's why I live each day not knowing whether tomorrow is meant for me!"

"You may think it's a joke uptown, but we see people like you released everyday. It's a seventy percent chance that you'll be back. Don't confirm the thirty percent rule that we have around here. It's a thirty percent chance that says you will not stay alive out there."

"That's not my problem. Now that I'm gone they will be having a lot more memorial services. Big Black, don't let it be yours!"

Before I could say anything else, the door slammed shut in my face. It was another set of steel doors that opened. I'd never been this far in the front of the jail since arriving. I took a deep breath because this freedom walk was real. We walked down a long hall through the control center and down the hill. I was walking out of this prison from hell with nothing but the clothes on my back.

"Sign here, Mr. Juan Bolden," the officer said, pointing to my release papers.

After signing she gave me fifty dollars, took copies of the signed paper and walked away. I kicked the double doors as hard as I could so they could swing open making a loud exit.

As I took my first step into freedom, I saw a long stretch Hummer limousine parked with the engine running. It had flaming stripes of fire on the side as a detail. Juvenile jumped out. All I could see was bare bodies inside. He had four women in the limo!

"Didn't I tell you I got you, Trigger!" he shouted, chauffeuring me inside.

Chapter 14

JUVENILE

"[He] put the wolves on you
[He] put a price on your head—
The whole hood will want you
Starting to look like bread."

Jay-Z, "Soundtrack"
The Black Album

Trigger was only home for a week before he and I went to Butter's house. He was hungry to get my image back from those who played a part in taking it. Finally calling her, today would be the day I get some information.

"Hey, Butter, how you been girl?" I asked, surprising her when she answered the phone.

"Who dis?" she asked, as if she didn't already check to see the caller ID.

"Girl stop playing, you know who it is, it's me, Juvenile."

"Oh my God, J! I've been hearing so many stories about you. I ain't know what happened since—you know," she said, not wanting to reveal what was secret, "That's why I'm surprised to hear from you? Oh my God...where you been at?"

"Taking care of myself. You know that's all I can do!"

"I know that's right! Where you at now?"

"I'm chilling, but you've been on my mind lately. You know I'm still feeling what you did for me. That's why I'll be up there later on today."

"Oh, you are?"

"Yeah, I got a couple ideas I wanna run by you to see what you think. I know you need some money, don't you?"

"Damn, right! So, why you haven't been calling me like you used to?"

"That's why I'm callin' yo' ass now! And you know you're the only one I would call anyway. I can't trust nobody else, but you."

"Well, if dat's the case then, what's taking you so long? You know a sista can stand a surprise or two."

* * * * * * * *

The night was still young, but a dangerous sense of calm lurked on those streets. Having other things to do forced me to think my way through this whole ordeal. Being careful is my first thought, so I took my time cruising to my first destination. Driving my old car, a dark blue Oldsmobile with all kinds of stickers on the back bumper wouldn't draw any attention. After passing through Pennsylvania Avenue, it didn't take me long to pick Trigger up. He was ready when I made the turn onto his street.

He ran down the steps and jumped straight in. Trigger was on fire and couldn't wait to burn. It's almost as if he couldn't wait to ask.

"You ready, J?"

"Yeah. I'm ready."

"We are about to make some shit happen, so let's go straight down there!"

It was winter in season and a fall night for sure. My black sweat hood fit the occasion. I thought I could do something that people say wasn't possible by walking away from the life, but now I have to admit I'm not all the way out—not yet.

We drove through the city in silence. Underneath this cover of darkness I watched the dread of a typical night and saw East Baltimore bodies move like dark shadows. Everything seemed to be playing in slow motion, like watching a movie. I tried not to be obvious, but I was driving almost in a daze. Each corner had its own players and each area gave birth to its own stories. Transactions were made up and down the avenues-- money from drivers and vials from sellers. Speed racers walked with change in hand—anxious to make a deal with any hustler willing to take short money. More desperate addicts used the curse words spare, borrow *and* lend. *Begging for spare change was another hustle, too. They were touting area products starting with their nods to the 'I'm high as shit' looks on their faces.*

"Yo, Trigger. I know you remember East Baltimore. This is where I parked the night I got shot up. I was around this corner," I said, pointing to the parking spot right in front of us on Greenmount Avenue.

"Yo' ass betta be glad you had that steel across your chest or I'd be looking for chalk marks showing where you took your last breath. Can you imagine what that would've felt like coming home? I ain't feeling dat' shit! That's why I'm gonna make 'em pay!" he said, angrily snatching the sleeve of his nine-millimeter.

"Man, it wasn't meant to happen!" I said, bitterly thinking back on that night and seeing my casket again. "It wasn't my time yet--you know what I mean?"

"Yeah!"

"That's why we're here. We gonna straighten this double cross' shit out!"

"That's how I've been feeling ever since you told me what happened," he said as we watched two fiends walked by looking curiously into the car.

"Well," Trigger said, "let's go see this bitch!"

Getting out of the car, he turned around to me and said, "Listen man. Give me your word—now!--dat' you gon' let me handle dis' shit?"

"Word! Dis' is your show," I said, pulling out my cell phone. "I just wanna find out who else was with it—even though we already know! Hold up. Let me call her again."

She answered right away. "Yo, Butter. I'm coming from the back way in about two *minutes." I really didn't want to call her from my phone because of what Trigger might do. The first thing Homicide will do is check phone records. I couldn't tell Trigger nothing like that because he would've thought I was tripping in my own fear.*

"Alright. I'm here—I ain't going no where," Butter said softly. "I don't know why I gave you a front door key because you've never used it!"

"Is the back door open already?"

"Yeah, baby—it's open," she said before I flipped the phone ending our connection.

"We in!" I said to my crime partner.

"So, let's do it!"

We quickly walked through the alley kicking trash along the way.

He said, "I can't believe dis' shit? Look at all this trash and food and shit! I used to have my jail cell clean—shiddd! I had wax on my floor because I hate dirt.

"I had my shit clean all the time. I come from that to walking through this!" he complained. *We walked through her gate pass more trash to get to her back door.* "Yo, I see why alley rats are so overweight—look at all dis' shit in Butter's yard!"

We quietly walked through the unlocked backdoor. I told him to lock it tight so she wouldn't get away. Nobody could get out of here unless they had time to move everything he put in front of that doorway.

"'Yo, Butter,'" I shouted, ducking under her makeshift clotheslines and walking up the steps. *In my mind, I wanted to play this out like Scarface would on the big screen. I'll be asking gangster questions while Trigger is holding her in fear. She had to pay like that undercover police did when Scarface shot him in the movie. She violated the rules. It's not so much that she violated the rules. She tried to and wasn't able to destroy me, so failing is going to cost her.*

"I'm up here in the living room," she said, sounding like she was already high.

I ran up the steps and walked towards her sitting alone on the couch. "Whatchu got girl?"

"I got some Hennessy and some smoke from Old York Road like I always do."

"Well, don't hold dat' shit," I said reaching, "Oh wait! I need to use the bathroom real quick."

I ran up the steps like I had to go to the bathroom. I wanted to see if anybody else was upstairs. She usually doesn't keep a lot of company, but I had to make sure. I quietly shut the doors to each room after checking them out and headed back down the steps.

"Who else is in here, Juvenile?" she asked as I came back down.

I stood in front of her and then walked over to the front door. Carefully looking out through the peephole was the last thing I had to do. I had to make sure nobody was coming.

"Nobody—why?" I asked.

"I just wanted to make sure 'cause it sounded like somebody was still down stairs. You sure it ain't nobody with you?" she asked, sounding nervous.

Trigger ran up the steps making noise while I stood there. He knew what to do. He signaled for me to move away from the door. After checking the lock, he placed a chair under the knob. I could feel Butter looking at me with confusion as I sat on my favorite barstool facing the front door.

"Who is dat', Juvenile!" she asked, jumping in shock. Her eyes darted back and forth, looking, trying to recognize this new face and looking to me for answers. "Shit! I ain't never seen him before?"

"You don't know him?"

"I thought you said nobody else was with you, Juvenile? What's going on?"

"I did, but what the fuck—nobody is telling the truth!"

He did it like we seen so many times before on the streets. Before I could really finish my sentence Trigger grabbed her around her neck with his left arm and had his gun in his right hand against Butter's temple. I kept my seat on the stool while Trigger did his thing.

"Now, bitch! We ain't playin' no games about what happened to Juvenile. We know you had something to do with setting him up. Now—if you don't talk they'll be reading about you in the paper tomorrow morning. Now talk!"

"You know I ain't have nothin' to do with dat' shit! I was in here with you, remember!" she shouted through the tears rolling down her face. "Now you gon' let him treat me like a fuckin' dog?!"

Trigger loosened his hold. Using his left hand, he smacked her letting her know this wasn't a game. Her whining screams started annoying me, but she got the message.

"Juvenile, tell him to stop—stop that shit, man!" she screamed before being smacked again.

"This crazy kid ain't playing with you, Butter! Now what the fuck happened?!" *I stood there pointing in her face and was at arms reach, but wouldn't help her. I wasn't lifting a finger.*

"They forced me, Juvenile!"

"Whatchu mean—forced you?" Trigger screamed, snatching her around her neck again.

"I'm so sorry because I shouldn't have gotten involved in dat' shit! Tavon said he was putting the wolves on you when he put a price on your head!"

"What?"

"He put a price on your head. That's why everybody was getting involved. He knew everybody was gonna be after you trying to get that twenty thousand."

"That's what you got paid?"

"Juvenile, I'm sorry, but Tavon told me to call him on the telephone when you were here again—and he'd give me twenty-five hundred dollars!"

"Dat's all you got, bitch, was twenty-five hundred— trying to get me setup! All dat shit we did together, all that shit Tavon didn't know about! Two thousand dollars?" I shouted in her face. "That's all I was worth!"

She broke loose of Trigger's chokehold, suddenly fighting wildly, scratching me across my face. Trigger snatched her from behind and slammed her to the floor after seeing blood dripping from my face. Her leg knocked over the expensive glass dishes she had on a standing display rack. Heavy pieces came crashing to the floor. The noise put me in a panic.

She tried to fight back while still on the floor. I quickly grabbed a cooking apron she had on the dining room table. We tied her up and dragged her toward the back door. He put the gun back to her head like he was about to pull the trigger.

"Juvenile, no! Don't let him do this to me—please," she begged. "After all I did with you—you gonna let this happen?"

"Who else was it then? Who else tried to set me up, bitch!" I screamed, feeling the blood running down my bleeding face.

"Please, I'm sorry!" she screamed desperately, "I can't breathe—Juvenile, don't let him kill me. I'm a tell you who else it was!" she said, screaming even louder. "Fast Money, too. He's the one that told Tavon and caused all this shit in the first place. We already heard that you were messing with Precious. Pretty put that out there, Juvenile! I swear I'm telling the truth!

"Dead-eye, too, and some guy named Rabbit who Tavon gave the contract to or something—I don't know!" she screamed, moaning in a frantic tremble. "Dat's all I know! Tavon said he would pay all of us, but Rabbit wanted to kill you for free! The rumor was he was gonna kill you no matter how long it took because you shot him before or something."

"Who else!"

"All I know is Dead-eye—he has a girlfriend who lives on Fulton Avenue and Lafayette and she drives a black BMW. He used to be up there on Pulaski and North Avenue. Juvenile I'm telling the truth, please, help me?" she screamed, "He was one of them who shot inside the truck. They were the ones who gave me the money to keep quiet. That's why I ain't say nothin'!"

True to my word, I walked out of the room with all the information I needed from her. Still, I couldn't believe she set me up like that. Whether I lived or died meant nothing to her. I guess—now--she regretted crossing me. That's survival, though. I might regret it, but regret is something you gotta learn to live with e-v-e-r-y-d-a-y in this game.

"Juvenile, please. I'll help you get Dead-eye back! I know everything 'bout him!"

"What's his fuckin' number?" Trigger screamed.

"Help me, please, Juvenile! I just don't want nothing to do with it anymore! It's 443—please let me get my phone book," she said, whining and begging before sounding like Trigger muffled her mouth."

POLICE BLOTTER
Woman's death ruled suspicious

Demetria "Butter" Haywood, of the 2100 block of Greenmount Avenue was found dead in her house after neighbors complained of a bad odor. When authorities entered her East Baltimore home they found her body in the kitchen near the back door.

Neighbors were questioned about her acquaintances. Her live-in boyfriend, Quinton "Donut" Anderson, was arrested after questioning pending the investigation and medical examiner's report.

Detectives gathered physical evidence, including the suspect's fingerprints all over the house, but would release no other details about the cause of death because the state medical examiner is performing an autopsy. Medical authorities are expecting to rule the woman's death a homicide. If so, this will be the city's 264th homicide of the year. "This toll is quickly approaching 300, but we are taking corrective actions to avoid another year of increased homicides," the mayor spokesperson said. "Our Mayor is committed to fight crime and will continue to deploy his forces to problem areas like East Baltimore to make our city safe."

Chapter 15

JUVENILE

"[Hustlers] will show you love.
That's how they fool thugs.
Before you know it...
You're lying in a pool of blood."
Jay-Z, *"Where I'm From"*
In My Lifetime

This evening was as good as any to check out what was happening at North Avenue and Pulaski Street. It was close to four o'clock. Nobody seemed to care if undercover cops were lurking around waiting to exercise a surprise jump-out, or patrol cars possibly coming through scattering the crowd. That time of the evening signaled one thing and one thing only for those working the corner: shift change.

Knowing this, we parked a little ways from the corner. We intended to watch all the action without being noticed. It was kinda chilly out but that didn't stop the open-air activities from happening. They were hustling like in the streets of New York where flatfoot bartering still seems legal. Older addicts stood still like medicated hawks watching whatever they could— soaking up corner action. Younger kids moved through the crowd soaking up corner profits feeding fiends their daily dose of street medicine for the same price they charged yesterday and the day before.

"Good Shit—Good Shit—Good Shit! Killer dope--two for five, y'all. Got dat' good shit! Get it while I got it!" the touter yelled, walking back and forth fishing in his one block territory. *This kid was a fisher with a net for trapping ill humans. Each time somebody wanted to try him at his word, starting with a nod of their head or the buyers throwing up a finger or two, signifying how many vials of* feel good *they wanted, he would run in and out of the alley making his constant sales, catching addicts in his human trap.*

"Pink tops—White bags—Pink tops—White bags--y'all! Right here—get in line on the wall with your money out!" another kid called out while openly counting his ill-gotten gains on the corner. *He had another kid beside him waving a gun. People started forming a quick line on the wall--like they probably did so many times before. They knew the program and followed it to a science.*

"Check dis' shit out? Look at how these young kids got those old heads acting like they in kindergarten—lining up like they're all waiting to go to the bathroom," I said.

"Blue tops, y'all—get dat' shit now!" another kid yelled as he passed by our car.

"I hear you Juvenile, but I want you to look at dat' shit. Look at those two cars right there pulling up on the corner," Trigger said.

The corner was smoking with action! All I wanted to find was that familiar face. "Where?" I asked, still watching the junkies forming their line on the wall and remembering Tavon's mother.

"Right there—look!" he said, pointing towards two sets of headlights.

"Yeah, I see them."

Two tan colored Crown Victoria's raced up from nowhere—one behind the other. Noise from the Firestone rubber tires controlled the strip when both cars came to screeching halts. Black letters had been peeled off, but each car had evidence of previously being used as Maryland State Trooper vehicles.

Fast action, direct orders and the presence of guns forced everybody to pay their respects. All eight doors popped open. Men dressed in dark colors jumped out. Each one had a white bulletproof vest strapped on them under their jackets letting everybody know what powerful gang they wanted to represent. Silver badges jumped around in the middle of their chest area. Those shiny pieces of metal gave them identity and clout. Everybody on the streets respected one fact when they came: it was their corner and their streets.

There were no sirens making a scene. Blue lights weren't flashing. From the looks of it, this operation wasn't being financed by taxpayers' money either. Regardless, the takeover was taking shape.

These deep-under-cover police gathered everybody standing around and made them lie face down on the ground.

"Juvenile pull off! Let's get the fuck outta here," Trigger said.

Pulling past all of the live action, I noticed a big, young officer looking like he could be no more than sixteen. He had the hustlers who once counted money and the other who waved his gun thrown against the wall. He started going through their pockets looking for whatever valuables he could find. He took money, the gun and phones without separating anything into evidence bag while his partner held what looked to be a sawed-off shotgun. Free of any hesitation, he quickly stuck the evidence in his jacket pockets like a shoplifter would some stolen goods.

Another member with a badge dangling around his neck snatched jewelry and money fiends intended to use for purchases. The other police checked the gutters for dope stash. I guess those officers must be getting tired of making less money in their war on drug dealers. Pay bonuses of those performing this sting operation were coming straight out of the pockets of these dealers who made plenty of dope money each day.

"Look! Look right there!" I screamed.

"It's some more coming at us or something?" Trigger asked in paranoia with his hands on both of his guns.

"No. Ain't no more coming. These fools ain't real because that kid with the gun right there is that stick-up boy named Chinese Anthony!"

"Where?"

"Right there taking that money out of his pocket," I said, while pointing him out, turning west on North Avenue, and gett'n the hell outta Dodge.

City Police make strange arrests

A uniformed unit of highly skilled tactical team officers patrolling a West Baltimore high-crime area discovered a team of men posing as undercover police.

Police interrupted what they describe as "a robbery in progress." A regular patrol of North Avenue and Pulaski Street ended in the confiscation of seven guns, body armor, handcuffs, and fake police equipment and two makeshift police cars. Both cars were previously used as state trooper vehicles and had been sold at auctions.

Without resistance, police separated robbery victims from those posing as undercover officers. "We unraveled a classic case of fake cops who were robbers," said police spokeswoman Carolyn Byrd, "We're calling them 'Police Bandits.'"

Police were already investigating complaints of recent hold-ups by rogue officers acting in violation of police procedures and refused to comment further.

Authorities are searching for two suspects that escaped through the alley. Six men, whose name have yet to be released, are being charged with imposing as Baltimore City's finest, false imprisonment, robbery and handgun violations. Other charges are pending. The seizure also included drugs packaged for street sale and ammunition rounds. Further scientific testing is required.

All suspects arrested are being detained, questioned and processed at Central Booking Intake Center.

Chapter 16

JUVENILE

"Stand there like you got a cape on ya'.
Fine! You'll be wearing a black suite a long time."
Jay-Z, "So Ghetto"
Vol. 3: Life & Times of S. Carter

"Juvenile, I didn't know that's how they carry it on the streets now," Trigger said, looking a bit confused.

"That's how they make it," I told him, driving further north on Garrison Boulevard. "They watch and wait--and just when they think you've made enough money, they move in for the kill."

I decided to ride up to the Jamaican restaurant up Park Heights to get something to eat. We needed to kill some time.

"Can I help you, my brother?" the tall Jamaican shop owner asked.

"Give me two orders of Curry chicken, rice & peas."

"What kind of sides you want?" he asked.

"Aaah, give me some fried plantain and steamed vegetables," I said a little undecided. "Yeah, that should be good."

"Do you need anything to drink?"

"Yeah, two bottles of cola champagne soda."

"Yo, I have no clue what the hell you just ordered, but you talk like you know your stuff. So, I'm gonna go with what you say," Trigger said, laughing as we walked towards a table.

"Man that's about the only Jamaican food I know, so I always order that."

We sat down at the table on the end where we could see everybody coming in and out of the restaurant. After ordering, it didn't take long at all.

"Two curry chicken and rice 'n peas?" an older lady with a Caribbean accent called out.

"Right here."

She put the tray down on the table and began serving.

"Wow, look at that steam coming off that stuff. You can smell the spices in this," Trigger said, looking down at the steaming plate of food before digging in.

I really had no appetite, but the food was hard to resist. "This chicken meat is tender. It tastes like Jameel's cooking to me."

"Damn, man. I didn't know this food tastes like this," he said. *I watched him for a couple seconds eating his spicy food real fast like he was still in prison.* "Slow down, man. That spice will kill you."

"I am eating slow."

That was my signal to leave that food issue alone. I had some other things I wanted to talk about. "Man, I know you be thinkin' about those rumors you been hearing? And you wanna know what really happened, don't you?"

"Juvenile, I was just worried about you being by yourself. That other shit didn't matter! Tavon put a price on your head. That explained everything to me!" Trigger said sounding adamant about his decision.

"I hear that man, but I'm still trying to figure out what to do with that tricky ass Precious, Trigger. I don't think I wanna run up on her just yet because I'm sure Tavon left some money in that house and had one of my cars in her name. The money and the car belong to me—and I want it!"

"Get all you can if that's what you want, but every one of them gotta account—even her!"

"I know she was tied up in this shit. That's why everything blew up on us! Now Tavon is dead and those that had a hand in this gotta pay!"

"Enough said! Let's go back down there and make shit happen!" he said, in a low but forceful tone, as he pushed back from the table.

We drove straight back to North and Pulaski. Unlike before, there wasn't a lot of activity going on all of a sudden. The traffic changed from a busy strip to a ghost town. The police must've been through this hot ass area again to sweep.

Slowly driving past the alley I noticed where all the traffic was. I spotted Dead-eye standing on the steps. He was running shop in the third house from the corner alley. Dead-eye was directing traffic through his workers like he was this superman and had them lining addicts up in the back alley. You could see his crew respond immediately to his commands. His workers ran to a girl carrying a brown shopping bag from the back of another house. One worker took money while the other one served desperate addicts.

As we pulled over to park, addicts started speeding out onto the street, one-by-one as they got their fix. Within a span of four minutes we saw Dead-eye's workers walked toward him with money in hand. All three of them rushed inside.

I saw a blue Toyota pull in front of the house. I couldn't believe my eyes. "Look right there!" I told Trigger, hitting him on the arm to get his attention. "You wouldn't believe who dat' is!"

"Who's that?" he asked.

"That's Rabbit going in there!" *I looked over and saw Trigger pulling pieces of steel from his waist. He was ready.*

"Yo, homie. Let's get 'em right now and put his boys in black suites! No more waiting—let's go!" he screamed in excitement.

"No! This ain't his area, so let's just watch. We'll follow his ass away from here," I said, banging on the steering wheel. I stuck my hand towards Trigger for a shake of confirmation and told him, "Just watch."

Rabbit ran in the same house where Dead-eye was. We pulled off and parked the car a little further down the block. After about ten minutes, they came back out and stood at the door exchanging some arrangements. After exchanging daps, Rabbit walked back to his car alone, got in and made a U-turn.

We made a lucky guess to park going his direction and it paid off. We were right there to follow...

POLICE BLOTTER
Baltimore City

Man shot on west side was identified by the US Marshal's Fugitive Task Force and the Baltimore Regional Apprehension Task Force through an advance laser fingerprinting system at Alcohol Tobacco and Firearms (ATF) laboratories in Washington.

Investigators believe Ronald "Rabbit" Tyler, 20, was shot several times after an unsuccessful robbery attempt. This incident happened only hours after authorities broke up a ring of robbery suspects posing as Baltimore City police officers in the same area. Authorities don't believe the crimes are related at this time.

"This is the second time my son was injured. The first time he recovered after being shot and was able to walk away," his mother said at University Hospital Shock Trauma where the victim was taken and identified. "This time he's on life support and may not make it. He never bothered anybody and was a good son, but those boys on the streets were jealous and shot him anyway."

He is listed in critical condition. Investigation into this matter is continuing.

Chapter 17

TRIGGER

"[We] got two choices y'all
Pull over the car or--
Bounce on the devil
Put the pedal to the floor."

Jay-Z, *"99 Problems"*
The Black Album

    Juvenile didn't think it was a good idea for us to put our name on what went down with Rabbit, so we decided not to show our faces for a minute. We already knew all those associated with him would be on the lookout for any information about who did it. That's just how this game goes. We came back with a new game plan.

    Flubber and Fruity, Junvenile's two brothers-in-law, were with us now because this next job took teamwork. We needed more guns because anything could go wrong with just the two of us versus such a busy spot.

    We used two stolen cars. Flubber was with Juvenile in the other stolen car in front of us. And I tailed closely behind in the dark blue Chevy Cavalier. It felt funny driving on the busy city streets again. From a prison cell to being behind the wheel of a car was a major shift. I'm used to being shackled with cuffs on my wrists and ankles. I'm hoping the police don't pull me over. If they did, I already told Fruity the game plan. I'm going to pull over like I'm cooperating. Then I'm going to put the pedal to the floor and bounce in a high speed chase!

After parking on different sides of the street, we sat in both cars on the prowl. Juvenile would give the signal when it was time to attack so we watched and waited.

"Look at Dead-eye's crew over there," Fruity said pointing. "They got to have some good dope. I don't know whether Juvenile told you, but I used to get high."

"He ain't tell me. Some dudes locked up with me know you real good and have a lot of respect for you," I said, looking directly at him. "That's how I heard." *I didn't want him to get too familiar with asking me questions or making long conversation while on a caper. I keep my mind focused on the perfect plan.*

"They always keep something good up here on North Avenue. I was just thinking of all that fuckin' money they getting up here!"

"I'm try'na get it—the money and the drugs!"

"Why don't we just run up in the house and take all that shit?" he asked.

"Have you been watching?"

"Yeah. I'm watching everything."

"Picture dis' shit! We gonna run up in the back door whenever we can catch them creeping in the alley. You see how some of them go through that side of the alley and take money?" I asked, trying not to point. "We'll run down on them with guns drawn and get in the back door without being seen."

"Alright—I'm with that'," he said, making sure he was ready for the signal.

"Just be patient and watch. We got this shit covered."

Both cars took turns circling the block. Sitting in a parked car for too long was a dead giveaway. With everything around us in motion, they had no idea they were being watched that day or several times before. Everybody's actions seemed predictable. I could see how easy these routines made it for the undercovers watching a drug ring. Just like the feds, *we were waiting for the right time to strike.*

Addicts were hanging around waiting for Dead-eye's runners to call shop open. They anxiously paced around in short circles so when the police pulled up they would be in natural movement. Standing still on a busy strip is a clear sign to police that they are involved in the trade. We watched the dead come alive each time the runners showed their faces.

The Bill Gates dope they sold was a clear sales pitch for a fiend trying to get high and a hustler like Dead-eye trying to get rich. Nobody knew the man. They just chased his image, and envied his multi-billionaire status.

Dead-eye finally came out of the house into the middle of the street to direct traffic. He organized his crew and the addicts and went right back in.

"That's Dead-eye standing on the steps--and both of them right there are his runners—those two standing by the steps," I told Fruity, pointing to them going back and forth in the front door.

Kids were playing innocently in the middle of the block without a care of what was happening around them. They watched everything, too. Today's activities would be stored in their memory banks and recalled when they grew older taking the places of those who were performing sales directly in front of them.

"I see him," he answered. "C'mon—let's make our move through the back door as soon as we see them come out again."

"Naw, man—not as soon as he comes out!" I snapped. "We gotta corner his ass in the alley so he can't run! Then we take his ass back in the house—and take everything!"

"I want that money they got up in there!" Fruity said, sounding like a greedy child.

"But I want him! He crossed my man."

"Hitting in the hole! Hitting in the hole—no ones and no change!" Dead-eye yelled to his runners, after coming from the alley way.

Right away one of his workers scream, "Muthafuckers, *Bill Gates. Bill Gates*--line up in the alley—now!"

What he said made the addicts run straight to the alley to form a line. A girl came out of a different house holding a brown bag and gave it to Dead-eye. Both of his runners were right behind him ready to make that money. They worked the line hitting one after the other. Fully working their system, they served the last waiting addict. After she walked out of the alley at lightning speed, Juvenile flashed his headlights two times.

"It's time to go to work," I said to Fruity.

We jumped out of our cars running and crept up on him in the dim alley like wild black panthers in total darkness.

Juvenile and Flubber took the lead. They came from the front and we came from the back. I thought he would've heard our footsteps kick pieces of broken glass and trash.

Counting money had him distracted. "Bitch, you know what time it is," Juvenile said, hitting him on the right side of his head with the butt of his gun.

"What da fu—" he shouted, turning around with a stunned look on his face.

"Get your muthafuck'n hands up, bitch!" Fruity screamed at the other walking beside him.

"Alright, Yo! Alright!" Dead-eye screamed, dropping the money, freeing his hands and grabbing his head. *His two workers stopped dead in their tracks, the shorter one dropping the brown bag on the ground.*

"See how much fun it is now that the gun is in your face, bitch!" I said, snatching the brown bag from off the ground. *If any of them moved wrong or tried to run, all three would be in trouble. The book of Baltimore's dead would be opened once again.*

"Juvenile—C'mon, Man. That shit was between you and Tavon, man. Why you putting me in it!" Dead-eye whined.

"I thought we were cool until you put yourself in this do-or-die shit! Now you getting your guys hit unless you give us what we're looking for," Juvenile told him.

As we marched all three of them toward the back yard, Dead-eye reached for his chain. Taking that off, un-assing his most prized possessions showed his cooperation.

"Bitch! Don't do shit until I tell your ass! Now give me the fuckin' keys to get in this backdoor!" Juvenile said.

"It's open already," he said, sounding like a scared little bitch.

Now it was my partner's turn to hold his ass at gunpoint. With Fruity and Flubber in tow, holding guns to their heads, we forced them through the back door.

"Get on the floor right now!" I screamed, taking control. "Flubber and Fruity go upstairs. I'll go down the basement to make sure nobody is down there. J, you got it?"

"I got 'em!" he said.

We ran through the house. It was nobody down the basement so I ran back up the steps into the kitchen after a quick search. We started searching bodies and taking jewelry when we heard a scream from upstairs. I ran up the steps with both guns drawn to see what was happening.

"Ahhhh! C'mon, man—please?!"

"Snatch his bitch-ass off that toilet!" Flubber screamed.

"C'mon, man—please!" the submissive voice said. "Tell me what you want and I'll get dat' shit?!"

"Where's the fuckin' safe?!" Fruity screamed.

"Don't kill me—man! Dat' shit is in the closet in the front room! The key is in Dead-eye's pocket! Just don't kill me!" he begged.

Fruity hollered, as he dragged his half naked prisoner down the steps, "Take the key J! Get that shit from Dead-eye so we can get outta here!"

I snatched the key from Dead-eye's pocket and threw it to Fruity. Snatching it out of the air, he ran back upstairs for the safe. It was somebody else upstairs hiding because fast footsteps ran into the front room. It sounded like a chair was pushed and a glass window broke.

There was a hard knock on the back door. "Boom. Boom. Boom."

Tip-toeing to the door, I peeped out to see who it was. Damn! It was that young girl working with them who was holding the brown bag. Snatching the door open quickly and grabbing her, I screamed, "Get your little dumb ass in here, bitch!"

"Ah, Aaaaaaaaaah!" she screamed in shock.

I slammed the door shut before throwing her violently to the floor.

"Dead-eye, for getting your stupid ass involved trying to kill me, you just killed yourself!" Juvenile told him. "You shoveled shit on your own grave."

I heard a loud, quick gunshot from upstairs. You could hear Fruity and Flubber running towards the steps and downstairs.

"I got the rest of dat' shit! It was somebody else hiding in the back room," Flubber yelled, as he made his way behind his brother past the hostages on the floor, and through the door.

"C'mon—now--let's get out dis' bitch, Yo!" Juvenile yelled, as he turned towards the door to run.

"Y'all take everything. I got it from here…I'm right behind y'all!" I screamed. "Let me finish shit up!" *Nobody was living beyond this heist.*

I turned to step closer to the hostages on the floor, but felt somebody violently snatching my arm for my gun.

"Y'ALL AIN'T KILLING ME!" Dead-eye screamed.

I snatched my body, pulling my arm free, but fell, losing my balance, against the kitchen cabinet. Juvenile turned and reached over to break my fall. I grabbed the other gun from my waist after catching my balance.

"BOOM!" *Juvenile hit him with the first gunshot.* "You wanna be a superhero—muthafucka!" Juvenile screamed at Dead-eye who was still rushing coming toward me.

I was finally able to catch my balance before shooting him with both guns and then the girl. His runners scrambled, in all the commotion, trying to reach the front door. Fruity let off a few more gunshots dropping them on the living room floor.

Pushing shit out of the way, we ran out the same way we came in—splitting up after we got out of the alley. Fruity was still with me. I started the car when he jumped in the passenger's side. I hit the accelerator before he had a chance to shut the door.

I drove like a madman behind Juvenile. The plan was to meet at Jameel's house since she was at some kind of church service—just in case we got split up or if the police came trying to pull us over creating a high speed chase. It didn't take long for us to park those stolen cars a few blocks away from his daughter's mother's house. We went through each alley watching for everything that could be watching us. Juvenile had his back door key in his hand so that got us straight into the house.

We stayed in the basement to find out all of what we had to split. Fruity and Flubber counted while Juvenile and I watched as the money stacks kept adding up. We hit the jackpot and walked away with about 17 G's, a diamond watch and rings.

Flubber and Fruity had enough drugs to wholesale for another four thousand dollars. Now that wasn't a bad day's work. That wasn't bad at all.

Police Blotter

Two Men injured in home invasion

A man was seriously injured last night in a Northwest Baltimore home in what police suspect was a drug robbery. Authorities were called to investigate "shots fired" by at least four armed attackers at a residence on Pulaski Street. Rico "Dead-eye" Amos, 23, of the 100 block of Pennsylvania Avenue, and three unidentified victims were found fatally shot by Amos' girlfriend who rents the property.

The gunmen entered through a locked rear entrance and robbed the victims of money and unknown valuables before fleeing the scene, witnesses said. Another victim was inside, but left the scene escaping through a second floor window.

Police questioned two black male suspects at a bus stop fitting the description not far from the scene. Both men were charged and being held without bail at Central Booking on multiple charges of murder, robbery, home invasion, and discharging a firearm with city limits.

The investigation is continuing.

Chapter 18

PRECIOUS

"I was dealt a bad hand.
What else could I do?
But keep something up my sleeve—
that'll help me through."
Jay-Z, *"Diamond Is Forever"*
The Blueprint 2

I know when enough is enough. And when things start getting as crazy as they are now, it's time for a change of scenery. I hustled too from off the streets, so I had to keep a fresh hustler or two up my sleeve that would help me through times like this. When one hustler won't, the other one will.

I'm beginning to feel like Charm City's thick walls are closing in on me. I have to get away. The only thing making me feel good lately are the drinks I sip all during the day because this is the longest time I've ever spent without somebody and it's driving me crazy.

Just last night, I was talking to my favorite cousin in New Jersey--telling her all the crazy shit that's been happening. Of course I wasn't prepared for her lecture, but what she said was nothing more than the truth. She wants me to come there and chill out for a while, at least until things settle down in B-More.

Dee keeps telling me the same thing. He wants me to pack my stuff and come up to New York with him, but I don't know about making that move yet, even though I could use the action. Deep down inside I've always wanted that constant New York action and it's been that way ever since I went there with Fast Money and Tavon.

Lately, all I've been doing is curling up in bed with my Hennessy bottle, a super size bag of sour cream and onion potato chips and this new book everybody keeps telling me to read. After reading so many chapters of The Wolf Trap *by* Dennis Wise, *I have to put it down because I'll finish it in a day. I'm trying to make it last, so in between I'm reading the latest issues of Don Diva, Ebony and Jet and any other magazine I can get my hands on.*

Between Henny sips and Coke belches, I actually enjoy reading—if I don't fall asleep. I always make an effort to go down to that new bookstore on Franklin Street to buy every issue of Don Diva magazine because it keeps me up with what's going on with other hustlers in the different cities. I've been reading this same page for I don't know how long now—dozing off to sleep-- and don't even know what's it about.

"Ring! Ring!"

"Hello?" I asked, wondering who may have been calling me this time since I'm not in the mood to talk.

"What's up, Precious?" the voice asked.

"Boy! You scared me calling me this time of night!"

"What's wrong?" Dee asked.

"The phone just caught me off guard—dat's all."

"See how fidgety you gettin'—even the phone scared the shit outta you!"

"Dee, besides me being sleep when the phone rang, there's a lot of thoughts running through my mind right about now."

"So have you given any thought to what we spoke about?"

"I've been really thinking about it Dee. It's getting crazy down here. I know you heard what's been going on?"

"Yeah, I' been hearing different shit, but what's going on now?"

"You already know that they got Pretty who was working for Fast Money. And not that long after they picked up Fast Money--right before Tavon got killed."

"What's happening with Fast Money now, B?"

"The feds still got him over the SuperMax jail because of that New York connect he was dealing with. Pretty is still over Central Booking since the house raid, but you already know about that, too."

"Since his connect is all in the news, he ain't coming home no time soon," Dee said.

"I know that, but that's not all. Lately, Tavon's workers are getting' knocked off, one by one. First, it was Rabbit. They say he definitely got set up."

"That's the kid that used to hang around with Dead-eye?" Dee asked, sounding eager to understand the city truth.

"Yeah. That's him. But, check dis shit out! Some dudes kicked Dead-eye's drug house door in and robbed him and his workers. But this is the kicker. I heard they gave up the money and still got murdered."

"How you hear all of this, Precious?"

"I got a call from over the jail and found out what happened to Dead-eye. The streets are saying it was a set up too because three or four guys crept in and got away with all that money. Everybody is saying that was another inside job."

"Oh, yeah? I keep tellin' you to get your ass outta tired-ass Baltimore. That place is like a deep hole. You have to get out while you can. It's one thing to grow up there, but you have to move beyond those corners to really live," he said, warning me. "If you don't, B--any hustler is bound for prison or six feet under. Those are the only two choices down there. That's why I left so fast. I saw it coming for me!"

"I know, but it's hard leaving my house and everything," I said. "I already know it's time to go because I had to beat this bitch down at the memorial for Tavon. She tried to step to me and I beat her ass to the ground! The police ended up locking me up for attempted murder—that's how bad I beat her ass!"

"I know you handled your business! But I got a question?"

"What?"

"Yo, B. What was the girl doing while you were beating her ass—getting a murder charge? It's hard believing your story because you're too soft to be fighting." Dee said laughing.

"Whatever. I know you don't believe me, but I handled my business out there."

I took a deep breath walking through my patio doors to my glass house. I needed something to help make up my mind if I should leave or not. I turned the flood lights on in the back so I could see the flowers I had in my mini-greenhouse. My enclosed back patio has become my place of peace lately. The smell of fresh flowers and the sound from my water fountain relaxes me each time I open these doors. This wasn't my first house, but it is the biggest one I've ever had, so it's hard leaving these memories behind.

"Precious, how good would you be with your pretty house if you get caught up like everybody else around you?"

"You right and you know what Dee? Fuck it—I'm ready. This shit is really getting to me," I snapped.

"Well, why don't you—" the call-waiting clicked in and interrupted the line.

"Excuse me. Hold that thought for a second, somebody's clicking on my other line and I'm waiting for Pretty to call. I'm talking to her on a collect call if I take too long to click back, okay?"

"Why now, Precious? We're talking about some important shit."

"I have to press "0" for my gurl, Dee. Now hold on!" I said impatiently.

He was right. I shouldn't be clicking over, but I've been wanting to talk to Pretty and this may be her call. A break from my deep conversation with Dee could clear my mind. Still, I wasn't prepared for the voice I heard on the other end.

"You have a collect call from—Craig Carter—at the Maryland Correctional Adjustment Center. If you accept this call do not use…"

I clicked back over before the recording finished because that was his problem. He had a federal charge, not me. I don't know about anybody else, but I have something against the prison-thing and these tired ass ex-hustlers. For one, I don't have time for a jailbird. It's true that me and Fast Money could've hooked up again before he got locked up, but he has nothin' to offer me now--not while his ass is locked up. All he's selling now behind those collect call walls are promises and a bunch of dreams. And I ain't having that!

"I'm back, baby," I said to Dee, walking back into the house. *My wet bar was calling me so I poured me another shot of my favorite drink. With that in hand, I took a few more steps in the living room over to my day bed to snuggle on top.*

"Was it something important? It had to be the way you cut me off," he asked, sounding a bit annoyed.

"No, it was one of those telemarketing calls, so I hung up," I answered, lying my ass off. "You know I didn't mean to cut you off, Boo. Now go 'head and finish."

"So, are you definitely ready, Precious—because this shit ain't no joke up here? I know you've been with those other kids getting change and shit, but this is the big time up here baby?"

"I'm ready, Dee. I keep telling you that you're the one I wanna be with, for real."

"You know—B. I can send da' fuckin' money to get your ass up here to stay with me like—right now! And dis' don't have nothing to do with business. You know it's been a minute since I taste that good stuff you got, gurl," he said, lowering his voice, trying to be sexy.

"Stop playing, Baby. You know you have a way of making me feel good, anyway."

The mood was getting so comfortable it forced me to slide my fingers between my hot legs. I was trying to bring myself to orgasm secretly. I wanted to experience feeling him again like I did before.

"Alright, that's what I wanna hear. How much you need?"

I was lost, listening to his voice, trying to get that old feeling back from when we last hooked up.

"Precious, you hear me?"

"Yes baby," I answered, unable to conceal my sounds of pleasure.

"Gurl, that's what I'm talking bout--rub that pussy for me. You know what, baby?"

"What Daddy?"

"You making me get hard! That's why you should be up her with me. All that pussy should be mine. Now rub that pussy like I like it," Dee said in a low, sneaky tone.

I moaned as my body shook from the excitement, enjoying the pleasure of his voice. "Ummmmh! Baby," I said, breathing hard, enjoying myself. "You know how to handle this pussy. Take it from me—you know how much I like that!"

I kept teasing myself, getting to that point, and then slowing down. I could feel him again all over my body.

"You want Big Daddy to hit that and beat that ass when you feel it, Baby?" he asked. "Tell me you do!"

"I do Big Daddy—just push it in me real hard so I can come for you! I've been a bad gurl."

"Do it then—and do it hard like I'm tearing that pussy up! And slap that ass because Big Daddy knows you've been a bad gurl!"

I started taking deep breaths, trying to fight it and make the feeling last longer, but I couldn't. Lightly rubbing in circles, pushing my pressure button, forced my clitoris to the point of no return. My body's energy rushed to my melting pussy, and exploded—taking me to another level. I exhaled, taking myself completely to that place of pleasure, screaming, sucking on my fingers, so he could hear me, "OOOowwww! Baby, that's it! Beat it up, Big Daddy! OOOowwww…I'm coming."

My body went limp as I laid there breathing heavily, already feeling mellow from my shots of Henny. I followed my body's command to collapse, allowing the energy and excitement to flow through my soul. Mini-sensations kept exploding as I slowed down and eased myself to a light-headed calm.

"Gurl, just tell me what you need so I can get that ass up here as soon as possible. I want that."

"Baby it's yours."

"Tell me how much?"

"Send about three thousand so I can do some stuff here before I leave. I wanna keep the place at least for a while and just travel back and forth—as long as that's alright with you. You know I'm a put work in for you like we talked about."

"Done. We'll talk about that later."

"Bye, baby," I said seductively.

"Hey! Hey!" I heard Dee say, just as I was about to hang up the phone.

"Yes, baby, I'm still here," I answered.

"I'm sending it through Western Union. It should be there some time today. I'll call you when I get it done so you can pick it up and have your ass here by the weekend."

"That's fine."

"B, just call me to let me know you picked shit up, Alright?"

"I will," I said, burying myself inside my warm mink blanket Fast Money gave me as a gift.

I have almost everything, as far as fashion, and all I've ever wanted—including expensive stuff I had back when I was with Dollar Bill. I'm surrounded by gifts like the ring Tavon dressed my left ring finger with before he died, to the cars, house, furniture and money I still have. The men in my life gave me so much to hold onto, more than just memories. I never knew the day would come when I'd leave B-More. But Dee was right and I realized that before dozing off...

* * * * * * * *

"Ring! Ring!"

"Shit, this damn phone keeps ringing." I said in frustration before answering. *'Who is it now?' I thought quickly to myself. I'm definitely not in the mood to talk, not after such a soul-searching conversation. I'd rather just lie down and let it all settle in my mind.* "Hello?"

"Collect call from…" I checked the clock and was surprised Pretty was calling so late. I waited for the recording to finish so I could accept the call.

"Gurl, I'm stealing a call," Pretty said, talking in an unusually low tone.

"Where you been? I've been waiting on you to call all day, what happen?"

"Gurl, we were on lockdown and couldn't make any calls. That's why I'll be glad when I get outta this shit. And that won't be too long from what my lawyer told me. He talked to the prosecutor trying to make something happen with the case. He should know what my deal is this week sometime. But we'll talk about that later. I just wanna make sure you're okay with all the crazy shit that been happening."

"I know, and I've been thinking of you lately in a lot of ways," I said, still feeling wet and sexual.

"Me, too, baby. That's why I snuck this call so I could hear your voice before I went to bed. You know when I get outta here I'll take care of you."

"I know Pretty, but you know this shit is scaring me because Tavon's old crew is gettin' knocked off slowly, but surely. It's almost like somebody is trying to kill them all."

"So what you gonna do?" she asked, showing some degree of concern in her voice.

"I'm looking to get away from this here and go to New York for a while," I said. *I was feeling more confident about leaving after making that statement to her. The more I thought about the madness that was happening, the more I convinced myself it's time to go.* "Plus, the homicide police have been around here trying to ask me some questions."

"I know dat's right. You sure that's what you wanna do, though?" she asked, with sadness in her voice.

"You damn right I'm sure!"

"Don't forget me, gurl. You know you'll always be mine—because I broke your hot ass in!"

"Dis' will always be yours, Pretty. But that's our secret. Just know I'm doing what I gotta do—for now, but I'll always take care of you." *She was my first, the woman who taught me a thing or two about a woman's love and men.* After a brief pause I told her, "I love you."

"I love you, too, Precious."

We said our goodbyes and I quickly hung up. I forced myself to let go before she had the opportunity to say another word, trying to convince me otherwise. I laid there thinking of what to take with me. I didn't need much because he had enough money for me to shop as soon as I got up there. I pulled out my Christian Dior suitcases and thought about how all our lives had changed almost overnight. I pulled my little safe from under the bed to get all my jewelry. I thought this life would never end, but it does.

Through our travels in this life on the streets we get separated. It's an up-and-down process. A lot of people want to see something happen to me. I'll be the first to admit that I was falling like that commercial ad on television. I was falling fast, but my beautiful black-ass was still alive and free enough to get back up. It will be the same game in New York when I get off my last train ride. A small adjustment is easy for me to make and I'll take extra steps to B-More careful moving at New York's speed.

The rest of the night was quiet. I went off to sleep hoping that phone wouldn't disturb me. While deep in my sleep, dreaming of moving to another state, I heard car doors slamming outside my bedroom window.

The first thought I had was, 'why are those cars so close to my house so early in the morning?' *It was 5:59am according to my digital alarm clock.*

'It's too early in the morning for this shit,' I thought, fighting my comforter and jumping out of my bed.

It sounded like something was going on outside of my front door. My second thought was having anything like this happen in this neighborhood was unusual. I almost tripped on the panties I kicked on the floor last night. In the midst of catching my balance, I reached out to the window ledge for support. After catching my balance, I quickly snatched the curtains like I was Moses parting the Red Sea and tried lifting my window.

My security alarm went off before I could process all of what was happening outside of my house. I heard this loud "BLOOOOOM!' crashing through my front door sounding like a small explosion...

Chapter 19

FAST MONEY

*"I'm not the snitch.
I don't go to the cops to get rich."*
            Jay-Z, *"Guilty Until Proven Innocent"*
                        The Dynasty

"Hey, Fast Money."

"Yeah, Gangsta. What's up?"

"What's your federal public defender talking about now? Every time he comes over here it's something different. He's always telling you some crazy shit 'bout your case."

"I couldn't wait to get back to tell you this shit!"

Gangsta sleeps right next to me. He has been here with me waiting to go to court on a federal drug conspiracy charge. He doesn't talk that much about his case because his is not as high profile as mine.

We grew up together on the streets. He was soldiering down on Monroe Street. That's why I talk to him about my case. I've shared some secrets with him that the feds don't know about. Raul didn't know everything—neither did Big Toney. As a matter of fact, he and I are going through the same things with friends uptown and lawyers downtown.

It's a lot of us hustlers sitting here on the federal tier waiting on court dates. Some of them are already convicted. They're just waiting for sentencing before they go into the federal system, do their time searching for a better connect, and get back on the game playing field. But it's just a matter of time before I go home.

That's right. I'm not like a lot of those other hustlers. I get money uptown and they don't. I had a bad break that I can recover from. My panel attorney said I should be going home because he can beat the charge—at least that's what he said when he was assigned by the judge. I have no other choice but believe him—even though everybody is saying otherwise.

"Gangsta, now check dis' shit out!"

"What's up Money?"

"My lawyer just handed me some papers with names on the back of the indictment. He was telling me that the federal prosecutor once practiced with him and is saying another witness came forward against me. He didn't have a name yet. Discovery is only listing the person by number. They're informant #519. All my lawyer knows is that they have been *informing* for the Baltimore City cops for a long time. Whoever it is, they are testifying against me for the feds.'

"Let me see," he asked, reaching for the indictment.

"Freedman is saying their testimony has something to do with the jewelry heist and the guns we were getting from Virginia. It has to be a dude snitching on me because no females ever knew about Virginia. I only had them going to NY," I said, after handing him the paper and stepping inside my cell. "Remember dat' broad I was telling you about that used to carry those things for me from New York to Baltimore like a pro?"

"Who are you talking about now? Wasn't her name Pretty Jenifer?"

"Pretty is lying to the U.S. Attorney. Now the feds are charging me with bringing those kilos back to Baltimore on Interstate 95."

"Oh, yeah."

"Gangsta, I know dat's a damn lie because I was bringing all my *byrds* back on the trains. My connect ain't want me to take none of his kilos on the interstate. His scared-ass was bragging one time about how potent our shit was. He said if the police pulled one of our rental cars using a K9, the dog would get sick and die. His scared ass said we'd be facing murder! I'm telling you, man. The cocaine we pushed came straight off the ship! That's why we never did the New Jersey Turnpike!"

"You was gettin' it from that dude named Raul like dat' dawg? What you say his last name was again?"

"Rodriguez. That's how heavy our loads were before other shit started happening! We were getting twenty five to thirty kilos at a time—sometimes more than that! I would even get Big Toney's shipment and bring that back, too."

"Whatchu get for doing shit like 'dat for Big Toney?"

"That meant an extra kilo or a few thousand dollars for taking care of that. Fast Money gets money uptown, boy! If you have it, you'll definitely get more. That's what was happening to me. Anything I touched paid off. But now I need me some of those *STOP SNITCHING* t-shirts for his ass and shit!"

"But that's what they saying about me, Fast Money. And I'm over here with you and shit. I'm not no fucking snitch. I ain't that kind of hustler. I ain't going to the cops to get rich," he screamed. "Dat's what the block is for!"

"That's messed up with this game. Shit ain't what it used to be. Everybody's telling whatever they can," I told him. "It ain't no love out there. It's like everybody's playing Monopoly, taking a chance, but wanna get outta jail for free at my expense."

"Fast Money. That *help-yourself room* ain't never empty. Now the game on this side of the wall is every man, woman and child for self! And still they can't get their lies straight, can they?"

"Hell, naw! I had the girl Pretty carrying long before my connect fell off. My man from Harlem named Reds was just starting to bring those bricks down to Baltimore. He was hitting big time dudes in D.C. with big weight, too. That's who was about to help me get on my feet before I got knocked off. I'd be way up on top if that didn't happen.

"They don't know all the rest of the people like Tasha on near Westside Shopping Center and Marsha from Edmondson

Avenue and especially Jackie from in the Village. She was bringing the most out of all of them when I think about it. That's the girl I was telling you about that live on Morley Street in Edmondson Village."

"Is that the one who lives off of Old Frederick Road?" he asked.

"Yeah, dat's her. She's still living at 1123 South Morley Street. So they don't even know what they're talking about. That's why I'm not pleading guilty to this. They don't have nothing against me besides he-say, she-say testimony."

"Hey, Fast Money, let me ask you this? Are they saying anything about the gurl, Tasha, you were telling me about?"

"Naw. They would have her address down here. She lives in the 2600 block of Lombard Street. She lives 2699 on the corner house to be exact, but they don't have it down here. My lawyer isn't saying anything about her either. She's still holding some money for me now. Between me and you, that's where I got a lot of shit that the feds were looking for at Pretty's house!" I screamed. *I was telling everything, but the truth. Nothing in prison can replace the lies. Besides, that's what keeps the time flying.*

"Hold up, Fast Money. Police are on the tier. It must be count time."

"I gotchu."

I watched the officers do count. They're always counting shit around here, so I kept quiet until they left off the tier. It's not good to let them hear about your life uptown because they will testify against you if they have to.

I knew I was broke and had no money or drugs. To make myself feel good because of my pain I lied a little about Tasha. This was my man Gangsta I was talking to. He knew what level I was on in the streets and would believe anything I told him. I wanted to change the subject anyway because other things were getting the best of me.

Nobody understands what I'm going through over here. If I could get out of the game and change my life, I would.

Everyday I live with regrets. I'm braggin' to Gangsta like I'm what's happening, but in reality that's not the real me. I know no judge will believe what I say when it comes to changing my life and getting a job, but I'm serious about walking away. I want out, but it seems too little, too late. My only hope is this lawyer handling his business in the courtroom and setting me free after court.

"Hey, Gangsta! Man, I was telling my mother and sister how we live in here. This place is a jungle."

"Did you tell her what your lawyer said the other week when he came to tell you he can beat your case?"

"Naw, I try keeping my mother's spirits up when I call. I don't go in to too much detail because her heart can't handle this."

"Money, they're saying you received profits from the sale of each kilo in Baltimore, right?"

"Yeah."

"They suppose to have all this evidence. So, why are they coming right back offering you a plea deal if you admit to trafficking?"

"That's why I'm fighting this, Gangsta. I ain't taking nothin'!"

"*Informants* are their smoking guns. Snitching is every true hustler's worse nightmare. Not even those STOP SNITCHIN' tapes being sold in West Baltimore can fight against the telling that's already been done! I'm hearing about so many of those guys I know. I had no idea some of them were snitching."

"How can we fight against that? And the worse part about it is they are everywhere! They'll tell just to get '*the man*' off their ass. Look at my case you can see that. Gangsta, you can't trust *no--by—dee*!"

"Hell naw! You right, Money—you can't trust nobody! And the shit we talking about gotta stay between us, too."

"Dat' ain't all. Rumors are flying about my situation. I've heard some of my homeys are saying I'm cooperating. Then

I'm hearing Big Toney is telling, but this was the bombshell. Raul, my New York connect, is the key witness in the whole case. My lawyer was telling me that Raul is still testifying before another grand jury telling them every detail. He's even telling them how I was using the cutt to multiply the weight he was sending me and how I still sold it for raw."

"Yo! That's crazy!"

"Ayy, Gangsta. Remember I was telling you how I went to Tavon about his gurl messing with his partner, Juvenile?"

"Yeah! Remember you let me see her picture."

"That's right. Guess what happened right after I got locked up?"

"What?"

"Tavon ended up trying to kill Juvenile. He got some dudes together and tried to take Juvenile out for messing with nasty Precious. Something went wrong with his plan and his ass got killed by the police. Of course she's not worth that, but every man makes his own choice in that game. We all knew it was more about trust than her."

While talking to Gangsta, I keep thinking about Black Face's warnings about Precious from the very beginning. It plays over and over again in my mind. She's a damn spider with a thick web and now she's claimed two more lives and the third is mine, so why am I still crazy about her ass? That's who I tried to call while we were out on recreation today, but she didn't accept the call. And never has.

"Man she must have some *killa* shit! She's got everybody going after each other over her?"

"Man, she's the shit alright! Precious ain't shit—and she ain't afraid to show it off either."

"Yo, Fast Money--let me see what other pictures you got of her so I can get my shit off over here?"

"If I showed you all of the ones she took when we were shopping in Los Angeles, the ones from the Hollywood West Hyatt Hotel, you'd be jerking off non-stop—killing yourself in there!"

"I don't care. Precious' body is off the chain!" he said laughing. "Don't try to keep it all for yourself—'cause I'm going to be back here for a good while now. Besides, your lawyer said you'll be going home!"

"Don't hurt yourself!" I screamed before sending some over. "Here. There's ten of 'em. Go ahead and have some fun because that's all that trick is good for now!"

Just that quick glance at her pictures instantly brought back memories of the very first time she freaked me.

'Ummm! Ummm! Ummm!' I'm lying when I tell people Precious ain't shit. Truthfully, I have to admit, even if I only keep it to myself, that Precious is the shit!

News Update

Fed Prosecutors gain other witnesses

The cellmate and former girlfriend of an alleged interstate drug trafficker with connections to the New York Police Department has both come forward with information detailing secrets of that case which one prosecutor calls "two bombshells."

A high-profile federal trial is scheduled to begin soon. Craig "Fast Money" Carter is alleged to have revealed intricate details about his drug operation to Tyree "Gangsta" Bradley and Precious Jenkins that federal prosecutors needed to seal his conviction. Investigators gained Ms. Jenkins' cooperation after a house raid netting money, an automatic handgun and paraphernalia hidden inside a secret wall compartment in her residence. "Items found in the house," she claims, "all belonged to the kingpin, Fast Money. And I will testify to that."

Federal and state investigators also set up wiretaps inside the SuperMax jail on Madison Street and, according to court documents, heard recorded conversation of those previously involved in this drug ring.

Prosecutors are seeking to withdraw a guilty plea offer and intend to seek maximum punishment of a *Life sentence* against Carter for his involvement in what prosecutors call the largest, most violent interstate trafficking scheme in recent history.

Chapter 20

JAMEEL

"Just me and you.
I love your point of view
Because you hold no punches."

Jay-Z, *"Song Cry"*
The Blueprint 2

"Tiffany, are you finished setting the table, sweetie?"

"Yes, Mommy, you wanna see it?"

I went downstairs to see what she was doing since she didn't want me to help nor did she want me in the dinning room before she finished. Everything was done just like I asked her.

"Good job, baby. Don't forget the napkins."

"Oh man. I was trying to do it right and I missed the napkins," Tiffany said, sounding really disappointed.

"That's okay baby--you're doing good."

Wednesday evenings are always family dinner nights for us. It's even gotten better now since Dorian has been spending more time with us. Dorian still goes out, but he has been in more than out. I worry every time he goes out with my two brothers and that Trigger friend of his. I just have to pray that he'll totally walk away from it all, in time.

"Ring! Ring!"

I wondered who this could be calling me? Those telemarketers always choose the wrong time to annoy people.

"Hello!" I said, speaking in an unpleasant tone.

"Baby what's wrong? Why you sound so harsh?"

"I'm sorry, I don't mean to sound that way."

"Have you been missing me all day? And don't lie," he asked.

"Oh, Dorian, stop! I didn't know it was you," I said, feeling giddy from his questions.

He's been making me feel so warm and so needed ever since he came home. That's what I've been missing in my life. "And to answer your question, *yes*, I've been missing you."

"Baby I'll be home in about 20 minutes. What are we having tonight?"

"It's a surprise. Why don't you just wait until you get home?"

"Okay, tell my baby girl I'll be home soon."

Although tonight is our family night, I'm gonna cut it short with Tiffany because I really need to spend some alone time with Dorian. I have to talk to him about the prospect of my new job after I graduate. I know he might try to eat and go to sleep, but we really have to talk.

I heard the basement door open and slammed shut in a hurry after going through about thirty minutes of anticipation.

"Who is that mommy?" Tiffany asked, looking startled.

"It's Dorian. You know he always comes in through the back door. I have no idea why, but that's your strange father," I said, poking Tiffany as I walked by her.

Whatever he was doing down stairs made a loud bang sound--like he loss control of the cover of the washing machine or something. Then I heard him running up the steps.

"What's up, Baby? How was your day?" Dorian asked, sounding out of breath. *He grabbed me around the waist and kissed me all over my face. That has been my evening greeting ever since we've started getting closer.*

"Mine was fine," I said. *He released me while grabbing at Tiffany.*

"And yours little lady?" he asked, chasing her around the dining room table.

Enjoying her father, she said, "Mommy—Daddy's chasing me again and I can't answer his questions."

"Just answer my question and I'll stop," he said, still playfully running after her.

"Daddy, my day was good, but I tried to call you—so I could talk to you."

"I didn't have my phone. That's why I rushed home so I could get that great big hug of yours."

Dorian has a gift with his daughter, a bond that I can't interrupt. Sometimes I can't figure out which one of them is younger.

"What we got here, baby?" Dorian asked, washing his hands.

"I made you a Cobb Salad with grilled chicken breast and shrimp on my George Foreman grill. I bought some Mescaline mix and your daughter sprinkled honey-glazed pecans over the blue cheese dressing you like."

"Umm-Umph. Cobb salad. That's what I'm talkin' bout!" he screamed, wiping his hands faster on the paper towel.

"That's what a woman does for her family, Dorian. I know exactly what you like."

Hugging me from behind with his mouth gently caressing my ear, he whispered, "I know I haven't said this before, but that's what I missed so much being out there. I missed you and my daughter." *He sealed his confession with a warm, wet kiss.*

We sat around after eating dinner talking and laughing and making fun of each other. The only thing we had left to do with Tiffany was check over her homework and sign off on her agenda book.

"Okay Tiffany, its homework time. Ms. Staten sent me a note saying that you have to read the rest of *Happy to be Nappy*."

"Momma, I only have about ten pages left. Can I read it to Daddy?"

"Girl, you know I'll listen to whatever you wanna read, so go get it," he said.

I stepped in the kitchen area to clean the dishes while they finished up. Tiffany curled up into her dad's arm and started reading to him. Each night on my long, living room couch we read something before our bedtime devotion. Sometimes I read her articles from magazines, just so she gets used to reading different things. Tonight was my chance to listen as she read with so much confidence to her father. She seemed so happy with Dorian around. You could see she was feeling her family. And so was I—Life had a plan for us.

"Tiffany, it's bedtime. Finish up with Daddy—and then get your shower. I'll tuck you in after you say your prayers."

"Okay, but I was gonna ask Daddy to tuck me in tonight, Mommy."

"Alright, baby. Read that last little bit and go get ready for bed."

Tiffany went upstairs to shower. She called Dorian about fifteen minutes later. He went up and seemed to take forever. All I could hear was loud laughing and giggling coming from Tiffany's room. I was about to go spank my two kids when he came running down the stairs.

"Jameel, I need to talk to you--just you and me."

"Can we sit over here on my favorite couch? You know I've been waiting for you to finish your fatherly duties and spend some alone time with me."

"I need to talk to you about something other than that."

I cuddled up beside him on the couch and asked, "Are you okay, baby?"

"I don't mean to bring anything to you, but you know I've been trying my best to get all the way off the streets. Gettin' out ain't easy Jameel. That's why I'm coming to you because you hold no punches and I love your point of view."

"And I'll keep giving it to you, Dorian, as long as you want it."

"That's what I need to hear right now," he said, looking deeply into my eyes, pulling me closer to him in comfort. "When I look at how you live, it seems so easy and that's what I want for my life. Tavon had all of our money in his possession and I don't have any money coming in. I wanted to use some of that money Tavon left. Then I'd be good until I found a job and get myself completely together."

"It may look easy, but it's not at all—not for me or anybody else, Dorian. I understand what you're saying completely, but the money Tavon left is not mine to use. I'm going to use that money to take care of his mother. I really didn't want to touch it, but his mother needed help getting into those programs. Other than that, I'm not using that money for anything other than what it was intended for. I hope you understand."

"I'm not saying it's not hard for you, baby," he said. "The only thing people like you have to worry about are bill collectors; me, I gotta watch my back at all times--kinda like I'm getting scared of my own shadow. That's why I don't have you or Tiffany around me more. The past is my past, but it doesn't always go that way. I'm tired, Jameel and I really want out. Being with you and Tiffany is all I want baby."

"Are you in trouble?"

"No. I'll work it out and make it happen."

"Make me understand?"

"I can only tell you I'm doing me. Besides, it's too much and you couldn't handle or begin to understand what's been happening."

"You have to give me the chance, Dorian. I want to be a part of who you are becoming. And I keep telling you how proud I am because I know you're trying to change. Not many get a chance to do that, Dorian. You have been blessed and *God* has *His* hand on you."

"I know baby, I know," he said, kissing me lightly on the forehead.

"It's kind of ironic that you came home in this mood tonight because I wanted to talk to you also. I guess we must have been feeling each other," I said as I rubbed his hands.

"What's on your mind, baby?"

"I really think we should get outta Baltimore. And since you're finished with the streets, it's time for us move on. Besides, we were just waiting for you to come back to us."

"*Whatchu' talkin' bout*, Jameel? You wanna leave town?" Dorian asked, sounding surprised. "I agree that we need to move out of the city, but leaving the state? Why can't we just move to Columbia or some place like that?"

"Calm down, Dorian. It's not final yet. Furthermore, we won't be that far away. It's just in New Jersey. I applied for a position with the *U.S. Health Care Coalition Against Domestic Violence* to be the executive director. Counseling women and children in my church ministry gave me the experience I needed. I'm almost sure I'll get it because I've already done two phone interviews and I know one of the people on the panel. She was a visiting professor in my psychology class. She encouraged me to apply for the position after she read a proposal I wrote in class. Think about it, baby? We could start a new life in New Jersey. You, me, and Tiffany."

"So when will you know if you got the job?"

"I told them I wanted to wait until after my graduation. I should find out not long from now."

We sat on the couch in silence enjoying each other's company and closeness.

"You know what baby, you're right. Going some place far from here is a good idea and you deserve to get whatever job you interviewed for."

"No, Dorian—we deserve it," I said to him, reaching to hold him in my arms.

"I'm so proud of you Jameel, I really am."

"No. I'm really proud of you."

"When is graduation, baby?"

"It's in June. I better make sure I ace these midterms before I start planning for a graduation. When I do walk across that stage you better not miss it!" *After telling him I rolled my eyes and twisted my neck to make sure he understood my point.*

"I wouldn't miss that for the world. I'll be there to see my superwoman walk across that stage. We'll be your front row cheerleaders."

Coming from him that sure made me feel good. I'm just trying to show him there's a better way to deal with life. He was finally coming out of the darkness stepping closer to the light. Change doesn't happen over night and I'm remaining patient.

"Dorian," I said with tears running down my face. "Your baby and I have been and always will be there for you. For a while, I had to practice tough love with you. It didn't mean that I didn't love you. I love you to death. I would die for you if you were doing the right thing, living the right way. I just didn't know any other way to get through to you.

"You were putting us in danger. And anything could've happened to any one of us. God knows we waited this long for you. And we're sticking with you until the end because we love you that much."

Dorian wiped my tears before sharing a passionate kiss. We cuddled, enjoying each other's closeness when he said, "I needed to hear that because a lot of thoughts are running through my mind. One thing I want you and my daughter to know is how much I love both of y'all for that. If it hadn't been for y'all, I don't know where I would be right now."

I felt like I was on cloud nine as we wrapped ourselves together in each other's arms. If I had one wish it would be having this feeling last forever. I guess we were both quietly reflecting on our conversation before deciding to share the rest of the night upstairs with the lights out. Feeling open and emotional, hot and steamy, because my monthly has just passed, if my man doesn't initiate making love tonight...then I will.

Police Blotter
Northwestern District
Drug Arrests

Acting on a tip from an informant, Drug Enforcement agents observed several drug transactions in the 3300 block of Belvedere Avenue. Officers raided the house and seized 33 ounces of crack cocaine, 19 ounces of raw heroin, more than 250 pounds of marijuana, .44 large caliber handgun and nearly $164,317.

John Wayne Brathwaite, 27, and Rupert Allen, 31, both from Kingston, Jamaica, were both arrested and charged with possession of crack, heroin, and marijuana, conspiracy and the intent to distribute. Brathwaite was also charged with possession of an illegal handgun. Both men face deportation charges at the Department of Immigration and Naturalization Services.

Chapter 21

FAST MONEY

"The jury got the[ir] brows raised
Listening to testimony about my foul ways.
Exhibit A...[There's no] Reasonable Doubt.
This is the first thing that turned the [jury] out."
Jay-Z, "Dopeman"
Vol. 3: Life and Times of S. Carter

This has been the longest six weeks of my entire life.
Going to court is mandatory early in the morning and each day
starts out at 3:00am. You can hear guards hollering your name
and cell number from a mile away. This was their way of letting
you and everybody else know you have another day in court.
Who the hell wanna get up that early? I sure as hell don't, but I
had no choice.

Before I even leave out the prison my bad day starts. I
first had to go to the bullpen after eating breakfast. I'm greeted
with an order to strip naked and hand my clothes over. Piece by
piece they search my clothes on a steel bench, underwear
included, while I stand naked, posing for research inside a cold
ass room. For however long it takes, I have to hold my breath to
avoid vomiting. This one small room has held thousands of
naked, sweaty asses going through this same process over and
over again to see a judge.

"Open your mouth and stick your tongue out. Turn around. Spread your ass," they scream—knowing this is the start of opposition. "Lift your arms—high enough to see each underarm--and turn around. Lift your feet up and then run your fingers through your hair. Anything you have between the crack of your ass will be released so let it fall. Squat and let your balls hang. Stand up. Lift your balls up with your right hand."

The next step is waiting in the bullpen for the U.S. Marshall's to come and rush me into their highly tinted cars. To describe it it's like a legal kidnapping. They snatch you up, tie you down in steel jewelry and legally take you to where the government says you must appear. These men are the biggest organized gang if you ask me.

It took a week to pick the jury. I wanted to take a plea bargain because of those snitchers testifying against me, but when Gangsta and Precious turned fed witness, the government withdrew their interest in a plea with me. Life is what they say they want for me now. But only a couple months ago they were offering me 30 years. I know it sounds crazy, but I would have taken that 30-year sentence. The hope of one day getting out is much easier to swallow than never going home.

Speaking of Gangsta, how the hell did he get involved in this anyway? He had his own drug conspiracy case. He had nothing to do with me on the streets. We saw each other from time to time but that was it. I just started talking to him since I got in here because he seemed like an okay person. Damn if he didn't fool me. The government allowed him to tell on me—and clear himself. One case had nothing to do with the other. He'll eventually walk away a free, snitching man. A man I trusted will walk away with my 'reasonable doubt' in his possession.

I couldn't believe it when I saw Raul take the witness stand. His testimony was Exhibit A. Following him was the person they called informer #519. That damned Rock almost made me fall out of my seat! His testimony was about my foul ways in the streets and how we made big drug deals. I swallowed a mouth full of mucous that gathered in the pit of my dry throat--

every time he said something real credible and damaging. I watched the jurors. My skin crawled as they raised eyebrows and got uncomfortable in their seats. Some jurors looked directly at me with eyes of conviction. Others tried to look away, but couldn't resist taking one or two "it's not looking too good for you" glances my way.

With his testimony alone, and his star informant credibility, I knew I'd be going to jail. He remembered dates and details. It was almost as if he was telling his own stage play, but I took the lead role. For some strange reason, to me, his testimony conveyed a lot of guilt. But that wasn't bad yet.

When I heard the name Precious Jenkins and looked around and saw her coming into court with cuffs I was just about ready to get up and walk straight back into that car and go back to prison. I squirmed down as far as I could into my chair. I couldn't believe they got Precious, too. Fuck, everybody was bargaining for their life and freedom and used my life as the "get out of jail free" ticket.

Each day of testimony showed me how the game had changed. At that point, I was looking around for just about any one to come put their two cents in. It wouldn't be surprising if my jeweler came in from New York to testify against me or some of the car dealers and business owners from different states that I've spent more than $10,000 with in any single transaction. Hell, nothing surprised me after Precious—not even when Outlaw and Pretty showed up. The whole game turned on me and it cut deeply into everything I was every taught, everything I ever believed in.

Yesterday when we were driving to my last big day in court, I heard the escorting agents talking in the front of the car. They both laughed at me because of the overwhelming evidence the feds have against me. It's not the physical evidence that is so damaging. It's those testifying against me that makes this case so solid.

I voluntarily turned my life over to the government. They tell me when to do what. From being paid and shopping on

Rodeo Drive in Hollywood to SuperMax prison on Madison Street in Baltimore. I went from counting more than $200,000 a day, to a prisoner spending limit of less than one hundred dollars a week for commissary. That's a helluva change, ain't it?

The funny thing about this whole thing is...we all made money by playing a part, making all of this happen...

If I can tell those in the joint, homey's who have been locked away for a long time, anything, I would say the game was my prostitute—and I was its pimp. I took the role as team leader and created corner opportunities for my players. That was my job and I did that well. Game rules and parameters was what I respected. I was the one who played it like it was supposed to be played and did it like it was supposed to be done, but, in the end, I got treated like the whore. And that's not how the game used to be...

I wish I would've gotten a job or went to another state to build another life. I tried to get out, but that just never happened either. I had options, though. I could've gone to college after being a sharp student at Southwestern Sr. High School or could've taken a trade to start my own business. All I know is life had too many other possibilities for this federal prison to be my only one.

Federal LIFE! Fuck! I'm gone...

Chapter 22

PRECIOUS

I'm a hustler, Baby.
I just want you to know.
It ain't where I've been...
But where I'm about to go!"

Jay-Z, *"I'm a Hustler"*
They Dynasty

    I've been sitting back on my bunk at this Women's Detention Center reflecting on everything happening in my life. Just a little while ago I was on top of the world and then Fast Money fell off. He quickly became a has-been. Linking up with Tavon and Juvenile was different for me, a dream come true, but Tavon got killed. Juvenile disappeared—and I'm really scared. I don't know what may happen if I see him again. I think he's the one behind some of these crazy killings on the streets.

    As soon as I decided to go to New York and was happy about my decision, my dreams came to a crashing end. As a beautiful black woman, I'm doing what I'm supposed to do. I used the good pussy I got to get what I need and want. But at the end of every rainbow is a big bucket of bad luck...

    In New York I would've started a new life, but the feds cut that short with the house raid. That stupid ass Tavon must've had a secret wall safe I didn't know about. That's where the money was hidden in the house. Instead of me receiving it, the feds got it all.

Before, during, and after my arrest, I knew I wasn't staying in anybody's jail. I'm a hustler. Everybody knows that about me. Materially, I've always had either 'a lot' or 'a lot more' from the hustlers I've been with because I play my part.

Even during the house raid, the first thing the feds questioned me about was Fast Money. The second thing they did was show me some signed papers with Outlaw's signature on it. With Outlaw's testimony and what they found inside my house, they said I was facing five years alone for the handgun. And the judge would add more time for the paraphernalia and unreported earnings—unless I cooperated.

If I became a government witness they had the power to convince the judge to drop the charges or in the least put me on probation with no jail time. I'd be set free after testifying for the government. They'd already had Pretty who I'd seen a couple times since being here. Federal agents had us down there for questioning at the same time.

Big Toney and the guy Raul were witnesses, too. It was no need of me remaining loyal to somebody who couldn't help me. Fast Money was going away for a long time and I was willing to help the process. It doesn't matter to me, one way or the other, what Fast Money gets. He was the cause of Tavon's death sentence away from the streets and being able to take care of me. He didn't care how that would hurt me—or Juvenile for that matter.

I know that plan for New York with Dee is dead now. He'll be the first to know that I testified in court. So going up there is out of the question. They'd eventually find me in somebody's alley. You know what? I've seen all that I could see hustling hustlers in Baltimore. That life ain't about where you've been. Fresh hustlers come a dime a dozen. Now, it's about where I'm going.

New Jersey, here I come. I'm gone...

Chapter 23

JUVENILE

"Summer to winter
Dead or alive--
24-7, 365."

Jay-Z, *"Never Change"*
The Blueprint

With my mission accomplished, it was now time for me to get out of this game. This life wasn't me anymore. Trigger was basically bouncing around enjoying his freedom and spending his portion of the loot we made. Fruity and Flubber jumped into the hustle and they were both getting' money in different parts of West Baltimore. They had become the center of attention now that they created their own crews and held down their own spots. It was happening for them, but it's nothing like what I was making with Tavon.

They changed status almost overnight. Before I put them on they were known as stick-up boys, every hustler's nightmare around our hood. But now they're in the game and blowin' up fast.

As for me, I've just been trying to show Jameel I can do the right thing. I wanted to believe good things would happen for us if I did it her way, finally. That was going to be a major adjustment for me. Still, I was going through the motions of filling out applications. I did that hoping Jameel wouldn't get too restless.

I was laid back down the basement watching the Thursday night movie on Fox Family when the phone rang. It's feels funny staying in the house with my daughter and Jameel all the time. I feel so safe in the basement that some nights I just lay on the Futon staring at the ceiling before falling off to sleep. That's how I get my piece of mind. I was in another world thinking of all of what I've experienced when my daughter called.

"Daddy, my mother wants you upstairs. She has a job man on the phone," Tiffany yelled down the steps.

"What man you talking about?"

"She didn't tell me. She just told me to tell you she wanted you upstairs for a minute."

I slowly walked up the step, not really wanting to answer the call. I was looking for a way out, but I still wasn't feeling the 9-5 option.

"Here you go Dorian," she said, handing me the phone with a proud smile.

"Hello."

"Hello, Mr. Canon. I'm Robert Rogers from the Electronic Warehouse, but you can call me Rocky. We are the largest distributors of electrical products on the East Coast—and I want to bring you in for an interview. Actually, I'm—" he said, before the phone clicked.

"Can you hold for a second?" I asked, appreciating the interruption.

"I sure can."

"Hello," I said, quickly. "Who's dis?"

"Yo, dis' is Fruity, man."

"What's up, man?"

"I need to see you and Trigger up here in about an hour," Fruity said. "Flubber is already up here. It's real important that all four of us get together to talk."

"And you need me? I was just up here chilling with your sister and Tiffany. You sure you need me?"

"Yeah, you! Whatchu' try'na to be smart?" Fruity asked.

"Yeah—and what?! You're disturbing my movie!" I shouted.

"What!"

"You try'na' to see me in some boxing gloves or something?" I asked playfully.

"Forget dat' shit. I need to see your lazy ass up here! This is serious."

"Alright, but this better be good. Did anybody call Trigger—since you need to see all of us?" I asked with a bit of sarcasm in my voice.

"Yeah, he already knows. This some hot shit we gotta talk about."

"I'll be there!"

"Let me speak to my sister."

"Hold on," I said, before clicking back over. "Did you say your name was Ricky or Rocky?"

"I'm sorry if I didn't tell you the first time, but my name is Robert Rogers, but you can call me Rocky."

"Rocky, an emergency just came up. I'm going to have to call you back. I have your number," I told him before clicking back over to Fruity. I knew she wouldn't be happy hearing my responses, but I had to answer Fruity's call. Before walking away, I said, "Jameel, your brother is on the phone."

Going down the steps to get dressed, I could hear her curt responses. She had no real clue about Trigger, but was always suspicious of me hanging out with them two. If she didn't know anybody else, she knew her brothers were up to no good. And she wasn't feeling it.

"Yeah, I'm usually in school on Thursday, but I passed in my major midterm project yesterday. I'm pretty much finished until finals come. Everything is all downhill. I'm just waiting to get closer to that graduation date. You and Flubber better not miss it," she said in a threatening tone. "Not to change the subject, but what do you need Dorian for this time?"

Although I couldn't hear, whatever he said she didn't like it.

"What are y'all up to, Fruity! Now he's trying to get his life together outside of that crazy stuff—and here you go calling him away from his family," she said, sounding very upset. She paused before speaking again. "You know what I went through and how I waited for Dorian, Fruity. Now you're calling trying to get him in the middle of something. I don't understand you."

I stood at the bottom of the steps still listening. He must've been trying to explain himself. Whatever he said, it wasn't working.

"Whatever--Fruity. He's getting dressed and is probably on his way," she said. "He's moving so fast that he's not even saying what happened with the phone call he just got about getting a job."

On that note, I went down the cellar, slipped on some sweats, strapped up with two guns, and headed out of the back door. It didn't take me long to get over there to see what was happening. Fruity was standing on his front porch waiting when I got there.

"What did you say to Jameel?" I asked, laughing as I walked up the steps.

"Shiddd, I was protecting yo' ass! She was asking questions about you!"

"If that was the case then why didn't she ask me anything?"

"Don't ask me. Ask Jameel. I was keeping you outta trouble," he said, shaking my hand. "Anyway, let's go straight in because you're the last one to get here."

I followed him down the basement where Trigger and Flubber were sitting around talking. "Trigger. Flubber. What's up, y'all?" I asked, interrupting their conversation.

"Ain't nothin' with me, homey. I'm just here—trying to find out what these two have up their sleeves," Trigger said.

"You'll find out in a minute, J," Flubber said, giving me daps before sitting back down.

"On a more serious note, the reason why we called this meeting was for all of us to get in on a big-money scheme. There is this really big spot we can hit. But we gotta' hit it soon. It's big enough to really put us over the top," Fruity said, as he paced the floor back and forth.

"Where is this?" Trigger asked with excitement in his voice. "How much we talking 'bout?"

"Man, there's this crew called the Jamaican Posse that we been coppin' from. We've been checking out the place when we go inside—and them cats are making a lot a money up there on Belvedere off of Park Heights. They have the slickest operation I've ever seen. Plus, they never run out of products up there," Fruity said.

"What's gotta be done?" I asked. *I looked at Fruity with eyes of surprise because I don't do stick ups. I robbed before, but it was to get revenge on all those who had a hand in trying to kill me. I taught them a lesson and that was already done.*

Flubber stood up and began to take charge. "It's a piece of cake because they hustle and get money from summer to winter. That Posse has been doing it 24-7/365, so there's always money up there. I mean, look how easy it was when we robbed Dead-eye. We walked away with more than 17 G's! That's nothing compared to what we can get in their main spot.

"Check dis' out," Flubber said, banging on the table where Trigger rested his guns. "All these dudes are illegal aliens, so the police gettin' involved or snitching is outta the question. They'll get deported in a minute and they ain't trying to go back home!"

"When I go up there to cop, they have all that shit sitting out—I mean bricks of it," Fruity said. "One of my homeboys told me how he heard the Posse gets big shipments straight from Jamaica. They used to smuggle dat' shit through cargo ships from Florida, but it was getting' knocked off a lot. He said the Posse was bragging to some dudes they trust—talkin' bout how the Coast Guard started shooting up the engines in their speedboats."

"For real, Yo!" Trigger said.

"Now, they getting like 200 pounds of weed and crazy kilos because they started shipments through our shipyards somewhere," Fruity said, still pacing around the room in circles.

"Fruity, why don't you sit yo' crazy ass down somewhere—you making me dizzy!" Trigger shouted.

"Man, fuck dat'. I want dis' money I keep hearing everybody talk about. That's cash that could be ours," he said before looking directly to me.

"Check dis' out, Juvenile? This is the slickest part of their operation. The one Jamaican dude named Rasta always talking about how a big green truck goes and gets the shit. Guess how they getting' it?"

"How, man, just spill it—don't start dat' guessing shit now!" I screamed.

"They have dat' shit wrap with heavy duty plastic in boxes and stored inside different trash bins. They say Baltimore City trash trucks pick dat' shit up—like every three days. They got them on the payroll, too."

"Damn, dat's the slickest way to smuggle crazy weight. They pick up and drop off large amounts of drugs to different drop-off spots, huh?" Trigger said, thinking out loud. "Fuck it! Let's get dat' trash truck since it's only square dudes--working nine-to-five with the city--probably picking dat' shit up!"

Flubber cut in. "Naw, man! Dat's crazy. We gotta get the money that comes with hitting the houses up on Belvedere. And the weed they got is called Green. A regular ounce is going for eight hundred right now on the streets! They're selling theirs for $1,200 and its selling like *crack* because their product is that good. They got three hand-to-hand crews up there on Belvedere. And right down the block another crew is selling weight only. So these cats got it going on—for real."

Now I could see what they were saying. The sting we committed before netted us a nice amount of money to split and no enemies I could think of. I had been up there to see the Posse before myself. I knew that much was true. And they were pulling in crazy money long before that incident happened between

155

*Tavon and me. Tavon used Fast Money's cash a few times to cop
here from them. They had some good cocaine with cheap prices
back then, so I knew what they are moving now.*

"Now check dis' out. Prices for kilos on the streets here
is about $25,000 per joint. New York was selling theirs for
around $20,000. The Posse is selling joints in town for around
$21,500! Plus, I see hustlers like Rock copping up there
sometimes, too!" Flubber said in excitement. "Yeah, I did my
homework."

"Ayy, Juvenile. You realize how much money we can
get outta dis' shit?" Trigger said, "We can walk away from the
game with what we'll get outta this. But it's your call, though."

"Yeah, it's my call, but at what cost?" I responded. *I
folded my arms and stirred at each one of them with serious
eyes. This wasn't a joke and each one of us had to know it.* "It's
been a while since I've been up there, but I know what y'all
talking about. The Posse is always moving around and never
stays in one place."

"It ain't that heavy, Juvenile," Fruity said, without
stopping, "I've been in there a lot of times copping, too. This is
how it goes. To get in the front porch man had to do a certain
knock. Once you get in, they pat you down inside the door
because it's another doorman inside. After getting pass him, they
have a big table in the dining room area, but it's set up like a
store. Money stacks are sometimes still on the table from the
transaction before.

"First you tell him what you want. Then they help you
count your money in stacks because they won't take it if it's all
mixed up. After that it's a wait. He always says something in his
native tongue to somebody down the basement. They send the
weight upstairs like clockwork. He puts it on the triple beam so
you can see the scale weight before leaving."

"That's still the same setup. So only the locations
change, but not the operation," I said, thinking along with
Fruity's observations.

"You know you getting the real shit because of the smell of the house. One time I was buying something. Another hustler was in there doing his thing. He bought four bricks and I could see the stamped cartel label wrapped up in duct tape with some Colombian Newspaper showing when they broke one open. Now that's some real shit! I know because we robbed some heavy hitters before and they had the same thing," Fruity said.

"Dat's probably what's coming into the U.S. through New Mexico. They have been pipelining a bunch of high quality shit through the West Coast," Trigger said. "I was reading about that in the papers before I got out. If that's the case then we should make out!"

"Before we go any further—cause' I'm down with this shit—I'm telling all y'all that Jameel's graduation is coming up. We don't have a lot of time to pull this shit off. I wouldn't be with this if it wasn't for me wanting to get her a diamond ring and finally do the right thing. Now, after this sting—I'm calling it quits!

"That goes for all y'all with other ideas that are in this room. My ass is history! Got it—Flubber, Fruity and you too Trigger," I said, looking at each one of them when I called their name. "This is my last one. There has gotta be a better way—and I'm with Jameel. I need a fresh start in a new state. Those streets will never let me change! I got my family. That's why I gotta go!"

"That's what I'm talking about. You finally giving that sister what she deserves because she's been there for yo' ass," Trigger hollered. "So, who's in—because I know I am!"

"It's our idea, so you know I'm down for whatever!" Fruity said, throwing his hand up like a City Council vote.

"You know I'm in, too," Flubber said, following right behind him.

"Well, for starters, we all gotta start copping from up there. We have to go in turns, so we can scope everything out," I said, marking the start of our plans to rob the Jamaican Posse.

We all agreed on needing everybody inside the house—two by two. We left on that note because I had to get back home with Jameel. I wanted to play with Tiffany, but I knew, by now, she would be fast asleep.

In The News
Baltimore City

Law Enforcement officials claimed victory now that another one of Baltimore's inner-city drug dealing gangs were taken off the streets. Federal Prosecutors are confident that they shut down a crack, heroin and cocaine ring stretching from New York to Baltimore that collected millions in profits.

Investigators believed this major pipeline funneled up to 50 kilograms of cocaine a week, according to federal indictments and witness testimony. The one major suspect from Baltimore involved in this major conspiracy was found guilty and is expected to receive a mandatory sentence of Life in prison next month in U.S. District Court.

Sources close to the investigation says Raul Rodriguez and several others who testified in this case were recently released at the completion of trial testimony. Charges against them were dropped in exchange for further cooperation against other key figures in this fallen drug empire in other East Coast cities.

Darnel "Big Toney" Carson, Pretty Jenifer, Gino "Rock" Silver, Tyree "Gangsta" Bradley, Precious Jenkins, and Vernon "Outlaw" Carey were key witnesses in what authorities are claiming to be the largest New York to Baltimore conspiracy in Baltimore's history.

Chapter 24

F.B.I./D.E.A.

"Money Ain't a Thang."
Jay-Z, *"Money Ain't A Thang"*
Vol. 2 Hard Knock Life

Classified Intelligence
Joint report prepared by
The Federal Bureau of Investigation
&
Drug Enforcement Agency

For the last thirty six (36) months several agents have been assigned to Operation Posse Takedown. This said drug organization's reach extends over United States borders and has direct ties to Colombia, New York, Florida and as far as Jamaica. Baltimore has become a hub for drug trafficking controlled by the Jamaican Posse over the last three years.

Intelligence, gathered through several enforcement agencies, reveal scheduled multi-kilo shipments of cocaine, South American (SA) heroin, and marijuana through the Caribbean corridor into Baltimore City, Maryland. Drug Enforcement Agencies have also identified two Arizona marijuana organizations as significant sources of supply to the local Posse Organization.

In a joint investigation, F.B.I., D.E.A. (Special Operations Division), Arizona State Police, Md. High Intensity Drug Trafficking Area Task Force, New York Drug Enforcement Task Force, and Maryland State Police have been able to identify several members in this group through the use of electronic surveillance, cellular wiretaps, listening devices, recordings and area informants.

The history of the Jamaican Posse originates with David "Clive" Anthony's arrival to the United States. Sources of intelligence have documented proof of his active involvement with a major drug organization while he resided in New York. He was involved in the Bedford-Stuyvesant section of Brooklyn for several months through a fraudulent visa before expanding his drug operation in the Park Heights area of Baltimore.

Clive has brought in several Jamaican immigrants into the country through Huffman & Brewner law firm under false documents. Most of these documents obtained during this investigation were acquired through falsifying government documents to gain approval of student visas at several local colleges. To date, none of those involved with this organization are or have been actively enrolled in higher education. Two prominent lawyers from the above-mentioned firm are also under grand jury investigation.

Clive Anthony was arrested without incident and charged with unrelated crimes concerning this continuing investigation after a *Terry stop-and-search*. Undercover Baltimore City narcotics agents, in conjunction with the Drug Enforcement Agency, confiscated approximately $373,000 U.S. dollars and seventeen (17) kilograms of cocaine. Inasmuch, he faces deportation and has been sentenced to a long term of confinement.

To date, Clive's Posse members are allegedly responsible for more than 1 ton of cocaine, ganja, and heroin in Maryland and surrounding states before his arrest. Several large shipments arrived in Baltimore and were divided and later shipped to New York, New Jersey, Philly, Delaware, D.C., Virginia and Connecticut through various trafficking methods.

Based on information provided by the Baltimore City Police Department and information gathered through high-tech surveillance equipment, this organization has grown to include more than twenty members ranging in ages since Clive's arrest. Each member has been formally identified since a new leadership hierarchy has been established. *[To note, area dealers who frequently purchase multiple quantities of illegal drugs from this organization have also been identified. Photos are available to the Courts upon request.]*

The younger cousin of *Clive Anthony*, the key subject of this investigation, has since taken charge of the powerful Jamaican Posse drug organization and has increased business with the inclusion of high grade heroin, methods of violence, and changed its system of distribution in the Park Heights area.

John "Rasta" Williams has been a major supplier to area drug dealers and has illegal ties to Baltimore City employees involved with his dangerous organization. Multiple kilogram shipment of high-grade heroin, coke, and marijuana are received at Dundalk Marine Terminal, the farthest inland port on the East Coast. Shipments are hidden in containerized cargo vessels departing from several Caribbean Islands. Surveillance has revealed how several Department of Public Works' employees are also involved in trafficking shipments in government vehicles, including trash trucks, upon arrival to the marina loading dock. They have also been identified and will be targeted as key witnesses in this case.

Arizona State Police, according to the Federal-wide Drug Seizure System, intercepted a tractor trailer delivery of marijuana (1,757 pounds) headed to Baltimore. This was one of the largest seizures of marijuana in the last four years.

To note, DEA's Domestic Monitor Program (DMP), a retail heroin and cocaine purchase program, tracks urban street level heroin, cocaine purity and pricing. The most recent purchase from the Jamaican Posse shows that South American heroin, produced in Colombia, purity was 42.8 percent. The level is significantly higher than the average of 6 percent. Baltimore remains highest in the Eastern United States where most of the nation's heroin and cocaine user population lives. Authorities estimate the wholesale purchase price per kilogram of heroin ranged in price from $40,000 to $190,000. According to the *Maryland High Intensity Drug Trafficking Area Task Force*, this is dangerously deemed one of the largest drug organizations in the last ten years.

The Baltimore City Mayor has been informed of our preliminary intelligence and a federal grand jury investigation is continuing in this matter.

Our collective method of surveillance and infiltration includes, but is not limited to, experienced intelligence officers from both the FBI and DEA. We have two agents posing as street dealers making several purchases. Informant #519 has been reporting positive intelligence on purchases and shipment information. A key member of the Posse was arrested for a related offense and has since become a confidential informant in our ongoing investigation and reports weekly before an Administrative Judge through a Baltimore City Circuit plea agreement.

Posse ties have reached as far as Florida in the United States where a multi-million dollar trafficking scheme via speedboats, cargo tankers and small aircraft carriers have been uncovered. Interception has been successful as a result of Coast Guard intervention. High-powered weapons have been approved by *Executive Order* to knock out the engines of speedboats suspected of being involved in this conspiracy. It can be safely estimated that multiple pounds of marijuana, heroin and cocaine saturate the streets of Baltimore City when this organization eludes capture. This matter is still under a full multi-jurisdictional investigation.

Each officer assigned to this investigation has testified before a federal grand jury and prays for sealed indictments of all those suspected of involvement in this case. *[Photos of this*

. . . .

organization's hierarchy are available to the Courts upon request.]

End of Report

Chapter 25

FLUBBER

"I'm from the school of Hard Knocks—
We must not let outsiders violate our blocks."
Jay-Z, *"Hard Knock Life "*
Vol. 2...Hard Knock Life

The first I heard of the Jamaican Posse was through word on the street. Rumor had it back then that Fast Money and Tavon used to get weight from them a while ago. In those days Fast Money was the man. Nobody knows this, but Fruity and I were hot on Fast Money's trail. We were trying our best to rob him because he was gettin' it! We robbed some of his workers, like that snitch Outlaw, but Fast Money was one of a few hustlers with money who slipped through our hands.

My first time up there with the Posse took my breath away. I went up there just to check it out with Fruity. Walking with him got me straight inside the door—no questions asked. That's when he introduced me to some their biggest members. How he initially got in to cop different amounts of weight through Rock was beyond me. To him, our hood is his comfort zone—and nothing or nobody takes him outside of there, but he started going up there to cop with his money after robbing Dead-eye.

I've been going back for myself since then and will cop for anybody else who wants some weight to sell on the streets. Of course, I get extras for puttin' somebody else on. Doing it in bulk *helped us with the Posse and made it easier for us to go in—whenever the time was right.*

Now the plan is in motion. I feel more confident about the robbery each time I going inside with Trigger. I'm still anxious and try to control it, but my sweaty palms start itching each time because I want that money. My job is to watch the guy Rasta. Nothing happened without him giving the okay. Everything was going through him, so he is our go-to-guy.

I'm inside here now trying to buy a half a kilo. I'm laughing and joking with them transacting business. I guess this is my gift—rocking people to sleep-- because I tricked so many other hustlers in the past setting them up. It's like I was born in the streets and grew up with that natural look of trust. I made sure I wore my diamond ring along with the iced out watch I borrowed from Juvenile. Rasta even offered me a quarter-kilo for it the last time I was here, but I played like I wasn't pressed.

I stood behind another guy who was buying two bricks. I was up next to put my order in. Looking around I could see where they keep their guns. Loud bangs on the door distracted me. I tried to memorize the knock because it's the same one each time somebody else comes inside. Rasta talked, so I could look around some more. I've never seen so much money and weight coming out of one place—and the key spot was down that basement.

I took notice to all of the new appliances stacked around each room. Maybe I was in the wrong hustle. They had big screen TV's, camcorders and several unopened computer boxes in separate piles. Come to think of it, I had seen the thief, Hollywood, trying to sell some appliances up on Park Heights the last time I was here. He's always using somebody else's identity to get what he wants. Hollywood and credit card schemes go hand in hand. Even he was trying to get on with the Posse.

"Rude bwoy! Where da' hell you been—cause' me thought you fall off de face of the earth."

"Man, what you talking about? "Dat's why I'm here Rasta-man! And I got dis' cash—that'll make your ass happy—won't it?"

"Who ya bring 'ere, blood?"

"Oh, this is my partner, Block!" I looked over to Trigger and said, "Block, this is my man Rasta."

I looked quickly over Rasta's shoulder as he talked to Trigger and then the other hustler who had just walked in. It was a hole in the floor with two sawed off shotguns just barely sticking out. Both were in short arms reach. Inside the desk, when he turned away to scream down the basement, I could see a couple handguns and money. Everything was in that basement and more than one person was sometimes down there. The cash was going down and the drugs were coming up.

Rock wasn't lying about how much coke, dope, and weed they had inside. Hustlers from all over town were in and out. I saw different faces each time watching the house and waiting to come inside. It was a constant flow of the same faces. That surprised me at first, but then I realized that Baltimore is a small town. And there are no secrets. Every one of us could be found in the streets—if that's how we're living.

Kicking the Posse's door in had to be strategic. We had only a few weeks to make as many transactions as we could before pulling this robbery off.

Baltimoreans hated on anybody from outta town who was cocky enough to come here and take money from out of our pockets. Outsiders, crews like the Posse, added fuel to Baltimore's fire. That's why Charm City became Harm City and Maryland became Murderland to some who thought they could violate our blocks. We were born into a hard knock life out there on the streets. That meant we had to survive by living off our land. This became our territory--each street, each corner and each block in a certain area belonged to somebody born and raised there. When it all boils down, nobody in the hood is safe because of how we prey on each other. We're like hustler crabs and Baltimore is our basket. That basket becomes caskets to so many crab hustlers.

That dude Rasta didn't have a problem inviting some of his customers to puff on a big-ass spliff! Each time he saw me he gave me a chunk of good weed to make my own. After getting what we came here for, Rasta called Trigger and me in the kitchen area where he was about to smoke from a coconut.

"What's dat?" I asked him.

"It's a coconut chalice. Dis' is wha" we smoke dem' from in Jamaica. Dis real shit."

"Oh, yeah?" Trigger asked.

"Carry it come and bring it 'tere," he said back to Trigger in a fast tongue. "It has three holes. One for de' clay cup. Another one right 'ere to pull de' smoke. Look 'ere?" he asked pointing.

"Yeah. I see it," I said, not really caring which hole was which.

"De' one right 'dere. Dis' free up de' dead smoke."

I watched him add water inside; he cut a round piece of nutmeg in half. He dropped that into the clay cup he called a kutchie. Next, he placed the cup into the top hole while he told Trigger to cut something he called cally weed.

"We give thanks and Praise to the Most High Jah Rastafari," he said before blowing big smoke into the room.

This seemed so sacred to him. He went through his ritual acting like we never existed.

Bob Marley's music could be heard in the background. "Get up—stand up. Stand up for your right. Get up—stand up. Don't give up the fight."

We all took turns as he passed it to us, but that didn't stop me from observing my surroundings. I noticed how they made it a habit, after each purchase, of leaving the front door open for a few risky minutes talking. The door man joked with the porch man and had casual conversation. Rasta never paid attention to anything other than the money coming in and the blow going out. Our plan could wait no longer.

BCPD Homicide Division

Police Information

Detective Richard Hunt of Central Homicide Division has announced today that they have issued an arrest warrant for a suspect in the fatal death of a woman found inside her house.

Demetria "Butter" Haywood was found murdered in the kitchen of her house and died after experiencing head injuries. Analysts with *the Maryland State Police Crime Lab* recently determined that blood samples taken from Haywood's fingernails and a bloody cloth in the basement both matched the DNA of one suspect named, Dorian "Juvenile" Cannon, of no fixed address.

As of the writing of this article Dorian Cannon was not in custody. Baltimore's Fugitive Warrant Apprehension Task Force is looking aggressively for this suspect. Anyone with information can call Baltimore City Police for a possible reward.

Chapter 26

JAMEEL

"Unless you was me---
How could you judge me?/
I was brought up in pain/
Y'all can't touch me."

Jay-Z, *"Never Change"*
The Blueprint

Tiffany and I both were in our separate rooms reading. It was another relaxing evening, the kind forcing me to lie around and snuggle up to a good book or magazine. I know I don't do it often, but I may even watch some TV. I was really hoping Dorian and I could do some adult snuggling tonight after dinner. My plan went out the door when one of my brothers called before we had a chance to eat.

I was lying on my bed flipping through a Young Bride magazine. Living our day, looking at all those classy wedding gowns and flowers, reading the different articles, made me feel warm inside. I know soon I'll have to really start visiting bridal shops and trying on wedding gowns because I really want this day to be perfect. The more time I take to plan, the less stress I'll have to deal with. It's so much to do, like finding a place, have somebody to do flowers, contract the caterers and the list goes on. I've always dreamed of using Martins West. I went to an anniversary party for Pastor and his wife there and haven't stopped dreaming about getting married there since.

With all my planning you would think Dorian and I already discussed marriage? Well, we haven't, but he knows this living arrangement is not going to last for long. I'm active in my church and most of all I'm going to set a good example for my daughter. That's the next thing on my agenda to talk to Dorian about.

'Hmmmm.' There's a company called Patsy's Classy Caterers that I'm thinking about using since they come with high recommendations. Our church has used them for different events. Maybe I will contact Sheila and Ms. Fossett real soon about some arrangements. And I'll probably hire Marlene to sing our wedding song.

Turning to the last page of the magazine, serious thoughts about Dorian's actions crossed my mind. I mean--it hit me like a ton of bricks. I usually sit back and mind my own business and try not to crowd him. I think everybody needs space and Dorian was no exception to this rule. And I have always given him that—even when he wasn't using it wisely.

Since moving in with me, things have been changing for us. He's still hanging out in the streets, but that's only when one of my brothers or Trigger calls him. He's really home more than he's out and is almost always there to tuck Tiffany in at nights. I know he's not selling or anything like that, but he needs to see for himself that he can do without those street corners and friends like my brothers.

One other thing has been bugging me. What is he doing in the basement when he first walks in the door? There is always some kind of noise when he comes through the back door. I know he wouldn't put us in danger, but I'm going to give it a quick safety check anyway.

His choice for private space was in the basement. He comes in that way, stays down there in his own world sometimes with Tiffany, and leaves through the back door after getting a phone call. I understood him and some of his reasons why he was using the back door in the beginning. But I didn't think it was necessary because all that street stuff had come to an end.

171

"Mommy, Daddy isn't back as yet?" Tiffany asked, walking into my room.

"No he's not. What do you need, baby?"

"Daddy told me he would tuck me in tonight."

"He might have just lost track of the time," I said gently, not wanting to disappoint her any more than she already was.

"Are you tucking me in after I say my prayers then?"

"You know I am."

"Go ahead and get your shower. I'm going downstairs for a minute. Call me when you finish."

"You want me to do it now?"

"Yes, Tiffany. I'll get the water ready while you get your night clothes out of the drawer."

"Thanks Mommy," she said as she walked out of the room. *I went into the bathroom and turned the shower on. I always have to adjust the water temperature. God knows that child hates hot water.*

While Tiffany was taking her shower, I gathered a load of clothes and picked up my little emergency flashlight. I could pretend I was about to do laundry, so if Dorian comes in while I'm down there, I can use that as a reason. It usually takes him a while to come back anyway, but I had to make sure.

When he comes in I usually hear rambling, like he's hiding something somewhere. And then he starts playing those loud video games—like a little child. I remember growing up with my brothers. They hid stuff under the steps, underneath the washing machine, behind the sinks and anywhere else my mother wouldn't ordinarily look. Sometimes they had me helping them do it because I had the smaller hands.

As I walked down the basement, each creepy step made noise. First, I looked around trying to figure out where to start. I decided on the storage place I have underneath the steps. That's probably where I'll find something hidden. I walked towards the door and tripped over those XBOX wires all over the floor. He had open cases of different games thrown everywhere. I have no clue what NFL Street is or Mercenaries. All I know is it keeps him occupied and in the house for hours at a time—and that's all that matters.

I opened the entrance door and used the flashlight to find the hanging light switch. I went through some tennis shoe boxes and a few bags of clothes he had. Those boxes seemed kind of heavy when I first lifted them. Looking through each one real quick, all I could find was the shoes that went with the brand name. Nothing.

I found a square safe hidden underneath the boxes. It wasn't really heavy, but it was big enough to hold what I may have been looking for. I tried to shake it for sound since I had no combination to open it. Nothing.

The bags of clothes had nothing inside either. He had a few leather coats and suit jackets hanging up. Some of the jacket pockets did have money inside. That's money he's probably forgotten all about. That's how he is. I find money in his pockets when I wash all the time.

As I closed the door to the storage, I realized that I didn't turn the light off. So I quickly went back inside pulling the string. He would really be wondering what I'm up to if he saw that light on because I cleared out all my belongings and gave him that space when he came here permanently.

The washing machine and dryer sat near the sink by the back door. I first checked the sink area and then tried moving that heavy washing machine. I took a piece of board and used it as a slat. I propped it up to see if anything was under there and then did the same with the dryer. Under the dryer I did see two thick strips of duct tape but nothing else.

I tiptoed around heading for the drop ceiling. I took a chair and started from the opposite end. I lifted a centerpiece of the ceiling tile and flashed the light. Right beside that was a metal box with a small lock on it. Pulling the box down from the ceiling showed it was actually unlocked. I grabbed that, lifted the lid, hoping to find out what was hiding inside. Dust.

My basement had no other closet space or cubbyholes, so the last place to check was under the couches. Underneath the *sofa there was a cut out. I reached into it and felt a heavy piece of leather with some straps on it. I was   pulling it out when I heard a voice calling me!*

"Mommy, I'm finished taking my shower and have my night clothes on. Are you coming up to tuck me in," Tiffany asked, standing about midway on the basement steps.

"Girl!" I yelled, upset for not hearing her come down the steps. *I was already scared, but she made my skin crawl.* "You scared me! Go ahead. I'm right behind you."

"You need some help looking under Daddy's couch?"

"No, Tiffany. Just go ahead and I'll be upstairs."

I let the couch back down on the floor. I was so nervous trying to straighten up before going back upstairs. I tried moving the couch, but it was too heavy and hard to push back. One thing I know about Dorian is he keeps everything in place, besides those games. Each piece of clothing, socks and underwear are neatly stored and he knows exactly where to find everything.

I wanted to finish, but had to make sure she was in bed safe. Really, I didn't want her to know what I was doing, so I turned the light off and ran up the steps. As I made my way up the basement steps I could hear her little footsteps running to get to her room.

"Tiffany, I'm right behind you," I called out. *As I got to the top of the basement steps I heard keys rattling. I stood still for only a quick second and realized Dorian was on his way in. I quickly shut the door. I started feeling a little guilty, to say the least, so I rushed up the second floor steps thinking he may have heard me.*

Tonight she got a quick tuck in because I was trying to listen to what was happening in the basement, except tonight there was no banging. As I closed Tiffany's bedroom door, I heard him coming up the steps from the basement. A combination of guilt and nervousness had me feeling jittery inside. I went in my bedroom pretending like I was ready for bed.

When he got in the room spoke first. "And what's up with you, Juvenile?" I asked awkwardly before sitting on the bed. *I realized how out of character it sounded after the words came out of my mouth.*

"Hey, who?" he asked, flopping on the bed beside me. "You don't usually talk that street stuff. What's up with dat 'hey Juvenile' stuff? When did I become that to you?"

"I was just kidding," I said, trying to laugh it off. "My mind was somewhere else."

"You wanna talk about it? You usually leave the streets outside. I can't remember the last time you called me Juvenile?"

"No, I don't. I just told you what's wrong. My mind was somewhere else, Dorian. It's not that serious, please!"

"Are you sure?"

"I am."

"Whatchu been doing?" he asked.

"Nothing. I just tucked Tiffany in and was about to go to sleep, why?"

"I just asked," he said. "Was that you or Tiffany downstairs?"

"Why do you ask?"

"I was just wondering what y'all were doing while I was gone because stuff is moved around downstairs?"

"I went down there to do some laundry, but I changed my mind. That's about it. You keep asking all these questions, what were you doing while you were gone?"

"I was with your brothers!"

"That's who you were with—not what you were doing? I know what my brothers are up to and it's never good. Dorian, what's going on?"

"There you go judgin' me again!"

"No, I'm not judging. I'm asking!"

"Yes, you are Jameel. How could you judge me without knowing my struggle? Or even imagine what I'm going through?"

"Dorian, let's talk about something else because this conversation never gets us anywhere! And I would hate for Tiffany to wake up to us arguing!"

175

"Well, let me ask you again, what were you doing while I was gone?"

"I was looking at this," I said, putting the magazine in front of him so he could get the hint. "With us getting ready to make that move, Baby, you know we have to start planning more sooner than later. You know my feelings when it comes to how God wants us to live."

"Let me see. What's in here?"

He stood there briefly, flipping through before turning away from me. He walked out the room to the steps still turning pages. Speaking under his breath, going down the steps, I didn't quite understand what he was saying.

I got up walking behind him before realizing he left wet, muddy footprints everywhere he stepped on the carpet.

"Dorian, please take off those boots! You are messing up the carpet," I yelled from the top of the second floor staircase. "And don't mess up that book, please? I still need it."

I heard no reply from him. I know he heard me loud and clear. And that was confirmed when he came upstairs to shower and sleep with me for another one of those hot, steamy nights.

Chapter 27

FLUBBER

"When you first come in the game
They try to play you."

Jay-Z, *"Encore"*
The Black Album

The speed of everybody's movement adds excitement in my city streets. Sirens sound off, one after another, because of repeated 911 calls by today's block-watchers. The funny thing about that is how these young "Nino Browns" secretly make most calls to police complaining about street corner competition.

On my block tonight you constantly hear loud pitch voices and disagreeing screams. Cars speed here like they're in a drag race. Drivers suddenly stop. Screeching tires and open car doors alarm everybody out here that someone is in need of our services. Passengers jump out and sellers make another transaction. Cop and Bop was old school thinking from an addict's point of view. We're new school hustlers, so our motto out here now is Push & Pull. Our purpose is to push the product and pull in the cash.

People always come to buy. They're either coming to cop from my crew or the other one across the street. I'm thinking of how crazy all this action is out here, and the chances we take, but this is the life we live. And I love it! What more can I say?

"Flubber," Ray-Ray said, walking towards me. He's the one who introduced me to this old playground area when I changed my hats and started selling. I agreed to let him and two

177

of his young homies run everything. He told me all I had to do is watch and count money. And it's been that way from the start. "About how many packs did we sell already?"

"Whatever it was, it wasn't enough money made yet! Why you wanna know?"

"Me and Corey was over there talking and he thought we sold seven packs. You know what Corey is trying to do—and that's getting with his girl Butter. I said we sold about nine packs—that's why I asked."

"It was about that. Tell Corey and Skinny Greg they better step dis' shit up. Butter will be seeing Corey's ass tomorrow if he keeps this slow shit going! Look over there!" I screamed, pointing across the street. "Andre and his crew are selling more shit than we are!"

"So, how much more do we have to sell, Flubber?"

I thought of a quick number and said, "Ray-Ray look! Y'all gotta step dis' shit up if y'all trying to get paid tonight."

My mind was traveling a hundred miles a minute. If things went according to plan, I would be calling my brother and Juvenile. It was time for me to put up more money so Fruity could cop something else from the Jamaican Posse.

"Just tell me and it's done, Flubber!"

"Sell about ten more packs. We can shut down for the night so y'all can get those outfits for the club! If y'all make it happen I'll throw in a bonus. And then y'all can really show off this weekend!"

"Done, Flubber," he said, running back across the street to the corner telling Corey and Skinny Greg.

I have a nice setup. I have Skinny Greg as a look-out across the street on the opposite corner. Ray-Ray and Corey are hitting and pitching as needed. The three of them take down more than five thousand dollars on a bad day. What's real is these young kids are hungry enough to sell ice in the winter if I tell them. The sad part is they don't know game when they see it.

Looking at them, it's hard telling one from another. They all wear their clothes baggy. Big t-shirts are bought and freshly worn each day. Jeans fit their bodies like extra loose sweat pants. Obeying the law of gravity, their pants fall down every three steps taken and have to be pulled back up like a holy ritual. That ugly combination adds up to today's fashion. The only good that comes from that is you can't tell a hustler from a regular homeboy. They all look alike.

Since setting up shop here, I watch the action from our side of the street on this old playground. Cars are parked on both sides. There's a mechanic shop, a hill, and road on the other side of the street with a back alley right beside the Cut Rate Bar. That's the side of Warwick where Kweli and his crew set up shop. We all get our drinks and lottery tickets right off of Baltimore Street.

Standing here against this brick wall, I position myself near the steps, with my back and one foot pressed against the old gray brick wall. There's another alley on this side of the street where we can run if the police comes. It's not really a playground. This is only where the playground once stood. Now it's an empty lot where we hang out. Kweli, from Annapolis, is pretty cool with me, even though he's my competition. He's been running this area for a few months now.

A black Crown Victoria with dark black tinted windows pulled on the wrong side of the street near the playground. "Yo! Police!" I screamed. "Shut shit down!"

Everybody started dropping drugs on the ground and running, but the car kept going. Walking over to the corner, now becoming the look-out, gave my foot soldiers enough time to find what they threw away and get back in place. Everything seemed okay before I walked toward the center of the playground trying to get Kweli's attention. I threw my hands in the air. "Ayy, Kweli--what's up?"

He pulled his fitted cap over his head and walked across the street in my direction. Not violating the hood's three step rule, he yanked at his pants up every three steps walking over my way.

"What's happening over there tonight?"

"Same shit, just a different day," he said, reaching for my hand. "You know what's up, though. I wanna get rich and have a million like you holding!"

"Look how raggedy this spot is. It don't seem like a million would come through here—no time soon!" I said, playfully shaking his hand.

"Dat's crazy—ain't it?"

"Yeah, that's why me and my brother try'na get that million because I'm tired of living like this."

"Did you hear about that freak I was messing with?" he asked, changing the conversation.

"Which one you talking about?" I asked, looking toward the bar. *A man was giving Ray-Ray the signal he needed to put another sale together.*

"Dat' crazy ass girl Khia," he said.

I listened but watched Ray-Ray walking our way. "I'm taking eight," Ray-Ray said, getting close enough to pass four fresh twenties in my hand and get what he needed from the stash.

"Make money, hustler," I told Ray-Ray. *I stood watching him walk directly to his intended before passing off.*

"Hey, Flub. She started messing with that kid Boogie Down from New York getting a few dollars and got pregnant."

"Word. She's pregnant now?"

"Word! She's about to have the baby," he snapped back. "He got her door kicked in and they locked her up because a lot of rocks were in the house. I'm glad I stopped dealing with her. That could've been my shit!"

"Was Boogie Down the kid we had problems with when we first started?" I asked.

This time Ray-Ray ran back to me putting two hundred dollars bills in my hand. Corey came right behind him with six twenty dollar bills.

"Yeah, that's him."

"They locked him up, too?" I asked.

"Nah! His ass is still hustlin' on the block. She's still over Central Booking trying to call my house collect!"

"Those chasers never learn that they end up holding the bag when the police come. It's the same ol' game just different players falling into the trap."

"Yo, Flubber," Corey said, coming toward me again. *He turned in the same direction I was facing and pointed to this pretty lady all dressed up.* "Dat' lady right there got a hundred dollars and she wants thirteen for that. Ray-Ray got the money already."

Really paying attention to his question, I asked, "Who you talkin' bout?"

"Her right there," he said pointing, "Can I give it to her?"

"Oh, dat's that trick Joann," Kweli said, picking up on our exchange.

"What's her name?" I asked.

"Joann the crackhead! Every time she comes she's always running game about being short. Then she got the nerve to tell you how many rocks you're gonna give her with the short money!" Kweli said in anger.

"Naw, she gotta pay for dat' shit," I told him. "Ain't nobody give me no deals when I was out there."

Kweli turned to Corey and *hipped* him to some game. "You haven't been around a long time, but when you first come into this game they try playing you for whatever extra they can get. Yo, you care too much. You should worry about what you suppose to being making for your man, Flubber--and not listen to crack head games. You tell her ass straight money! You the one in control, not her. It's not the other way around!"

"But she gonna take her money around the corner," Corey said. "We try'na finish these packs for the night so we can hang out."

"Fuck it! Give her money back! She'll be back because our shit is good down this playground," I screamed. *He threw his hands up in frustration and ran back across the street.*

Before walking back across the street, Kweli said, "We gotta keep teaching these kids this game, Flubber. I'll holler at you later on. I gotta make this run to re-up real quick."

"Ayy, Flubber," Corey said, running back over and handing me the hundred dollars. "She'll take the ten."

"Alright, Kweli," I said, taking the money and walking back to my wall. "I'll holler at you later."

* * * * * * *

I'm the oldest of three. I haven't had a chance to have children or establish a relationship. I've been too busy in the streets trying to perfect the hustle. This has gone on most of my life. From the age of 12 my mother couldn't control me. I spent most of my juvenile years living under true hustlers on the street. They taught me the game through old street stories. Stickup artist like Kessler and those Shotgun Bandits made me want to do that shit myself. My motto comes from New York. Those suckers on the streets hustling make it. I, on the other hand, take it. It's just that simple.

I don't play when it comes to life and death because I've seen it too many times. That's how my Pops got killed. He got into a fight after drinking at the bar around the corner from our old house. After getting a mutual friend to end the disagreement, he was shot twice on our front steps and died in my mother's arms. I never forgot that story growing up. I always imagined what it would be like if my father lived beyond that incident. Maybe that's why I play the role of the father for my brother and sister.

Before all this stuff happened between Tavon and my soon-to-be brother-in-law, I was still sticking up to make ends meet. My stings were for pennies because I was hitting around-the-way hustlers. Robbing them was easier because we knew each other.

* * * * * * * *

Corey and Ray-Ray kept the sales coming, but I needed to make a quick run like Kweli did. It was time to call Fruity and Juvenile, get this money off of me, and pick up some fresh packs.

After being gone for about twenty minutes, I was back with more fresh packs, holding my side of the playground down again. I settled watching all of the action in front of me. All of a sudden I heard a loud argument coming from the alley behind me.

"I'm clean! Dat's right, Fingers, I'm home—now!"

"Yeah, right. You think that shit is supposed to mean something because you're home, now?" the skinny crackhead man said.

"All this has got to stop, baby! C'mon, now--that's the last thing my son gave me before he died and I'll-be-damned if you're gonna sell it for some crack!" she screamed, trying to pull the television out of his control.

"It would've been okay to sell before you got clean," he said. "As a matter of fact, yo' ass would've been telling me to bring it down here—with yo' dope-fiend ass!"

"That was then, Sticky Fingers. All that shit is changed!"

"Shit ain't changed out here because you got some days clean! Dis' ain't the first time you tried to change—and it ain't gonna be the last time. You're a goddamn crackhead like everybody else we get high with! So, if you knew how good this shit is—you'd be trying to sell this piece of shit television, too!"

"If my son was here--he'd beat yo' ass, bitch!"

"Now you think you're better than the Fingers, P-nut! Don't forget…we shot dope and smoked the rocks we stole from your son the day before he got killed! Now you think you betta' than everybody else. You watch! You'll be smoking dis' crack and selling bits and pieces of ass in no time gettin' us high!"

"Thank God my son ain't here!" P-nut screamed. "Now gimme my fuckin' TV—and I ain't asking you no more!"

"P-Nut, you ain't shit without your son! He was the reason why Fingers fucked with you in the first place!"

"Main man! Give her the TV like she said," I screamed, walking up to them in the alley-way. "Dat' shit ain't happening down here!"

I could here Corey and Ray-Ray running behind me.

"Dis ain't her TV, though," he said, trying to believe his own lie. *He sat the TV down and looked at me with total disregard.*

"Who da' hell you think you're playing with!" Corey screamed before pounding on his frail body.

"Beat his ass, Corey!" Skinny Greg hollered, running toward the fun.

I let it go on for a quick second so word would get out that we don't play. "Alright, y'all! Dat's enough now!"

"But dat's Tavon's mother, P-Nut, he's messin' with, Flubber! Dat shit ain't right—dat's why he's getting fucked up!" Ray-Ray said, hitting the old man a few more times for practice.

"Alright, y'all—don't hurt him bad!" P-nut screamed. "He ain't hurt me or nothing. He's just got a problem and I wasn't having it!"

That's how that goes, but I didn't want the old dude going to no hospital. That would interfere with business because the ambulance would draw attention and the police would come down here asking questions and harassing whoever they could.

"P-nut! You alright?"

"Yeah, Flubber!" she screamed.

I had to watch out for Tavon's mom. The beef he had with my brother-in-law had nothing to do with me. Besides, I understand what she went through back then putting her only son in the ground. "P-nut, take your stuff and go! Skinny Greg walk with her and take that TV back to her house."

"Alright," Skinny Greg said before turning to Fingers. "Don't bring your dumb ass around here no more tonight or I'ma kill you myself!"

"Flubber thanks," she said, lifting her man off the ground. "Alright, Fingers! Now get your crazy ass up so we can go!"

"Do that. Make sure that TV gets to her house," I said to Skinny Greg, "But come right back!"

Things can get out of control just like that. "Corey and Ray-Ray! Y'all had y'all fun. Now get back out there and get dat' fuckin money!"

Chapter 28

FRUITY

"Ladies are pimps, too.
Gon' brush your shoulders off."
Jay-Z, "Brush Your Shoulders"
The Black Album

I wanted to go shopping to get what I needed to enjoy the night. I was now gettin' *it, so I wanted to be the talk of the club. Ray-Ray, one of my brother's workers, took me to the mall to find top of the line clothes since I didn't know where to start. Mondawmin was the perfect shopping place for the latest fashions.*

Walking inside one of the more exclusive men stores in the mall, we were greeted by several beautiful women, but one in particular grabbed my attention.

"Hello. My name is Destiny. Are you looking for anything particular today—or are you just browsing?"

"My man gotta whole lot of money that he don't mind spending a couple thousand for something nice," Ray-Ray said, trying to impress Destiny.

"Yeah, I got some parties set up and I want some nice outfits to show how I'm livin."

"What's your name?" she asked.

"Mine is Fruity. This is my man--" I tried to say before she cut me off.

"I already know Ray-Ray. He comes up here shopping all the time, but I never see him wearing the tight outfits I help him pick out."

"Well, show me some of the stuff you'd like to see your man in. And costs don't matter. Don't worry about the prices," I bragged. "Just make me look like the man you'd want on your arms at a nightclub. In other words, just show me off!"

"Even though I have a man, I can do that for you because I like what I see. We can start over here and work our way to the middle. Here we have the more expensive shirts that I love seeing men with hairy chest in."

"I like these."

"Open your shirt and let me see your chest?" she asked.

Unbuttoning my shirt, I let her see what she was asking for. "Like this?"

"See, you have the kind of chest that fits perfect into these colorful leather Robert Cavalli shirts off of this rack, right here. The tops are four-hundred and they come in all colors."

"Oh, yeah, well, I'll take that blue one right there. And give me that cream one right behind it."

She grabbed them and walked me over to another section.

"And over here we have some stylish *Rocawear* shirts and Sean John linen pants. In this other section," she said pointing, "we carry Versace dress pants to match the tops you're buying."

In all, she showed me different dress pants styles. The black Sean John outfit was tight, but not really what I wanted for tonight. "What else would you like to see me in?"

"I would love seeing you in some cuffed Versace pants to go with the shirts you just picked," she said smiling. "Or if you wanna cool out and look *flyy* then you should pick this Roc-A-Wear outfit. And when the night is finished, after wearing either one of these outfits, I'd like to creep over your house when my man is working at night or have you in my bed so we can end the night."

"Well, pull your phone out. Put your number in my phone and we can make that happen one night real soon," I said. "Now show me your shoes."

"I'm sorry, but we don't have a good selection of shoes. If you go over to that store across the mall you can find what you're looking for," she said, walking me to the cash register. "Don't worry about my friend. I control that. You can call me whenever you want to make that happen."

I left with Destiny's phone number and about three bags full of outfits. I had enough to start my closet. We walked to the shoe outlet across the mall. Buying the matching Versace slip-ons ended my quick shopping spree.

I've been eating pretty good since we started hustling. Earlier today I gave money to one of my female friends. I told her to put an expensive rental car in her name just for the weekend. If that works out I'll lease something later.

She called me on my cell phone to tell me she picked up a light blue, four-door Jaguar. I had no idea that my outfit would blend in with the rental car. Before ending my conversation with her, Flubber clicked in. We made arrangements to meet up about ten o'clock at my mother's house.

Chapter 29

FLUBBER

"I understand all that, but now ain't the time.
I came to the club to get that off my mind!"

Jay-Z, *"2 Many Hoes"*
The Blueprint 2(The Curse)

Fruity picked me up around 11:15 p.m. in this pretty blue Jaguar. It felt different for us because life had changed. Knowing this, riding with my brother, had me feeling on top of the world as we headed downtown. We hadn't talked too much about anything other than plotting the Posse heist. On our way to downtown Baltimore, it was time to bring the conversation up again.

"Now this Jag is you, Fruity! If we keep taking down, then you'll have your own and not some Enterprise rental. You can get something in your own name."

"Yeah. That'll happen in time. We gotta keep sticking together in this game and a whole lot of good shit is gonna happen for us. And then we can take care of our family."

"I'm right there. Besides, where am I going anyway?" I asked in a loud tone.

"Man, I'll be glad when Juvenile says the word. We're going straight at that Posse," Fruity said, as a police car flashed its blue siren lights behind us on Mulberry Street downtown.

Knowing the routine, he started pulling over and reaching toward the glove compartment for the rental registration.

"What da fu--?" he said, quickly checking his pockets and finally buckling his seat belt.

"We alright! Stop panicking!" I screamed. "Be calm."

"Flubber, I got a gun and too much money on me—dat's why I'm saying that shit! Plus, I got these Philly blunts," he said in panic.

"Look at yo' scared ass!" I said as the police pulled around him and sped by. "I can't believe dat' shit. You take all those crazy chances on the streets and scared of the police! You went through all that and they went right by!"

"Man, fuck you!" he said, knowing I was telling the truth.

We moved through the city without much conversation. Passing through downtown, I watched the night lights glow, lighting the path at the beginning of each new block. 'The City of Baltimore invested a lot of money to make this entertainment district look more attractive,' I thought.

Car traffic was bumper to bumper. The streets were filled with people searching for something to do after a long week of work. The night was coming to life.

A few blocks down he made a left onto Charles Street. Passing all of that activity had him ready to talk again.

"Ayy, this writer from here is having his book release party tonight down the Belvedere Hotel. It's some old hustler talking about Westside and how he was getting paid back in the days," Fruity said.

"What's the name of the book, anyway?"

"If I ain't mistaken, the flyer Jameel gave me said something about fast money and the life," he said. "Reach into my jacket pocket and get that flyer outta there."

I dug down into his jacket pocket and pulled out money, his Philly Blunt and a green flyer. "You talkin' bout this right here."

190

"Yeah! That's it," he said, scaring me. He was looking my way and driving at the same time.

"For the Love of Fast Money book release party—they're having it at the Belvedere Hotel downstairs from 9 tonight until. They talking that dress to impress shit on the flyer—no jeans, Timbs or tennis. You're dressed right, but I'm not. So you either have to take me back home and change real quick or pass because I'm not getting in thugged-out like this!"

After reading the flyer the title hit me and I started singing my mother's old Ojay's music. "For the love of money—Some people got to have—well, well. Some people really need it—awww—let me tell you y'all. Hey, Fruity. I remember when Momma used to play that song over and over again."

"Me, too," he said smiling. "Jameel told me he had a book signing up Coppin during Black History Month and talked dat' shit about how he got out of the streets. So she gave me that flyer earlier," he said, hitting me across the shoulder.

"I guess that's where she met him at. It says here that he's got a bookstore downtown on Franklin Street. Now that's slick!"

"Yeah, that's smart, but fuck dat'," he said. "Somebody should be writing one about us! That's how we carry it on these streets. We should be the ones writing a book and call it Blood Brothers or somethin' like that!"

"You try'na hang down there after we stop on Charles Street?"

"Naw, I ain't trying to get with that type of crowd, yet," he said.

"Aaaw, man," I said, changing the subject. "Don't forget we gotta call Jameel tomorrow because she's having a dinner for Momma over her house."

"Ain't forget, Flubber," he said, but I knew the opposite was true. *My brother forgets everything besides what's happening on the streets.*

We rolled up near the club trying to find a parking space. I hadn't been inside one in a long time. I was always in the parking lots setting people up for robbery. I remember one of the last times it happened...

I got a call in the wee hours of the morning saying some D.C. ballers with big money were inside Blue Crest North. I heard details of the cars they drove at Fast Money's Platinum party and the jewels they flashed. My homeboys had a plan and needed my help making this heist happen, so I immediately got ready and jumped into my buddy's car.

We all knew that our clubs in Baltimore have door searches for guns and knives. So, if you were already inside— nine times outta ten—you couldn't be armed. We approached them D.C. dudes in the parking lot when the club was letting out. I guess they were smarter than we thought because one of them dudes pulled out a gun as soon as we approached them and started firing directly at us.

We fired back. Bullets went everywhere. The next day I heard a girl, a mother of two, was shot in the line of fire and innocently killed.

* * * * * * *

Parking a half a block away, we stepped out of the rental car about the same time. While walking toward the club, somebody started walking directly toward us.

"Hey, fellas," the nicely built girl said in a sexy tone. "How y'all living?"

She had taken some steps away from the two young women she was standing with. I noticed she was wearing a tight pair of torn blue jeans showing her features. Her short cut orange shirt was tied to her side and showed no signs of a baby or body fat.

"We livin' large—that's how we living! Who da' hell are you?" I asked, knowing she was one of those project chicks looking for something to get in to.

"I'm Kiesha. That's my girl Shampoo and that's Doll over there," she said, pointing to her friends directly in front of us. "Those are my two homeys from our click from up Westside!"

"Yeah, well, we're trying to get into this club and see some people. Dat's how we livin'!" I said.

"Well, I know y'all ain't trying to be caught without your gun inside the club--especially if y'all living like that? It would be busted if those people y'all trying to see is strapped and y'all ain't," she said. *She pulled a long hail from her blunt, blew smoke in the air and stepped closer to us.*

"Kiesha, right?" Fruity asked. "What you trying to do about us getting shit inside the club?"

She continued, "You know you can't get it inside. That metal detector will go crazy and the bouncers will, too. That's why y'all need me!"

"Need you for what?" Fruity asked.

I stood there with an idea of what she was trying to offer.

"To get your gun inside the club—that's what!"

"What's it gonna cost us?" Fruity asked in return.

"The Pleasure Posse ain't asking for too much. Pay our way in the club and a few dollars. That's what's up. Give me your word on that...and I'll play my part," she said, exhaling more weed smoke in the atmosphere.

"We don't know you from a can of paint, so how can we trust your ass?" my brother asked. "Who da' fuck are you?"

"I told you who I am. Give me the gun and I'll show you what I'm about," she said, throwing her right hand in the air. "Y'all gonna have to just trust my work! Dat's my word."

"We ain't giving you shit!" I said, walking around her.

"I don't know why. I'm trying to help y'all stay safe in that club."

"Alright, we gon' put you to your first test," Fruity said. "You fuck this up and that's your ass! I will beat your little bad ass like a man!"

"Ayy! Shampoo," she screamed to her girls. "Hand me that Prada bag and watch my work."

She snatched her bag and walked toward the Jag with Fruity.

"Make sure you unload dat' shit before giving it to her," I told Fruity openly. *I pulled out fifty dollars from my pocket when my cell phone rang. I wasn't about to take my eye off Kiesha or her hood partners, but answered the phone.* "Yo."

"Hey, where y'all at, Fruity?" Juvenile asked.

"We down the club on Charles Street—getting' ready to go in. Fruity got some *chicken* carrying the heat inside."

"I tried to find something to do with Trigger's ass, just to get him out. And we ended up all the way over here to see some dude he was locked up with! Trigger got me down here in no man's land--over in D.C. at Club H2O!"

"Well, we hangin' out over this way."

"You be cool with Fruity until I get there. It'll be a little later, Flubber, but I'll try to get up there before y'all leave."

"Alright, but we try'na go to the hotel with some of these honeys up here. Before we do, I'll holler."

Standing there, near the alleyway, I was torn between the piss smell offending my nose and the both of them getting things together in the back of the car. I became distracted because of the noise behind me. I looked back there before I stopped, but didn't see anything or anybody. Now I had to jump out of the way because somebody was trying to make a move on me!

My heart jumped and my instincts were on fire! I turned around real quick! Somebody was coming at me from the alley and all I could think of was being setup by these tricks.

"Whatdahell!" I screamed, jumping in defense.

"Can I get some change? I haven't eaten all day," the homeless man asked. "Can you help me?"

"Damn! Man, get away from me with that bullshit!" I blurted out after being caught off guard. *I had to play it off because Doll and Shampoo were looking.* "You scared the shit outta me!"

"No, we saw yo' scared ass jump out of yo' fuck'n skin!" Shampoo said before hearing her and Doll screaming in laughter.

I calmed myself while still watching my brother and Kiesha come back from the car. "What-da-hell you laughing at Doll—with 'cho ugly-ass?" I asked, fixing my clothes, trying to gain my composure.

"I don't care how ugly I am. I saw what she saw. Yo' ass would've been downtown by now! Dat's how fast you were moving!"

"Whatever—because both of y'all are crazy!" I screamed in defense, changing the subject. "Can I get in with this sweathood on?"

"Yeah, scared ass, you can get in. Just follow our lead in the door."

Kiesha had the gun because she kept adjusting her clothes and then fumbled with her pocketbook to cover things up.

"Y'all ready, Fruity?" I asked.

"Let's go everybody. Stick together going inside," Kiesha said. "That's the only way this will work."

I took the lead and hoped Flubber knew what he was doing. We all walked inside the front door in our small crowd to the security post. We stopped in front of the metal detector, waiting for instructions.

The door bouncer looked suspiciously at my brother, then me, and said, "There's a ten dollar cover charge."

Kiesha walked straight to the mirror, avoiding the metal detector, where the other bouncer was standing and looked at herself. She touched her hair and brushed her shoulders off before turning toward the bouncer.

"Women get in for free right, handsome?" she asked, rubbing the front of his pants. "Every time I come here you look better and better. You just might get what you want from me-- if you keep it up!"

"Kiesha, I'll get with you in a minute. You and your girls go 'head, so we can get to these two," he said in a different voice. "Women are free tonight."

"Come on Doll and Shampoo. You heard the man—ladies are free tonight."

He looked back to us and said, "Y'all gotta get patted down after going through the metal detector. Kenny, search them two. Take that body scanner to search his hoody. Make sure they don't' have nothin'—and I mean nothing on them!"

We walked inside after paying the cover charge, scanned the crowd and found what seemed like a safe place to stand.

"Hey, y'all. Y'all thought I was bullshit'n, didn't y'all?" she said laughing, catching our attention, before putting her hand out. "Now since I got in for free, that's another thirty with that because you didn't have to cover our door charges!"

Stepping behind my brother next to the speaker, she passed the gun while I stood in front of her. As the music sounded off, she reached into her pockets for the shells.

"Here you go—with your crazy ass!" Fruity said, counting her money in her hand.

Rocking side to side to the beat, she threw her free hands in the air before showing her dancing skills. *"Awww! Dat's my song. Fat Joe and Remy Martin is da' shit!" she screamed.*

"Got a date at 8. I'm in a 7-40-fi-zive. And I just bought a bike so I can ride till I die. With a matching jacket. Bout to cop me a mansion..."

Fruity and I checked her out while she did her thing. This girl had flair and a go hard style making her sexy. The music banged louder and she danced harder.

"We gangsta. And gangster's don't dance with boogies, so never mind how we got in here with weapons and hoodies..."

Fruity motioned her to come to him.

Still dancing, she stepped his way and said, "Yeah, you're interrupting my flow. What's up before I go over to the bar with my girls?"

The music was still going off and so did she. "Listen we don't pay admission and the bouncer don't check us. And we walk around the metal detectors... Lean back. Lean back. Lean back. Lean back."

"Where you think you going unless you gonna get us a two bottles of Armadale?" he asked.

I heard what he said so I pulled out another stack of money out of my pocket. "Kiesha, go get us two bottles. We only drink top shelf! Know what I'm sayin'?"

"I hear that!"

"Bring your hot ass right back! As a matter of fact, I'm walking with you," Fruity said, "so we can bring Shampoo sexy ass back!"

The club music beat inside my chest. "Shorty, you fine. Boomp! Make me wanna hit dat'. Boomp! The way your booty shake—Boooomp! I can see it now—You're off the hook! Booomp!"

I was still standing next to the speaker when someone tapped me on the shoulder.

"Your brother told me to bring this bottle to you!" she screamed, handing me my bottle of Armadale."

"And what's your name, girl?"

"I'm Alize, but he just told me to bring this over to you—that's all," she said before dancing right in front of me.

I stepped away from the speaker and put my hand out there to see if Alize would follow my lead. She didn't resist.

"What's your name handsome?" she asked.

"Flubber. What's yours?"

"Alize."

"Where's your man or are you here by yourself?"

"Tonight, you got me all to yourself."

"Word."

"Yeah, but first I have to run to the bathroom. I'll be back with you in a few minutes," she said, taking a few steps in the other direction. Stepping back to me she said, "Hey, Flubber. Don't try to run away because I will catch you."

"Alright! Make sure you bring your ass back. I'll be right here by this speaker waiting for you."

The DJ sounded off in a serious mix. "Park Heights, R & G, Greenmount, Barcley. Booomp! I wanna rock right now! Booomp! Westport, Cherry Hill, North & Long, and Dolfield. Booomp! I wanna rock right now! Boomp!"

"What is the world coming to!" the voice shouted.

"Who you talkin' to?" I asked blindly, turning in his direction. Then, noticing a familiar face coming closer toward me for a handshake and hug, I said, "Damn! Boy, what's going on because I ain't seen you in a while."

It was true. I've been hearing things about him, good things about getting' money, but hadn't seen him in a while. What I did know was how much weed and coke he was buying from the Jamaican Posse. He was known for handling something like ten to fifteen million dollars a year.

He shook his head in disbelief standing directly in front of me. "I ain't never seen y'all out in the clubs—unless you and your brother was trying to heist somebody," Rock said in a joking way.

"Rock, my main man," I said before giving him daps.

"The last time I ran into you and your brother was up Park Heights copping from the Jamaican spot. I'm the one who introduced him!"

"Look how fat your ass is getting! You look like you're sneaking pork chops and bacon in bed late at night!"

"I gotta invest my money somewhere!" Rock shouted in laughter, still holding two drinks in his hands. "I heard the women love big men anyway! The first thing they do is kick this extra weight out of the way...and the rest is freaky history!"

"I hear that shit, Rock. But tell your girl to stop feeding you that pork—because you look like you about to explode!"

"I see your brother, Fruity, over there chillin' at the bar with those two fine ass females, but that other one must've crawled from under an old rock," Rock said on a serious note.

He pulled back on one of his drinks to finish it off before setting the empty cup on the speaker. He pulled a blunt out of his shirt pocket and set it to fire.

"I think her name is Doll," I said.

"I didn't know you and your brother was this cool!"

"Why you say that?" I asked out of curiosity.

"Fast Money didn't trust y'all. He ran y'all stickup history down to me and told me not to ever trust y'all."

"Fuck Fast Money! He's the one who couldn't be trusted. Talking like dat'—he better be lucky he's over the Supermax and not on the streets because I would deal with him!"

"I wish I would've known that a long time ago. I would've been tried to turn y'all on to some work. Being on my payroll ain't bad—right about now. You feel me?"

"Have you heard from Fast Money?" I asked as he passed me the blunt.

"I hadn't seen him in a while before everything happened. The feds had information about the time when he working for me. They had me down there trying to use scare tactics to get information, but that shit is tired! I ain't tell them nothing! Plus, you know it's bad luck going in a courtroom if you're hustling, so I did what I had to do and left."

I heard both Rock and the music, peeping down at my watch real quick. It was about 1a.m. The bass had the building vibrating. "He don't know how we livin' now. Tell him, if you ever talk to him, that I don't chase money—now money chase'n me! Tell him to picture that?"

"He wouldn't call me anyway," Rock said, "because of how he did his thing before he got locked up. When he used to work for me, I was teaching him shit! I was teaching his stupid ass the game—uncut, but he blew up and got bigheaded. The feds called me down to question me about him while he was on trial. I ain't no snitch so I ain't have nothing to tell them anyway!"

"Damn, Rock! The feds pulled you in that conspiracy?"

"They tried to, but my lawyer got me off—and shit!" he said, grandstanding and playing with his nose. "Guess what I heard about his case?"

"What?" I asked curiously.

"I heard a lot of people were testifying against him—and shit, especially his connect and people from Baltimore."

"Oh, yeah?"

"Yeah—all of them guys that were with him got knocked off, too. Fast Money trusted too many snakes out there. And all of them testified against him in court. I'm telling you, the game is fucked up because everybody is telling trying to get a deal. Most of them out there are working for the police helping them identify people, places, and things as they happen. The streets are even saying I was testifying against his ass. Picture that shit—with all the money I'm making?"

"I ain't here that! Most of what you're saying is news to me."

"Flubber, you know Fast Money was down with getting Juvenile hit. And Precious, too. Tavon had Fast Money and Precious on his payroll."

"I heard a rumor one time about Precious having her hands in it, but we found out about dat' snake, Fast Money, almost from the start. He told that fuck'n lie about Juvenile messing with that girl."

"That shit is old and done." *After speaking, he put his arms around my shoulder in friendship.* "I heard y'all are doing shit now. Put my number in your phone and call me so we can make things happen together. It's enough for all of us—and I'm gonna get mine by any means necessary."

"I wasn't gonna let you leave without 'em. It was a reason why we came in here. It ain't no mistake, is it?"

"Hell-naw," he said, taking his cell phone out of his pocket. "Here, take my cell phone and plug your numbers in it so I can call you. Boy! I'm telling you I got the bomb shit!"

"Let's walk over here a minute, Rock."

"Look," he said loudly in my ears. "If y'all looking to cop some weight real quick just give me a call. I deal with some of the dudes that are getting big weight all around town. I'm still getting shit from the Jamaican Posse, but they're too hot up there! I still do when I have to, but not lately because I got another source."

"A'right. Just holler at me or my brother."

"I can call you at any one of those numbers and you'll get right back to me?"

"Yeah. One of us will call you right back."

"Since y'all are just jumping out there, I'll give you a big break!" he said while giving me daps.

"Before you step off, let's tell my brother what's happening with you."

I took the lead walking in Fruity's direction.

"Hey, what's up Fruity? Come here!" he screamed over the music.

"What's up Rock?" Fruity asked. *He immediately walked away from the sandwich Kiesha and Shampoo had him in.* "What's happening with you?"

"E-ver-y-thing!" Rock said, smiling, showing his diamond fronts.

"Boooy! You been around a long time up on Edmondson Avenue selling weight and weed," Fruity shouted. "Gimme dat' blunt, Rock! Stop being so tight and pass it!"

"Let me get you a fresh one so you can really feel it," Rock said, passing him a fresh blunt from his jacket. "I got so much of this shit it ain't funny. I was born to get money and it's gonna stay dat' way! I was just telling your brother that I've been able to put my hands on a lot of weight! You feel me? I got a new connect."

201

"Whatchu try'na do for us?" Fruity said, sucking hard on that blunt.

"If y'all tryna' get on—since y'all started doing y'all thing real heavy—just get in touch with me. I gave your brother all my numbers and I got his. Plus, I can get the Hydro, Purple Haze, and Arizona at a cheap price—straight from New York. I can put y'all on to the connect once you get your clientele built up—like I have up on Edmondson Avenue."

"Alright, my man. Dat's what I'm talking about! Get my numbers from Flubber and I'll talk to him tonight to see how much money we can put together for some weed. I understand what you saying, but now ain't the time—know what I'm saying? I came to the club to get that hustling shit off my mind and have fun with somebody's daughter! And now I got two or three. So I'll get with it sometime tomorrow."

"A'right, Fruity! Do your thing!"

I grabbed Rock by the shoulder and guided him back to the corner so we could talk. "My brother is zoned out with all them women right now, but you'll be hearing from us Rock."

"Alright! I'll holler at y'all when it's time. As a matter of fact," he said. "Call me tomorrow, so we can set something up right away. They give it to me for about nine hundred a pound. I bring it back here on Edmondson Avenue and sell it for about two thousand a pop! I'm telling y'all...selling that weed is better than selling dope! I'll make sure I give you a good price and send some of my sales to you, too."

"Alright, just listen out for our phone call."

Chapter 30

FRUITY

"12 a.m. on my way to the club
1 a.m. DJ made it erupt.
2a.m. now getting with her
3.a.m now splitting with her."
        Jay-Z, "Do It Again" (Put Ya Hands Up)
                Vol 3 ...Life & Times of S.Carter

I was feeling the night. The music was pumping and everybody in the club seemed to be enjoying the night. I haven't been to a spot like this in a long time. I don't know whether it was the weed we smoked with Rock, the Armadale, or Kiesha. It could be a combination of everything. Whatever the reason, I had this on top of the world feeling and wanted to seal this early night with some fun.

Shampoo and Doll was cool—giving me the eyes like they wanted it, too, but Kiesha was the truth. She spent all night acting like she was my girl and had her girls catering to me, too.

I didn't have to know her history and I'd be a fool to let her just walk away like that, especially since other hustlers were trying to whisper in her ears right in front of me. I was really hyped from the time we met outside of the club. And I can just imagine her nasty ass in bed. I'm getting hard just thinking about it.

"Hey, Kiesha," I said, tapping her shoulder, "Come 'ere—let me talk to you for a minute?"

"Alright. What's up?" she asked, grabbing the back of my shirt, walking behind me toward the bar.

I found a comfortable spot right next to the lounging area where other people had the same thing in mind. The lights were dim, setting the mood. Plush living room love seats set the tone away from the busy crowd dominating the dance floor. I sat down first.

"You know I love diamond jewelry, especially that watch and medallion," she said, sitting on my lap. *My erection was unmistakable, so she got my point.*

"It's only the jewelry your thug ass likes?"

"Naw, I'd be lyin' if I said 'yeah'. I've been feeling you ever since I saw you outside. I'm attracted to go-hard thugs like you—and have always been. That's just me."

"Now that I know you're down for whatever, and you're feeling me…what's next? That's if you trying to hang?"

"I'm with that. You seem like you know what you're doing, so I follow your lead."

"What time do you have to be in the house? You know it's about 2 in the morning?"

"House! I'm grown as shit! I'm grown enough to see 2 in the morning—plus some. Besides, I get down for my crown—even if it takes all night," she said, blushing, twisting her neck and sucking her teeth.

I held out my hand and asked, "Let me see a driver license. Let me see for myself how grown you are?"

She fumbled in her pockets and pulled out two pieces of identification. She flipped pass her Social Service card and handed me her age of majority card. I looked to see if she had one of those side profile shots proving she was underage.

After dropping his drink in front of us, a guy bent over as if he was about to fall. His drink splashed while his arms quickly wrapped around his waist. "Uuuuuurmph," he growled, throwing up the contents of his stomach.

"Now, what you gotta say?" she said, sliding off my lap, pulling me away from the sofa.

Walking behind her, now following her lead, I said, "Oh, you are twenty-four. Excusssse-me!"

"Yeah! So what's up now? This *pretty young thang* can hang!"

She lead me to sit in another seat closer to the front area. "Now if you really are trying to impress me then show me some more of what you working with?"

Ignoring all the other people standing around, she placed both of her hands on my knees. Slowly, Kiesha started her lap dance routine. "I'm only doing this because you are a soldier and you know how to get dough! This ain't for everybody." *She ended her routine by bending over and touching her toes-- sticking her ass in my front of my face and jiggling those cheeks.*

I don't know what it is, but this girl has got me wide open. "It's more than that, Kiesha. Can you freak as good as you dance?"

"Everything about me is da bomb including my head— so if you ain't down for real, then don't try me 'cause I'll have your ass strung out. Plus, I'd work you and your homeboys, too. I'm warning you! I know how to use every hole on your body and mine," she said, using her hands and head to make her point clear. "You betta asked somebody about me and my posse."

"The Jaguar is outside."

"And so is my car!"

I just looked at her and licked my lips like I wanted to taste her. "You make me wanna take your hot ass to the hotel right now!"

"You're wasting time still talking. Let's go if you're try'na have some fun! My skills go wherever I go. So what you waitin' for?" she asked, drinking the last of my bottle of Armadale. "But first I gotta get my girls."

"What! Your girls?"

"Yeah, we get down like this together, so you get the whole package tonight unless they're going off with somebody else. You get three at one time 'cause we freak for money from the first to the thirty-first!" *She stood still, looking at me, making sure I understood what she was saying.* "Can you handle all three?"

"You and your girls do it like that? I'm with it, but y'all gotta be freakier than the Fruity!"

"You'll see. They call us the Pleasure Posse. We freak with rubbers, without rubbers; it doesn't really matter to us how you wanna get down because we get ours the best way we know how! I'll be right back," she said, walking back through the crowd to find her girls.

I walked over to Flubber who was still hanging out with Alize. They looked like they were in deep conversation. I put my hand on his shoulder and said, "Now this is what I'm talking about. This is the life!"

"Excuse me, Alize. I'll be right back."

"Boy! I'm gonna have some fun tonight. Kiesha and her two homegirls are going to the hotel."

"Word? I know that chick was for real when she stepped to us man," he said, being two-faced.

"I'm tellin' you. She just put on a show for me! I'm taking her hot ass tonight."

"You'd be a fool not to. I think you should keep her closer than the rest! She's a soldier—somebody I can see right by your side. Here, you gonna need these," Flubber said, as he stuck his hand in his pocket and handed me two pills.

"That's what I needed. I gotchu."

"Fruity man, I'm starting to love this life and the money we be gettin' with Juvenile and Trigger!" he shouted, trying to talk over the music.

"What you mean—and Trigger? Trigger ain't helping nobody do nothin'! All he wants to do is play with his guns," I said.

He pulled me a little closer so I could really understand his point of view. "Yeah, but we still need him. We're all hustler's in love with the same thing—Money! If he wasn't around we'd be splitting even more money! Every time we meet, I see how he's always trying to impress Juvenile!"

"We gotta find a way to get rid of his ass." I said slyly. "We'll deal with him later. For right now, we need to get this second party started. That's what you should be concentrating on. I got my hands full with the Alize!"

"You know what I'm trying to do tonight with her and her girlfriends. So you know we goin' to the Hyatt, right?"

"I'm with that! I'm taking Alize. She's gamed for hanging out the rest of the night because I gave her money to take care of her overnight babysitter. Plus I gave her a few hundred dollars for spending the night with me. You know how crazy I can get with a female. I warned her, but she was tellin' me how wild her ass gets. So I'm try'na see, tonight!"

"I hear that shit."

We all left the club at about 3 in the morning. Flubber and I rode in the Jaguar. Alize and Kiesha's crew drove in separate cars following us to the pharmacy.

"You betta take those Viagras, Boy!" he said, as we walked into the 24 hour Rite Aid store.

"I got that right here in my pocket. That's why I'm getting one of these big Pepsi's to wash it down."

"Now we gotta get them raincoats near the prescription window."

"I had that already in mind."

As we walked to the back of the store, Flubber started talking about Alize. "You know I keep thinking about that girl's name. It's something about her name that I remember. It keeps ringing in my head."

"I was thinking the same thing, too," I chimed in, "but we did so much shit I can't remember sometimes. The only thing that rings a bell is that pregnant girl that we stuck-up in those apartments."

"You talking 'bout the girl I pistol-whipped because she wouldn't tell us where the rest of Outlaw's money was. All I remember is getting' mad as shit because she was willing to die for that dude. Come to think of it, she does remind me of that chick we robbed on Hollins Street a little bit, but that was a while ago!"

"I don't know. But she's probably not the same girl anyway. And even if it is, she's your freak tonight. Deal with that robbery after having your fun tonight."

With that in mind, we got back into the Jaguar and headed to our destination...

Chapter 31

FLUBBER

"And when he come up for air
With a mouth full of hair.
Just grab your Coach bag
And get the f*ck outta there."
Jay-Z, "Show You How"
The Blueprint 2(The Curse)

I had the rest of the night already planned when Fruity
dropped me off at the front desk.

"Hello, do you have VIP suites?" I asked the lady at the front desk.

"We sure do have them on the 14th floor, sir. However, those are usually booked in advanced. Would you like me to check if we have any available tonight? We might, even though it's such short notice."

"I would appreciate that because tonight is a big night for me."

"Okay, seems like you're in luck tonight. We have one available, so I can accommodate you and your party."

"What's in it?" I asked, trying to sound intelligent.

"It has two bedrooms, a living room, entertainment center, dining table, a fully stocked wet bar, and parlor bathroom. And the rooms can be separated for additional privacy."

On such short notice, Alize became my partner. She
walked in my shadow and grabbed my chest area underneath my
arms. She stood behind me, caressing my body, like a wife would

209

a husband. I watched everything in front of me, especially the front door—just in case the police came to interrupt.

Kiesha walked in with a big brown knock-off Louis Vuitton bag capable of holding a weekend's worth of overnight clothes. All I could think of is how ready these freaks are for Fruity—and Alize was more than ready for me.

"Are you ready Big Daddy to give me what I need?" Alize whispered.

"Am I—shiddd! It's coming faster than you know it!" I answered, still giving my attention to the front desk clerk. "How much is that VIP room?"

"That would be $700 per night, plus taxes."

"Is that all?" *I spoke loud enough so Kiesha, Shampoo and that ugly-ass Doll could hear how big we were spending.* "I'll take that."

"Can I see your driver's license?"

"Sure."

"Will that be cash or charge?"

"Let's do it cash—just let me know how much it is," I said, handing her my bent up piece of identification.

"Is this rental only for tonight?"

"Give me the whole weekend, shit. It's only money," I said, taking a glance over the contract. "Fruity, come here."

"How much is it?" Fruity asked, walking up to the desk.

"The rental for the suite is seven. I need you to give me about eleven or so. We can keep it for the rest of the weekend."

"What's the total," Fruity asked.

"That'll be $2,205 including taxes, sir."

I waited on Fruity to give me his share. "Give us one second to get this right," I said.

"I'm gonna show you how to have fun!" Fruity said in a low tone. "I'm taking all three of these freaks tonight!"

We paid our bill in full and gave her something extra. She gave me the swipe card for the suite and the details for room service. All of us followed our concierge to the elevator.

"Come 'ere Kiesha," Fruity said, pulling her close to him on the elevator. *While the rest of us watched, he stuck his finger down her pants.* "I'm letting all three of you tricks see how the rest of the weekend is going down!" Fruity said, laughing.

"That's how I like it!" Kiesha said throwing her body on Fruity.

Just as we stepped off the elevator, my cell phone rang. I looked at the caller ID and saw it was Juvenile.

"Yo, J!"

"Where you at?"

"Shit is happening down here at the Hyatt, homeboy. We got the suite on the 14th floor and we about to have some freaky fun! Fruity got three of them and they don't mind sharing! What's up?"

"Man, I got Trigger's drunk ass inside the car with me. I'm on my way back to Baltimore. After I take him home, I'll be going in because your sister keeps calling me trying to find out what time I'm coming in. Be safe down there and have some fun for me and tell Fruity that he's the man!" Juvenile said, laughing loudly.

"Alright, J! We out, son!" I said, following our escort to our room. "Hey, Fruity. Juvenile and Trigger are down for the count—so you're on your own with them three!"

Fruity looked back at me and winked his eye. "I can handle being superman after drinking that Pepsi, know-what-I-mean? I'm going all night! You gonna have to check on them, not me!"

Fruity and his crowd took the larger side of the room. As we settled on the other side, I watched Shampoo walk across the room, topless, toward Doll. Grabbing her by her hair and pulling her head backwards, Shampoo used her tongue to do a search for Doll's tonsils. Shampoo turned around with a lustful look to see our response as she squeezed Doll's ass.

"Y'all may want to be over here. This is where the freaky fun is!" Shampoo said seductively before walking over and shutting the room divider.

Without words being exchanged, Alize knew what the night was all about. Shampoo gave her a clear demonstration.

"Have fun over there. I got him all to myself," Alize told them in a soft voice.

Now that we were alone, I stared at Alize with explosive lust because I'd been feeling her all night. I watched her as she threw her Coach bag on the chair and stood by the window. Excitement raced through my body as she undressed. The moonlight shined through the parted drapes reflected off her skin. Her body sparkled. Lust could climb no higher. Even though it wasn't time to touch her, both of her erect nipples watched me watching her.

Walking into the bathroom naked, she asked, "After being in that smokey club, I have to get my body right. So, can you turn the water on so we can get clean?"

"Can't I just stand here and watch you?"

"If you want to, but I wanna watch you, too. I wanna see what I'm working with."

I walked inside the bathroom with her. I pulled the sliding glass doors apart and adjusted the temperature. "You like it hot?"

"Yeah. Real hot."

She would be the first to get in. I was already feeling myself pointing skyward inside my pants and I wanted her to see it, so I pulled everything off and went in to get wet. I let the water run on my head and down my body—hoping this moment could last for a long while.

"Ummm, look at you! You must be really feeling me, huh?" she asked.

"Waiting like crazy to see what you can do."

I watched the hot shower water dancing on her skin. Now looking at her body from head to toe, she was more attractive without those clothes. The only thing that could be seen was a few stretch marks, but her body was tight!

Moving to my chest area—pressing her lower back against my navel, gyrating her body against me like she did on the dance floor, Alize was master *at transferring her boiling body heat to mine.*

"Oooooh, shit! I want to feel this dick inside of me," she moaned while holding my sides with both hands from behind her.

My erection was her target, but she didn't stop there... Reaching for her toes, she bent over, massaging me tightly between her cheeks. She used her smooth ass crack like handcuffs—arresting my erection before wiggling like a fish out of water. Alize was taking me on a trip, a trip to a physical place of pleasure with twists and unexpected turns along the way.

To add fuel to the fire, I gave my right hand a little more power to take pleasure to another level. "Wham!"

Feeling me slap her naked ass, she screamed in surprise. "Eeeeew. That's what I like. Slap it again, Big Daddy!"

Slapping her again, I could feel the sting on my hand. "Oooow!" she screamed. "Hurt me Big Daddy. Grab my hair and show me how it's done!"

As I grabbed her, pulling her hair, she braced her body locking her arms on the glass. I could feel her pushing back against my body as hard as she could—almost knocking me down. I tried to handle it, but she was going for a ride and doing it her own way.

She turned toward me after turning the shower water off. Still breathing hard, Alize locked her eyes on my hairy chest. She knew what I wanted. One nipple she pinched with her left fingers. The other she trapped inside her mouth. Stooping, her tongue traveled south, taking the long way, sucking the small of my back and then my navel.

"You want me to take all this, Big Daddy?" she asked, looking up while stroking me with her hand. *Like a pro, her little hands grabbed me by the ass—pulling all of me inside her mouth.*

Without a response I gave her what she needed to become silent. With her mouth now full, there were no more words, just moans from my pleasure.

After getting me started...she turned me around, away from her, and started licking the rain drops off my thighs and running her tongue between my sensitive circle, tossing my salad...setting me on fire. This was way more than I expected as I pushed off the glass doors of the shower to brace myself.

She knew exactly what she wanted me to do to her. She got up to put her back against my chest. The cold water beads only added to my tingle. She grabbed me from behind her—putting her right arm around the back of my neck.

"I want you to play with my pussy so I could feel it," she said between moans, using her tongue to search for my eardrum.

"You want me to play with it, baby?"

"Yes!"

"Then tell me!"

"Take this pussy, Big Poppa—take it like it's yours!"

My fingers rubbed her nipples first. I tried my best to make her feel each pressure point. Now moving past her chest, I searched to find her tamed jungle of soft hair, the diamond cut I'd seen since seeing her strip naked.

I slid my fingers slowly, slowly, taking my time finding her secret garden. My circular movement separated hair and then lips. Her silky moisture was like lotion-- soon softening my rough fingers.

Her thighs tightened and her body became intense. Suddenly she reached forward, grabbing what separated my belly from her back, and guiding me between her legs.

Just like she would a pony...she rode me, forcing me to discover how deep she was. Thrusting until her body jerked without control, she told me her deeper desires. Grabbing me by the waist with both hands, she screamed, "Go faster, Baby—faster! Push it harder!"

Her body jumped in quick motions. I couldn't contain my body's reaction any longer. I squeezed tighter, feeling the screams of my body's pleasure, each drop we worked for, pulsating inside of her. With each release, my body became limb and powerless and suddenly free.

I wanted to do something different with this woman. She was giving it up, free of any inhibitions, and making me feel real good. Going again was my intention, but I had to do one thing that turned me on. With that in mind, I washed my body and gave her further instructions. "Clean it up so I can do something special for you."

"Uuhhm Big Daddy," she said like a kitten, washing her body under the shower water. "Now, if you don't know what you're doing I'm gonna talk about you! Don't let me have to give you instructions because that turns me off!"

"I'm gonna give you something to talk about and it won't be bad! Plus, you gotta keep this between me and you."

"Well, I'll be finished in a minute. Set my Coach bag in here so I can fresh'n up real quick."

After drying off, I was still heated and full of excitement. I was already enjoying the thought of what was about to happen, so I started rubbing myself, resting on top of the sheets, impatiently awaiting her arrival.

"C'mon, gurl. What's taking you so long?"

"I'm coming, Baby. I'll be right out."

She used an enticing body spray in the bathroom tempting my instincts. She soon followed...wrapped in a fluffy white hotel bathrobe, walking slowly out of the door. Her presence filled the room with a sweet-smelling watermelon fragrance.

She walked up to me. Untying the wrap separating me from touching her natural beauty, I began squeezing her and then rubbing her body communicating my willingness to go even longer. After dropping her robe, I lifted her body weight, so she could easily wrap her legs around my waist.

"Damn, gurl. Do you know how sweet you smellin' right now?" I asked, guiding her toward the window when she stopped me.

"No, let's stay right here near the end of the bed. I wanna see what you're doing. You have a treat for me, so I went in the bathroom to get a treat for you."

"So, let me taste you?"

She led me behind her, turned to face me, and slowly sat on the end of the bed with her legs open wide. I kneeled in front of her, assuming the position without a second thought. Firmly, she placed both of her hands on my shoulders, grabbing me, getting ready for the ride.

While chasing my urges using my fingers to stimulate her body's response, I began kissing her inner legs. Her body heat warmed my mouth and each soft hair follicle massaged my tongue--while the position itself tickled my fantasy.

Her excitement ran through my body--touching the fetish that made me nasty. She guided my head movements, pulling me closer to my destination. Each nerve ending on my body pulsated, letting me know I was more than ready. My arrival, finally reaching her creamy middle, provoked more moaning and had her body moving to my rhythm, especially reaching her wet pussy.

"Uuuhmm, that's what I want..." she said, letting my shoulders go, reclining back on both hands, finding a comfortable position. "You like what you taste?"

"Uhmm Huh. Watermelon Jolly Rancher."

Scooting more to the edge, exposing all of what underwear and pants were meant to shield, she lifted one leg and then the other across my shoulders, finally bracing herself for all the stimulating tongue and finger tricks I had in store. Flowing with me, reaching that place of pleasure, moaning and giving in to lust, her body trembled and her breathing quickly became quick screams before shaking uncontrollably in my face. That was just the beginning...Freaky Flubber had more in store.

Chapter 32

FRUITY

*"Got a project chick
That plays her part.
And if it goes down y'all
That's my heart."*

Jay-Z, "Girls, Girls, Girls"
The Blue Print

Now I've heard of a ménage trios, but I had to find another name for what we were about to get into. Since I didn't want to think orgy, I'll call this a ménage qua!

Walking around, soaking in this life that is different for me, I got a good look at all this space. The smell of fresh flowers filled the room. A colorful bouquet dressed the dining table VIP style. Sitting on top of the kitchen counter was a tasty fruit displayed on a shiny silver platter. The lounging area felt like somebody's home. And the granite bathtub was big enough to hold everybody at one time.

"Hey Fruity," Kiesha said, grabbing my attention. "Look at this little kitchen with all this food we can cook when we get hungry. If I had the money I would live in a place like this—shit—this is top notch! We should take some of this shit home."

"And they got a bar with a little bit of everything over here," Doll said, *grabbing something to her liking, pulling back on the small miniature bottle and drowning it.*

Shampoo walked behind me looking around. "I'm glad you got this suite for the whole weekend because I ain't leaving here until its time to check out. My five kids and their different babysitters will just have to miss me this weekend—because the fun for me is right here! I need this break anyway."

"I hear that shit, but y'all better make this worth my money," I said before stepping out on the balcony to a totally different view of the city. *This was a different city view from the one I know. Downtown was lit up, offering a safely strange night life from the one I was used to. There were no dark allies or dangers lurking around every corner. Florescent night lights advertised day business. The blue from the Aquarium and the red from Rusty Scupper and the sweet taste arising in my mouth from the Domino Sugar sign was automatic. The streets look like dinner plates and the harbor water would've went well with ice, showing off the beauty Baltimore wants all to see. And, for the life of me, I couldn't find one blown street light...*

Turning to see if they wanted to join me, I saw Shampoo turning toward Doll, allowing her nipples touch hers, and kissing her passionately before inviting Flubber and Alize over to our soon-to-be-steamy side of the suite.

"Y'all may want to be over here. This is where the freaky fun is," she said before being refused. *She should've known Flubber and Alize had other plans.*

Even as she closed the room divider, they were still putting on a show. Shampoo was already topless, exposing her large nipples. Unable to wait for my slow commands, satisfying their own personal needs, they started taking each other's clothes off.

The carpet in the entire suite was so plush your feet tickled with each step. Without hesitation, Kiesha stripped naked, ready to enjoy the night.

"With this carpet alone, we don't need no bed, do we girls?" Kiesha asked as she bent down to lie naked on the soft carpet floor.

"Hell naw. This carpet is soft!" Doll answered while looking over to me. *She walked up behind Kiesha, squatting, opening her legs grinding her wet, sloppy lips on her back in search of erotic satisfaction.*

Just watching and being around these girls was keeping me hard.

After seeing the carpet action and walking toward me, Shampoo asked, "Fruity, you ready for all of this?"

"Shiddd, Am I?"

"Well put the cash on the table, Big Money, and anything goes after that," she said, taking some clothes off my body.

Now this was the life people on the streets respect. All I did was change careers. I moved from a bad boy sticking up people to having my own little operation which now makes me a money spending bad boy. Everything seems to be about dollars and sense. If your talk is not backed by dollars, then shit you say don't make sense.

"You got it!" I said, pulling a wad of money out of my pocket and peeling ten fifty dollar bills. "Plus, I'll add another hundred so everybody'll be happy and I get freaked the hell out. I wanna see some nasty Joe Pro shit in here tonight! No tongue should be still and all lips should be moving!"

I was still buzzing from my drinking and that weed Rock gave me. After getting off the floor, Kiesha walked up to me and undressed me completely.

She led me to the end of the bed--whispering in my ear. "Your show is about to begin."

Licking me across my chest and running her nails on my warm skin, Kiesha looked up to me seductively and said, "Step back and let me see what we're working with. And then we're gonna make our own Joe-Pro movie for you!"

Kiesha stepped to the side. Shampoo came around in front of me, bending over with her feet apart, showing all that she was offering.

Shampoo pulled Kiesha closer, slapping her on her left butt cheek and then giving her a long, ice cream lick. "Let's get this party started," she said, turning back to me.

With expert handling, Shampoo grabbed my hard dick. She excited me with a quick teasing suck while Kiesha reached around getting her hot and steamy, exploring her body from behind with finger play.

Soon they climbed on top of the bed where Doll was zoned out, playing with herself, waiting for action. Kiesha slid behind Doll at the top, Shampoo positioned in front of her and Doll behind Shampoo. After organizing their bodies, catering to my request, things started getting really sloppy. The moans from tongues to flesh and the sound of pleasure sparked the Viagra inside of me. I stood there, believing what I was seeing, heart beating fast, breathing hungrily for action, trying to record every detail, like a movie director—watching this Fruity-Pro movie play out.

Satisfied with what I was seeing...made me wanna join in. Viagra now had me unable to control my urges. Holding its effects in my right hand, I used my left fingers and thumb to explore Doll's wet body parts that no longer contained its moisture.

Turning around, grabbing some ice from the bucket not far from the bed, Doll slid chips inside her mouth and ran her chilly lips all across my chest. Reaching downward, rubbing my leg and grabbing my hard dick tightly in the wrap of her hand, she pulled on me in a slow, jerking motion before using her tonsils to slide across my throbbing penis head.

"Uh! Uh! Uh!" Kiesha screamed in pleasure, shaking the headboard wildly, not wanting to control herself.

Shortly after, I could feel Shampoo and Kiesha slowly licking on my legs and taking turns tossing my salad. My body shivered with excitement when I felt Kiesha bowing in front of me, taking Doll's place.

Doll walked over to their weekend bag pulling out a metal trick. Grabbing Shampoo, leading her back to the bed and placing her on all four, she started pinching and flicking her breast before opening Doll from behind with her big, battery operated toy.

Hearing Shampoo's pleasure, enjoying her wild moans, Kiesha started going wild trying to bring me to explosion. Feeling her, giving her what she's begging for down there, almost reversed the effects of the pills I'd taken. This was an all night movie and I was going the full distance.

This was more, way more, than I expected. I knew these club girls would be fun, but not like this...

Confidential
Internal Police Memo

At 10:30 am, neighborhood informant #519 reported that two brothers, Flubber and Fruity, who were previously involved in drug related robberies, are now involved in a major drug ring. These suspects are said to be expanding their operation to reach more drug areas. Informant #519 gave this officer several contact numbers belonging to one of the suspects in question.

On the night in question, the sibling suspects arrived at a downtown nightclub driving a blue, late model Jaguar. Previous information and intelligence provided by informant #519 resulted in several positive leads and state and federal convictions. New intelligence, which includes addresses and relative information, has been forwarded to the Drug Task Force. More information is expected as this investigation continues.

End of Report.

Chapter 33

JUVENILE

"My life is getting too wild.
I need to bring some sorta calm to it.
Bout to lose it…
*Voices screaming **"Don't Do It."***

Jay-Z, *"This can't be life"*
The Black Album

Over the last week I've been really having second and third thoughts about this heist. I was for each robbery when it came to taking revenge on all those double crossing me with Tavon, but I was never a stick up guy for money. That shit is certainly not my style. When I think about the dangers of what we were about to do, I couldn't stand losing any one of them. One of us, any one us, would probably get killed trying to pull this Jamaican Posse heist off!

They had too many guns. And their security was tight. It would be four of us. Three would go in while one secured the front porch. Still, getting by the front and even getting inside the house didn't guarantee entry into the basement.

We could imitate the knock on the front porch and could do the same like Rasta does at the basement door. That's where the money is stashed, so we have to make sure—if we go—that we make it down there at a record speed. But my conscience keeps bothering me—speaking in my head over and over. 'If risks and consequences outweighed the reward then it isn't worth it.' Intuition was saying something to me this time—and I don't think anybody else would listen.

Trigger seemed to be born of the streets. This life is something he was excited about, but this decision was on me and would be on my conscience after deciding to pull this off--and something goes wrong. Trigger doesn't care, but I do.

Man, this whole thing is gettin' old. Puffin weed, drinking, carrying guns, another day of merely existing on these streets, just to see if we're gonna see another day, is a waste of time.

Life had to change. The time had to be now. I had to calm down because all this is too wild. Regardless of the fact that I don't have the amount I wanted before quitting this game, but I'm not planning on dying trying to get it either. Besides, I couldn't imagine seeing Jameel in pain after losing her brothers or me. Tiffany's pain from losing her father or two uncles was too much to imagine her going through.

Jameel had been speaking to me about that all along. My history guaranteed me certain employment because I could pass the background checks since I had no felony conviction. Her thing was having me quit before it came to that point. In a way, she was right. She always told me, 'If you quit, if I was man enough to walk away, God had prepared a better way for me.'

Seeing my life flash in front of me really changed my thinking. I have everything I need. I have a woman who should've been my wife. I remember when Tavon used to say that all the time about me having a family that loved me and I'll use my last, the only money I have, to put that diamond ring on Jameel's finger.

I'd done too much harm in Charm City to just think I could stay. Besides, the game just ain't right without my old partner anyway. We've already loss him and that's way more than I could really bear.

Now, this! You would think with all of the violence I've seen and promoted on the streets that I would be able to make this call and get it done. The only way I can get that dirt off my shoulders is to call it off and walk away. Life really has to change before I lose it. One thing I have to admit is: Saying goodbye to the game ain't easy. I'll miss this life and the rush that comes with taking chances, but all this shit comes second to life and my family.

I'll be calling this meeting. It'll be like the first one Flubber and Fruity called to ignite this Posse plot. My call will be my chance to call it off and tell all them, "Don't Do It!"

Chapter 34

JAMEEL

*"Thank God for granting me
This moment of clarity."*

*Jay-Z, "Moment of Clarity"
The Black Album*

Tiffany and I had been out shopping for graduation outfits most of the day. We went out Owings Mills to Hecht Company, but ended up finding me a beautiful sequins dress in Saks Fifth Avenue. I couldn't wait to get home to show Dorian.

Something has been bothering him, but he really didn't want to talk to me. I tried to get him to open up, but his answer was staying in the basement. Questioning him about my brothers and why they hadn't been calling wasn't a good idea. Something was wrong and I felt it.

Coming inside I had a million and one things to do. I knew washing and ironing had to be done and balancing my checkbook. First, I had to check on him.

I shouted down the basement. "Dorian, wait until you see what I bought for graduation! I'll be down as soon as I change, okay?"

"Alright, Jameel," he answered, sounding sleepy.

I rushed upstairs with my twin Tiffany trailing right behind me.

"Momma, can I change to show Daddy what I have, too?" she asked walking into my room.

227

"Sure, sweetheart. You know Daddy wants to see you what you have."

I was truly excited about having him see me. "Baby, give me my dress out of that bag, please?"

"Here you go."

Both of us quickly changed. I let the Princess go first, walking like royalty down each set of steps. My dress drew a reflection from the night light in the hallway. Going through the kitchen and down those creepy steps, we found Dorian staring in space, deep in thought.

"Daddy, turn on the brighter light so you can see how I look."

"Jameel, turn that light on for me?" he asked.

"Don't I look like a Princess? I got this dress just so you could see me and Mommy dressed up."

"C'mere baby—and give Daddy a hug?" he said, trying to hold his composure. "And you, Jameel—let me see you?"

I smiled briefly--trying not to upset his attempt to come out of what deep thoughts he was into. "See, how do I look?"

"Baby, you look like a Princess, too—just a little older than this one I'm holding real tight before she goes to bed."

"Can you tuck me in, Daddy?"

"When it's time I'll race you up there," he said, letting go of his little Princess and pulling me close.

It sure felt good having him home with us. Having him hold me, and touch me, had me never wanting to let this man go.

"Baby, if anybody deserved the reward for hard work, it has to be you. That's what I was just sitting here thinking about. I wouldn't miss your graduation for the world."

"Well, after you put your daughter to bed, can we celebrate early by spending some quality time together?"

"I was feeling the same way, too. Y'all go ahead and change. I'll be up and ready for that. Just give me a few minutes."

He didn't take long before coming upstairs. He went straight inside the bathroom to play with Tiffany. She was brushing her teeth, getting ready for her prayers. After finishing with her he came inside my bedroom.

Sliding under the sheets, we held each other tight. Tonight we'd be communicating without words. Freeing myself of underwear, kicking them somewhere between those sheets, allowing him to peel my big T-shirt off of my body...let him know I was his for the taking.

This time instead of making love, we allowed love to make us do some specials things in celebration of our life to come...

* * * * * * * *

I showered after loving my man for what seemed like forever. He went off into a deep sleep, snoring loudly, while I went in the extra room to iron clothes and downstairs to wash. The quietness of the night sparked thoughts about life. I was already feeling good all over and traveling deep into my thoughts took me to a quiet place, a place of peace.

I had already changed the last load for the night and set the dryer temperature. I walked softly up the stairs not wanting to disturb them from their sleep. Just as I was about to iron my last little bit of clothes, something startled me.

"Aaaaaaaaaaaaa! Nooooooooooooo!" I heard Dorian screaming out in his sleep.

"D-o-r-i-a-n! Are you okay?" I shouted, running to the room.

"Mommy!" Tiffany screamed, waking from her sleep, "What's wrong with Daddy?"

"Nothing baby—just go back to sleep!"

I went inside the room and saw Dorian sitting straight up, looking confused and scared, trying to recover from his dream.

"What's wrong?"

"I keep having these crazy dreams, Jameel. All these strange men keep chasing us, trying to hit us and get inside the house with knives and pipes."

"Who is it?"

"I don't know. All their faces are strange. That's why I keep waking up. It's like they keep trying and trying and won't give up. And I keep running."

I held him tightly. "Dorian, everything will be alright."

"I know I said this before, Jameel. But I'm really tired of doing it like this. It's too many of us dying and too many other hustlers trapped just waiting to be buried six feet under," he said, whining in my arms.

"We'll be out of this town after graduation and it'll all be behind us. God knows, this will be behind us, Dorian."

"Back then I just didn't care. Now, I want more for our family than this, baby," he said, squeezing me for more support. "I love you and I need you, Jameel! I need you and Tiffany to make my life complete. That's why I'm finally saying this to you. I'm ready for all of what we've talked about."

"God answers prayers!" I said in happiness. "Thank you God for this moment of clarity."

His change, his transformation, had taken time. Sometimes I felt like it had taken too long, but it had finally come. Moving was the solution. No matter what, whatever was coming with change…Tiffany and I will be right by his side.

In the News

A federal agent, who is also a plaintiff in a federal discrimination lawsuit, was indicted and arrested today on several charges. A twelve-count federal indictment alleged that Mr. Andre Cousins was heavily involved with a Westside drug crew. Charging documents accuses Mr. Cousins of obtaining illegal handguns and false identification for several associates to gain access to shooting ranges and high powered firearms. One of his alleged associates was killed in a police involved shooting after discharging an illegal firearm. Authorities are also still investigating allegations of gun trafficking.

"We have to research the government's case before we take a position. As of today, he is officially resigned from the Federal Bureau of Investigation. My client is part of a large civil suit against the FBI agency. We think this is why he was targeted," said Attorney James Lucky.

Authorities countered defense arguments denying that these charges have anything to do with the civil class action lawsuit Mr. Cousins was previously involved in.

Chapter 35

TRIGGER

"Or get a gun, a mask,
an escape route--
Some duct tape will make 'em
take you to the house."
              Jay-Z, *"Show You How"*
                    The Blueprint 2

It was up to me to rethink this strategy since Juvenile flipped our plans and backed out. He's talking about moving and graduation and all that other weak shit. All I keep thinking is a scared man can't make money. He doesn't understand how hungry I am after being away for all of those years. He was a family man and all and I wasn't, so he's probably better off not being around, anyway.

That's just how it is nowadays. I think the decisions of the streets are about living for the moment, living each challenge as it comes without planning. I intend to show Juvenile just what he's missing after robbing them cats of all they have—and I mean everything. This life is do or die and you gotta be in all the way! There's no room for a halfway thug.

* * * * * * * *

We drove three cars to Hilton Street near the reservoir off of Liberty Heights, so we could park one as our getaway car. After parking it near the dark alley, we huddled in the darkness

232

of the night. I took the time to go over the plan one last time. There would be no other opportunity to rehearse. This was it.

We drove up to the spot in Park Heights in two cars. As we got closer to the turn, we moved at a slow creep. I gave the instructions to pull up in front of the house.

Fruity's female thug had proven herself, so we had Kiesha as our first driver. I was in the front seat with her. Flubber and Fruity ducked down in the back seat.

We had Alize driving a second car. Alize was thorough, but she wasn't as rough as Kiesha. That's why we had her park right across the street from the Posse's spot. She was there just in case something went wrong. This shit was going down! And it was going down tonight!

We were only a couple blocks away from other Posse members who were handling hand to hand streets sales. My plan was to have Flubber cover the porch once we go in. He'd be in position to shootout with whoever tried to be a hero tonight.

Both cars sat in position for a few quiet minutes. It felt like life was taking its own moment of silence. It was over when Alize flicked the headlights one time.

"Alright—check your guns. We can't fail at this shit, y'all. When that door opens again, we gotta move quick, fast, and in a hurry!"

"Got it, homey. Dis' shit is on!" Flubber said in a low, deep voice.

"Scared money don't make none, so let's get this shit done!" Fruity screamed while cocking the white pearl handles on his matching guns.

"Those two guys are going in. Now you know they are gonna keep the door open for a few seconds when they come out. It's on after that," Kiesha said.

We waited, with ski masks ready, as the two guys came out of the house with two bags. They got into different cars. Once they pulled off we made our move.

"Alright y'all. Be careful," she said in a scared voice.

All three of us ran up toward the house. As soon as we got close, I ran directly to the porch man and jammed him with my guns. I had him at gunpoint, holding him around his neck. Fruity stood watching, looking around, making sure we were safe.

Flubber and I both worked to duct tape his mouth and pushed the porch man toward the front door. We hit the peephole with clear fingernail polish. They would be able to see the image of his face, but not a clear one.

I still held my gun to his head. "Knock on the door, muthafucka!" I said in a low, forceful tone, holding him tighter around his trachea.

He did the knock we heard so many times before. I held my gun to his side—forcing him to put his face at the peephole. Once the door started opening, Flubber hit him across the skull, using the butt of his gun to put him to sleep.

Fruity hit the door, pushing straight inside, overtaking the inside door man.

Flubber, running quickly past that commotion, went straight for Rasta and the money table. By surprise, he caught another member running toward Flubber trying to protect his leader, Rasta. Reaching for his gun, making a fast movement for his waist, he was seconds too late.

"Bloooom!" Flubber shot him, point blank range, knocking him to the floor in front of Rasta.

With money still in hand and visibly shocked from all of the action, Rasta finally tried to reach for his gun. Flubber had him covered. "Don't move motherfucker or I'll blow your head off!"

"Lay down! Lay the fuck down!" Flubber screamed. *He pushed him away from all the stuff he had on the table making him get on the floor. He started snatching the money and drugs they had laid out on the table and was impatiently stuffing the black backpack.*

With the first floor covered, I took the lead hitting the basement door. Fruity was behind me. Kicking the door and racing down the steps we caught the Posse scrambling.

"Oh! Shit!" a dark skinned woman screamed. *She was nervously packing a bag full of kilos.*

"Bumboclaat—a whey dem 'eeddiat yah up to!" the Jamaican guy screamed in panic, reaching for his gun on the long table holding money neatly stacked in piles.

Our fast footsteps stopped them in their tracks before they were able to get to the back door. After getting down the stairs, Fruity fell forward, tripping over something on the floor, with his guns in his hand. I was still able to hold the two at gunpoint.

"Mutha-fuc-ka! Where y'all going?!" I screamed, ready to shoot if I had to. "C'mon motherfucka, get up and help me tape 'em up!"

I could hear Fruity get'n up as fast as he could. I looked out the corner of my eyes to see boxes with big black stamps on the side. Pulling the duct tape out of his hoodie, he snatched her up, wrapping her quickly. Stacked in columns not far from where they were sitting counting money, were blocks of weed wrapped up in heavy plastic.

After taping the girl, Fruity threw the guy against the wall strapping him down.

"Look back there! Hurry up!" I screamed. "I got this up here!"

We had the whole house at gunpoint.

"Now where da' rest of the fuckin' money at--bitch! Cause' I know it's down here," I screamed, holding the gun in his face.

Snatching the tape from her mouth, I screamed, "I'll blow your head off, bitch! Now tell me where the money is!"

"De money's in dere!" the girl screamed, pointing her head directly in front of her. *The only thing in the corner was this heavy wooden chest sitting flat on the floor.*

"Whatchu talk 'bout bitch," he shouted. "Ain' no bloodclaat money in yah!"

Fruity ran back to me with some bricks of weed, stuffing it inside his bag.

"Check over here inside this chest," I told him.

He moved with quickness and was able to open the chest without trouble. "Jackpot!" Fruity said, pulling bags of money out, stuffing them inside his bag.

"Fill dat' shit up. Hurry up, so we can get da' fuck outta here," I said before *pistol-whipping* the leader.

"I got enough of it! The rest can't fit!" Fruity screamed. "Alright, let's go."

Fruity threw the bag on his shoulder running up the steps. I could hear some scrambling upstairs with Flubber. Reaching the first floor, I screamed, "What da' fuck!"

Rasta was having a fit down on the floor. Fruity had his foot on top of Rasta's head trying to control him, but he was kicking anything in reach.

We ran around the hostages on the floor as Flubber grabbed his duffel bag, heading for the door. The plan was to cover the front door. Making sure the coast was clear, snatching the door, crouching down like I had seen on TV, I was only letting only a small part of my face show. If anybody was out there, I would see them first.

Stooping out on the porch with my guns ready to fire, I screamed, "C'mon. Get da' fuck outta there!"

Kiesha had the car doors open. Fruity was right behind Flubber running with guns in one hand and bags in another. Flubber and Fruity jumped in the back of the car. Alize had pulled the second car right behind her.

Running across the grass, I could see some Posse members running in our direction with guns drawn, screaming shit I really couldn't understand. Everything seemed slow-motion until I started firing in that direction.

"Sphlwooow! Booom! Booom!" sounded off. *Loud gunshots were tearing through the frame of the car as I dived inside. The back window exploded. Other shots made a funny noise bouncing off of steel car parts. Fruity and Flubber ducked down to avoid getting hit.*

Kiesha pulled off at a full speed. Alize was in the stolen car speeding behind us like the police in hot pursuit!

"Go! Go! Go!" I screamed at Kiesha, shooting again out of the busted passenger side window.

"Which way!"

"Just drive this shit! Get the fuck outta here!"

Loud bangs from Flubber's gun returned fire. As I looked over to my right I could see the crowd ducking to take cover.

Trying to get away, I knew one thing. We had so much shit it would be hard to count. We raced down Belvedere and safely reached the light at Reisterstown Road. We ran dangerously through a red light making a left turn. I could see Alize speeding closely behind.

Kiesha avoided another light by turning into the Amoco gas station and then onto Garrison Boulevard. The light was green when she turned left on Wabash speeding straight ahead.

Fruity looked to see if any cars were following us.

"Oh! Shit! Flubber shoot that car trying to ram Alize!" Fruity screamed.

Flubber extended his body out the passenger side window firing again--this time making contact protecting his girl.

Screeching tires and the sound of a two car impact disturbed the quiet night. "Scurrrrrrrrrt! Booom!"

We made a right at the school and sped across Liberty Heights, this time not stopping.

"Keep going straight!" Fruity screamed. "Fuck dat' other car, shit! They might be still behind us!"

"Where am I going!" Kiesha screamed in panic.

"Just keep on going straight!"

Alize was still on our heels driving with a shattered windshield. We turned left illegally on Clifton Avenue and drove up near Longwood Street, quickly abandoning the stolen cars.

We all got out, ducking behind parked cars, running toward Poplar Grove. Noticing a set of lights behind us, we tried to see whether this white van belonged to a Posse member who could've been following us from a distance all along.

We had pointed guns, covering the slow moving white van, ready to fire just in case. The van turned down Longwood with only one person in it, but it was driving too slow to be watching us, I guess.

A few vehicles were coming down Longwood, but we started running again toward the alley with the bags and guns still ready in our hands.

We ran down the alley, making it towards the other end, getting closer to Poplar Grove. I thought I saw another white van. I wasn't sure if that was the same one, so I followed the crowd into the yard. All I cared about was being home free. Everybody was safe in Jameel's backyard. We pulled it off!

Banging on the back door, Juvenile was in shock when he found us all trying to rush inside.

"Whatdafuck! I know y'all ain't bring this shit to Jameel's house! I told y'all I ain't want nothing to do with this! And y'all still did it anyway—and now this!" Juvenile screamed again. "Why y'all bring this shit in here, Trigger? Fruity and Flubber—this shit ain't smart at all! And then y'all got these girls, too. Oh, hell no!"

"Man, fuck dat! Just get us the fuck in first!" I screamed, pushing inside the basement door.

In the News
Baltimore

Police are concerned with a DVD that is circulating in the city. "Stop Dat' Snitchin'" video is sparking controversy because city enforcement officials are unsure whether it will expose the reportedly "secret identity" of star, confidential, neighborhood informants.

The subject of these tapes is centered on a key witness in a recently decided case concerning a New York to Baltimore drug conspiracy. *Alpo "Rock" the Bull* is alleged to be the reason why local dealers are angry. Authorities are holding him in at an undisclosed location for his protection. More on this story as it unfolds.

Chapter 36

JAMEEL

"It must be sad,
Though it hurts to say...
You deserve better."
Jay-Z, "Soon You'll Understand"
The Dynasty

I can't believe it! I thought this day would never come. I've finally met all my requirements to graduate from Coppin State University. Going back and forth to campus studying has become a part of my life. I'm so used to going to classes four nights a week that I'll actually miss my soon-to-be-called alma mater. But I'm ready to take my life, my baby and Dorian to our destiny. I know God has a plan for me—and I'm willing to take my family out of Maryland to find it.

It's been a while since I've admired myself in this bathroom mirror. Usually I'm rushing, but today I'm taking my time because it's mine to celebrate. Oops, I almost forgot I had something to do to satisfy my curiosity before leaving here today. My body has been going through some changes, lately.

"Tiffany."

"Yes, Mommy—I'm right here."

"Do Mommy a favor?"

"Yes?"

"Bring me that Rite Aid bag with that purple and white box inside. It should be down there on the dining room table."

"I got it," she said, running up the stairs.

"Here you go, Mommy," she said, pushing the bathroom door open.

"Thank you, sweetie. You can set it on the hamper next to the sink."

'I can't believe how overpriced these things are,' I thought to myself, breaking open the box and pulling the small wand out. I bought one because I've been missing my cycle for the last two months. I know my body and I know when it changes. It didn't take long for me to follow the instructions to do the test. Now, all I have to do is wait.

Dorian, Mr. Procrastinator himself, waited until the last minute to get his clothes so he had to run out to the mall this morning. Isn't he a trip? I told him he didn't have to wear a suit, but he insisted.

"Dressing any kind of way on your graduation won't do," he said to me this morning. "This is the day I have to represent, so only the best will do."

I've been praying for a new car—because I sure need it. This piece of a car has been holding up for some time now. We're going to need a new one once I get this new job. We can't be traveling back and forth in what I have now.

Tonight, after graduation, he and I are going to have a sit down because it's time to talk about tying the knot. We've been in each other's lives for some years now, but we still only call each other friends. We have to grow into responsibility. And I'm ready for what comes next.

I left out of the bathroom to go out and get some air on the back porch. It's a sunny day and perfect for a celebration. I still can't believe I'm finally graduating from Coppin. I remember starting out with my counselor with no credits at all. Now having more than 120, meeting my requirements, took a lot of work.

I can see why Saturdays in the months of June and July were for family reunions, cookouts, weddings, and graduations. Today, mine would be held at the First Mariner Arena. I know that's the new name but we still call it the Baltimore Arena.

Momma is going. She and my baby wouldn't miss this. I invited Ms. Emma and Mr. Paul, my two supervisors from the Post Office. Both of my brothers are coming, too. I only had those six tickets. People from the church wanted to come, but I had none left.

I stepped back inside. I took my time getting dressed. My daughter watched me from start to finish. Tiffany does this all the time and is treating this day like it's my wedding.

She was even more excited when she started putting her clothes on. She was looking cute in her favorite white dress with pink polka dots, a pink hat to match and gloves.

Tiffany spinned around like a model. "Mommy, this is my special outfit for you."

"You look beautiful. And I did this for you. This is your special day, too. You helped Mommy complete school, so what I should be saying is congratulations to you," I said, giving her a hug before stepping out of my bedroom.

"Thank you, Mommy," Tiffany said, looking at me giggling.

I glanced at the clock on the wall in the hallway and couldn't believe how time had passed by so quickly. Rushing pass the bathroom, I took one quick peek at the results of my test and put it back inside the box.

Hurrying down the steps straight to the front door, Tiffany and I got outside walking to the car like two supermodels. I opened her door first to let her in and eased in my side of the car like it was a stretch limousine. My heart was beating fast in excitement. I took deep breaths trying to gain control of myself before pulling off.

Our first stop was getting Momma and then to the Baltimore Arena to meet everybody else.

Momma started as soon as she got inside. "If your father could see you now," she said, grabbing me before getting in the back. "I'm just glad to see things work out for you 'cause you deserve it. You and Dorian have to do what's right."

"Momma, now—I'm not trying to cry and mess myself and this pretty dress up before the graduation."

"Well, chile'. I'm just giving y'all my blessings, but you know what's next. This town gave you birth, but you have to go where the good Lord leads you and your family."

"I'll get to that with Dorian tonight. Thanks, but can this wait until later?"

"Okay, but not too much later." she said. *Momma was spoiling some of tonight's conversation about marriage I expected to have with Dorian.* "Where is he anyway?"

"He'll be here."

After arriving downtown, we parked in the garage directly across from the Arena. We walked inside to find our seating spaces. Both of my faithful supporters were already there and had saved seats for everybody else.

I walked up to them and said, "Thank you, Mr. Paul. I was telling Tiffany already, you and Ms. Emma played a part in this, too. If it wasn't for both of you helping me, I wouldn't be here."

"Don't talk like that, Jameel," Mr. Paul said, hugging Tiffany and reaching for my embrace.

"No, I have to today." *I embraced Mr. Paul and finally grabbed Ms. Emma.* "I have to thank both of you. I remember those days when I was so tired from studying and you both helped me. I couldn't keep my eyes open and could've lost my job so many times, but you both hung in there with me. Thanks so much!"

"No, thank you, baby," Ms. Emma said in response.

"Come 'ere, Jameel," Momma said, pulling me to the side.

I was still feeling nervous and happy inside. "Yes, Mam."

"First of all, Momma's so proud of you." *She squeezed me and wouldn't let me go.* "If anybody deserved a day like today, it's you. I raised you to be a strong woman—and that's what you are."

243

"Thank you, Momma." *This time I was unable to control my tears.*

"Well, I'm so glad that you're receiving Dorian—and putting your family back together. He's a good man and needs you just like you need him. Y'all started a family and he's head of it just like your father was with us before he got killed. Sometimes you gotta look past a man's fault and deal with him where he is. Love is taking you places. And having him with you and Tiffany is going to change your life. I guarantee it."

"Thanks, Momma. And I heard every word you said."

"All graduates are needed. Please assemble backstage for final preparations. We are about to get started. Thank you," the voice said from the loudspeaker."

"Now go'on up there and make your family proud, Chile," I heard Momma say as I reached for Tiffany.

Holding the love of my life in my arms felt good. "Thank you Tiffany. And baby never forget how much Mommy loves you, okay?" I told her. "Gimme a kiss?"

"I love you, too, Mommy," she said with a kiss, "And congratulations."

"Thanks everybody. I have to go," I said passionately, "The program is about to begin."

"You, go girl," Ms. Emma said.

"Jameel, you go 'head up there and do your thing. Don't worry about your late-as-usual brothers and Dorian. They'll be here. You know how my boys are—they're always late."

I had no idea where they were. And Momma was right about my brothers. They're always late, but I was looking for Dorian to walk in the door at any moment.

The walk-in processional didn't take long. The President of Coppin had already begun with his opening remarks when Dorian was ushered to his seat. I continued looking up at our seating area trying to get his attention. Each time I looked up...he was smiling and sending kisses down to me. He just doesn't know how proud he has made me. He's even having that effect on our daughter. She's the happiest I've ever seen her and can't stop smiling--even if she wanted to.

Now my excitement was directed at our international guest speaker. Everybody in class was taller than I was, so I had to hop up and down over their heads to see the former President of South Africa walk onto the on stage. Not believing my eyes, unable to stop my tears of joy, I can't believe how good he looks. Ever since I heard about his life, his struggle and read his book I've always wanted to meet him. Now, I'm sitting here in front of him. 'Unbelievable,' I thought. 'My dream while on this earth was to one day be in his company. And that was happening.'

He gave a strong message of hope and endurance and self-pride. As he explained it, we had a social responsibility to serve with our higher degree of education. Education is the catalyst to change and I couldn't agree more.

I watched with pride as so many of my friends and fellow classmates walked across the stage receiving their degrees.

"Even though I was standing next in line, ready to proudly walk across the stage, it still startled me when I heard the President call my name over the microphone: "Jameel Jackson."

"That's my baby girl," I could hear Momma screaming.

"Yeah! Jameel! Baby we're proud of you!" Dorian screamed.

I walked across shaking numerous hands before reaching my dream. "Be proud of your accomplishment, young lady. Your future awaits you," our guest speaker said to me before posing for our picture.

I choked on tears of joy because he seemed to be looking into my future. I could still hear loud clapping coming from our area. "Thank you so much and be proud of your accomplishments, too."

"Go ahead, baby. I'm so proud of you! Thank you Lord!" Momma screamed out loud like she does in church.

After completing the list of candidates, the announcement we'd all been waiting to hear was made.

"Ladies and Gentleman. I present to you the graduating class of Coppin State University."

I really couldn't talk long when I did walk up to him to introduce myself. I got a signed autograph photo of the former President of South Africa. I hugged and kissed so many of my friends and teachers as I made my way back to my family.

I had to accept my brothers not being here. It happened too many times before to mess up my day. They stayed in the streets. Being out there prevented them from being a part of my life growing up.

"Alright everybody. Are we ready to go?" I asked.

"Yeah, all that clapping and shouting made me even hungrier," Mr. Paul said.

"I know dat's right," Ms. Emma said with a smile.

Dorian was still hugging me, holding me close to him. He was celebrating and I could feel him. "The Cheesecake Factory is not that far, Mr. Paul. Y'all just say the word, and we're there. My truck is parked right around the corner."

"Let's go to the Cheesecake Factory. We all can meet down there," I said.

We walked through the happy crowd to the parking lot. Sitting inside the lot waiting to pay and get out, Momma started expressing herself again. "Jameel, I so happy for you, baby?"

"Momma, I'm happy too, but I sure missed my brothers."

"This is sad, baby—though it must be said. You deserve better and you better not stop until you get it. Don't let anybody hold you from your dreams and reaching for the top, especially your brothers. We'll deal with them later."

"I know—"is all I could say before she cut me off.

"Girl, if I was you--I'd spread my wings like God wanted me to and fly," she said, turning to Tiffany. "Grandbaby girl, are you okay, sweetie?"

"Grandma, I'm just hungry."

"Well, we're almost there," Momma said, "And you can eat whatever you want."

"Do they have a kid's meal?"

"I'm quite sure they do," Momma said. *We went straight to the restaurant after finding a place to park. Ms. Emma, Mr. Paul and Dorian were already waiting for us at the front door. We walked inside together and gave my name. We were seated right away with water and menus.*

"Welcome to the Cheesecake Factory. My name is Janae, and I'll be serving you this evening. Are you ready to order?"

"You can have whatever you want, Jameel, since this is your day," Dorian said.

"I'm hungry as I don't know what, too."

"Girl you better get the biggest celebration meal you've ever had," Mr. Paul said.

"Go ahead, Janae. Take her special order first," Dorian told her.

"Let me have the seafood platter and a sweetened iced tea, then."

"And I'll take the kid's meal!"

We all had big portions. Most of our food was put in containers because it was so much. All I really wanted to do is now was get home and continue my night with Dorian.

Dorian walked us to the parking lot. Momma got in the car with Tiffany while we made plans for the rest of our night.

"Dorian, did you hear from my brothers today?"

"Naw, not really. I did talk to Fruity briefly last night, though."

"Oh?" I replied sadly. *All kind of emotions ran through me.*

"Jameel, listen to me. Don't worry about them. They're big boys. What I want you to do is concentrate on the rest of your night."

"What are you up to?"

"I gotta make a run to pick a really big surprise for you. I have to leave now because I was supposed to be there already."

"So, what do you want me to do, Dorian?"

"You and Tiffany drop your mother home and I'll be there in a minute. Okay?" he said before kissing me. "You set everything up at home."

Rolling down the window, Tiffany sang, "Daddy and Mommy—sitting in the tree—K-I-S-S-I-N-G."

"Oh, be quiet," I said jokingly as I got in the car. *I drove off with all kind of thoughts. My mind wandered...*

"Why you so quiet?" Momma asked.

"I was just thinking about us one day getting married. Momma, I have a feeling that's the surprise Dorian has for me tonight."

"Gurl, didn't I tell you that man is gonna do right by you," she said, acting like she knew something I didn't.

"Mommy, can I be in the wedding?"

"Just like today was our graduation as a family. That day when we get married it'll be your wedding day, too. Mommy is going to need somebody special to be by my side to help me get dressed, walk down the aisle, and wipe all those tears."

"Okay, Mommy."

I half way listened to Tiffany and Momma chatter about what role they'll play in the wedding. I thought about what was needed for another interview coming up in New Jersey. Really it was to discuss my offer letter and benefits. I've even negotiated my salary—and that's at $63,000 a year. That's more than enough to take care of my family and go back to college to get my master's degree. I wanted to tell Dorian this tonight before I shared it with anybody else. I'll miss Momma, and pursuing a singing career with the church choir, but Baltimore is not the answer!

Baltimore City Digest

Siblings shot on Westside

Two brothers were injured in an apparent argument with at least three other men who jumped out of a white van. The three suspects escaped the scene after shooting the pair several times Friday night. Details of the argument are sketchy.

Emergency Medical Services responded to a 911 call and found both victims suffering from non-life-threatening gunshot wounds. Andre "Fruity" Jackson, and Carlton "Flubber" Jackson were both rushed to University of Maryland Hospital.

Authorities have no motive and no suspects in this case. Anyone with information is asked to call local police.

Chapter 37

JAMEEL

"I'd do anything
I'd give anything—
Anything for you!"
                Jay-Z, *"I'd Give Anything"*
                VOL. 2...Hard Knock Life

We said our goodbyes to Momma and got back in the car. I wanted to get home before Dorian so I could light some candles and get ready for tonight. As I hurried home all I could think about was how everything in my life was beginning to fall in place.

'It took some hard work and tough choices to get to this point in my life, but I was determined to make it.

"Tiffany. You know what?"

"Yes Mommy?"

"Mommy loves you and I'm so happy that you were at my graduation. Now I have to wait some time, but I'll be happy to come to your graduations."

"How many do I have?"

"You have quite a few. And you know what?"

"Yes Mommy?"

I'll be at every single one of them. I promise."

It took a few minutes for us to get through the North Avenue traffic. Each time I drive at night the same thing happens. It's almost like a magic trick in the car when things get quiet. Tiffany falls asleep.

We made it back to the neighborhood. The darkness of the night scared me when a police rushed through a red light onto Poplar Grove. He had his lights flashing, but cut his noisy siren on and off—making that irritating sound. I pulled to the side for a moment until he faded into the darkness of the night.

I turned onto my street and found a parking space directly across the street from my house. Pretty soon, if all goes well, I hope to be pulling up into my own driveway.

"Tiffany. Tiffany," I called softly until it broke into her nap. *After unfastening her seatbelt, she stepped out of the car and raised her arms overhead to stretch. I laughed to myself as her tired body trembled in response.*

"You okay, baby?"

"Yes. I'm still sleepy."

"We're home, see?"

I saw this white van parked in front of my house. With the lights on and the engine still running, it looked like two guys sat in the front compartment. Glancing that way again I noticed the red firefly from a lit cigarette moving on the driver's side.

That's just how things are here. Strange people and vehicles appear around this way all the time. At one time, it used to be familiar faces of people we knew and grew up with. Now, anything goes. It's so crazy that guys sell right in front of the corner store on Poplar Grove right off of Clifton Avenue. My baby has to see this every time she goes outside.

I walked up the steps behind my groggy child to the door. I thought she was still sleepwalking until she asked me her question of the night.

"Mommy, can I go to Coppin State University when I grow up and go to college?"

I'll still answer her question knowing she wouldn't remember anything tomorrow morning. She'd probably ask me again. "You're tired baby, but you sure can go to Coppin or any other college you want to."

These doggy bags from the Cheesecake Factory, flowers and the some smaller graduation gifts I received had my hands full. I reached the top of the steps and fumbled with my key ring trying to find the right one. My ring had all kinds of memories on it. My favorite was the plastic keepsakes making the usual noise. It was a kaleidoscope that had Tiffany's photo with me inside a little square tube. That day with her at Disney World was a memory that would last me a lifetime. Some other nick-knacks on my key chain came from other trips to Universal Studios, Kings Dominion and Six Flags.

"Mommy, are you and Daddy really getting married?"

"Yes, Tiffany. We are sure," I said, laughing as I opened the door. "Go 'head, baby."

Tiffany stepped inside the threshold after I pushed open the door. She said, "I want to be the mini-bride."

Suddenly, I heard noise behind me. Fast footsteps came quickly behind me. My reflexes forced me to turn around quickly in the darkness. It happened so fast I could only respond in shock, dropping the things I held in my hands.

I wanted to scream, but a rough hand was around my mouth. I didn't want to holler out for help for myself. I wanted to scream at the top of my voice for Tiffany.

"De damn Yankey bways dem kick dung mi door an tek a whole 'eap a money. Dem tek me last!" the angry voice shouted.

I had no idea somebody would ever handle my girl child like that. Whoever it was snatched her violently in the hallway. I could see the strong muscles of man's arm wrapped around my baby's neck. The same thing was happening to me. Angry muscle pressure was so strong around my neck it felt like it was about to snap. Whoever this was, they had the nerve to do something like this to us on my front porch. I could feel the bodies of maybe two others brush pass me in a hurry to get inside. One of them snatched my keys. I could hear them running up the steps.

This wasn't funny. Whoever this was could rest assured I would be pressing charges—once this was over. I hope to God that his was a joke being played by one of my silly brothers. That would just be their way of apologizing for not showing up at the graduation, but none of them would play this rough. Then, again, it may be Dorian and one of his friends.

That guy had better get his arms from around my baby like that. I hope this is one of those nights when Dorian is hurrying home because I need help. I wasn't resisting being forced up the steps behind my daughter who was kicking and trying to scream through the man's big hands.

No questions were asked while they were doing this, but I was trying to talk between his fingers. Nothing understandable came out, but I still tried to mumble my pleas.

"Dem bumboclaat nuh know who dem a fuck wid! It's gonna be bloodshed fe mi money in yah tonight!"

'Oh, my God!' is all I could scream inside when I saw the guy throw my baby down on that hardwood floor like she was a lifeless doll. He pointed the gun at her head. I'd give anything—I'd do anything for this not to be happening to my baby. It killed me inside. I couldn't stand to see him stick his knee in Tiffany's back. 'Oh, my God!' That was my baby crying in pain and reaching for me to help her over and over again.

One of the guys searching snatched each drawer out of the dresser. He was looking for something. I had no idea what. If I could help them I would.

"Bitch, me gwine let your mout free. Now whey de fuck'n safe."

He freed my mouth. I screamed for my baby. "Oh my God! She can't breathe! You can get anything you want, but let my baby go, please! She's just a little--"

With hate-filled fists, he hit me with blows that sent me falling backwards. I could feel my body shivering in fear as I tried to fight my way back, but he used tape to tie my hands behind my back.

"Aaaaaaaaaaaaah! Please help!" I screamed, taking the chance before he quickly shoved something inside my mouth. *I could hear him snatch a long piece of tape from his hand, run over top of me on the floor, and tape my mouth shut. That thing inside my mouth and the thick tape holding it stopped me from talking at all. My body was shaking and my water escaped as my bowels gave way.*

I'm trying to plead for this to end, but nothing came out besides more mumbles. I just wanted to beg him so she could breathe. I tried to reach out to Tiffany. Suddenly, my face was crashed against the floor with a strong force.

My vision became cloudy, but I still could see my baby's face on the floor in front of me. I was dying looking into her eyes. Fear gripped her because she was experiencing a danger that would never-ever go away. When this is over—oh, my God-- we are gonna need help to get over this.

"Oh, my God, Please don't—" I screamed.

I could see his big boot pressing up against her face and then toward mine again. The sting from his kick to my forehead almost made me pass out. For a second everything turned black.

Her desperate screams would haunt me forever. There was nothing I could do to set my baby free as he slapped some gray tape over her mouth before throwing her back against the floor.

Why in the world is he handling my baby like that? She's a good child and would listen if he just spoke to her. I know because I raised her.

She was a good baby from birth and I tried to be a good mother. When Tiffany was hungry I'd feed her. When she was crying—like she was now—I would be the one to give her what she needed. The guy turned my face away from my baby.

I don't understand. If it was money-- I have some for them. Payday was yesterday and Mr. Paul gave me some money in an envelope as a gift. God knows I would've given them that at the front door. I would've signed my check on the dotted line and let them walk away—just go and never look back! God knows I wouldn't tell anybody!

I want to beg him, beg them all to stop. I moaned and pleaded from behind the tape while my baby fought and moaned right in front of me. If I could talk then maybe I could communicate this deal to them.

If y'all leave right now—just let us go and walk out that door—then I won't be calling anybody. Just leave me with my baby. Whatever happened between us would be our secret. Not another soul would know. There would be no police, no prosecutors. I would do an excellent job in not remembering anything. God is my witness—I won't tell anything, but they can't hear me.

'Oh! My God! Where's Dorian?' I thought.

My ribs weren't bothering his feet. God only knows why he used those heavy boots again to shatter my sides. If I could tell him that I was pregnant, maybe, just maybe he would stop. I screamed at the top of the tape in my mouth. I saw the other guy standing over top of my baby. She was at his mercy as she laid face down. Her eyes were blood red from straining—trying to get away. He snatched the top of his gun to make it snap.

I could hear someone running up the steps. As he entered the room she said.

"Mi nuh fine nutten man, so let's jus' smoke de madda and de pickney an' get de hell out. Dem t'ree wi get de message—part two next!"

I tried to break the tape that was holding me. I'd give anything for this not to happen—and it felt like it was coming loose. I pray to God for this not to be real. He could take me and let my baby run free. I wanted to tell him that before he snatched by baby from the floor!

"Blooooouw!"

Shock paralyzed me. Adrenaline stiffened my body as I watched my baby's head hit the floor and bounce back up because of the impact. Her blood splattered across my face.

I felt like I was having an out-of-body experience because a part of me died instantly. Tiffany was lying on the floor, lifeless, in a pool of blood. The flash and blood in my eye was blinding me. He stepped towards me and got right in my face.

"Whey yuh Bumboclaat man dey, whey 'im dey. Mi a go teach him nuh fe' mess wid a Yardie," *he screamed before spitting in my face.*

In one flash, my child was watching God. In one split second spark of light, my heart—my baby girl Tiffany, was gone! 'Oh, Jesus, please, help us!'

I could feel him violently grabbing me to lift my head off the floor. I had no fight left in me.

'Oh! My! God!' is all I could say behind the stuffing inside my mouth.

In the second flash of light, me and my unborn child were following my daughter in the next life. And all of a sudden all of our eyes were watching God.

Author's Notes

The old saying goes: "Live each day as if it's your last." I had many cliché-ish titles I could've named the spin-off to my first novel *"For the Love of Fast Money."* The title did finally come from a prophetic message from a minister of God concerning my nephew Tarik Lateef Walker. It was from his message the title *Business As Usual* was born.

After enduring all those years of hustling on the streets, I finally changed my choices. I spent years wrestling with the life I lived. I trained myself, month after month, year after year, on how to "unravel" the knot I was used to tying for myself. The way I used to live, those layers of get-rich-quick schemes, was that of an onion. I was searching for a better way to live life, but there were certain qualities I could not deny.

I couldn't shed my hustler's spirit—and still haven't. I had to transform that natural skill into a legitimate ability to make money. Selling was here to stay, but I did aggressively peal off years of suicidal tendencies and forced that old part of me to die. Neither could I divorce multi-tasking and taking risks.

As I was trying to recover, my nephew, Tarik a.k.a. "Todd", was by my side during the different stages of my changing life. I'd talk to him from time to time about how different things would be if I followed my dreams and freed myself from everybody else's expectations.

On the other hand, he, like others, had high expectations of my "reactivation" into Baltimore City's dope game. I was expected to return to the lifestyle and choices of selling drugs in the streets. I was to selfishly harm hundreds of addicts and their families just to feed the hungry mouths at my own table. I was expected to take Similac, Pampers, and food from babies whose parents chose to spend essential living monies for self-important highs. That was "the onion life" that had my soul stinking.

Peeling back each layer and reconstructing my hard knock life took years of work.

Anyone who has ever been in that life knows there's a particular area where temptation is too powerful to deny, a corner or street that's too hard to divorce. I had one place to stay away from in Baltimore City: *Fairmount Avenue and Franklintown Road* in *West Baltimore.*

Again, I was expected to use the monies of fathers who are supposed to be providing food, clothing and shelter for their families to provide myself harm's material things. In my life before, I hustled for a selfish cause I wholly believed in and didn't mind stealing the dreams of each addict coming before me. Anybody who knows me will agree.

Today, I have a conscience and a plan. Long past the risk age of 16-35 years old, I chose life over death. My head was full of visions. One of those visions was writing and publishing novels through my own publishing label. In order to do this I had to put a halt to my habits, remove the bracelets from my wrists and force the cuffs on my compulsion. Without violating any principles or game rules, I was determined to do what I absolutely could not do for so many years: *I walked away!*

Writing was my way out! It took some time for me to accept how *words channeled through me* moved people. That's why I would eventually name my retail stores: *Words by Wendell.* It was at that point of no-return when I began to accept the gift I've always had. I wrote poetry, short stories and articles for my college newspaper to try to find my way through the confusing maze. It was my private comfort zone. All that changed when I shared some personal pieces with a woman I now call my wife. It was through her influence and sacrifice that writing became my life.

Having my own line of greeting cards, selling African-American art, and books in my store added purpose to each waking day. That was my way of saying 'yes' to my life. And when I made that commitment, there was always something more to do, more requirements that kept me busy. Selling candy to babies was more rewarding than taking their candy because of their parents' addictions. Choosing life over death helped me to define my selfhood and individuality.

Actually, it was those brothers like Wayne Brewton and Ronnie Hunt who taught me how to live. I was a dreamer. And they believed in my dreams. I was told, "Don't run from your gift...run to it! That game is not your life's destiny. Living life is." It was Wayne and Ronnie, men caught up in the system, who helped me to understand my gift.

For me, it was better to tell fictional stories of the life I lived instead of selling fictional substance again. Living life on these terms, creating opportunities for myself and others to follow, would help more people than the lives I would destroy if I got back in the game.

On this journey before my dad passed, I had a strong woman behind me, my mom and dad as cheerleaders, the spirits of men and women I call friends beside me, and destiny in front of me. My mother knew more could be done to define the dash between my life and my imminent death. She constantly told me that I had to give myself a chance. Before my father passed this life he also believed in the dreams I had of book publishing and a gift store. To him it sounded like his son finally had a plan that could work. My children needed more than an example of misguidance and so far failure. It was my promise to make it happen for them. Stepping out there, one fact remained and it could not change for me: "*In order to gain anything...you have got to give something up.*"

My first book was going through the final stages of publication and I finally opened my first store. I was on my way and I wanted to show my nephews and my sons that there was more to life than hustling. I wanted them to dream, have faith and hold on like I had told so many others in my family who looked to powdery substances and get-rich-quick schemes to get them out. I knew that their "out" wouldn't work and would only draw them further into the fires of failure.

Like any hustler on the street, I looked for opportunities. My business and street skills coupled with my writing talent and publishing vision would get me out. I knew that. My thoughts assured me that "what I was in to" would get us all out, eventually.

With much less funding than needed, I opened my first store in a bad location. After more than a year, this particular June 30th would mark the closing of my first gift shop and the search for a new location to open my second. In the meantime, I took a chance vending downtown at an outside stall. This Monday was a slow one since I was the new-kid-on-the-block in Baltimore's world famous Lexington Market.

I had finished a day of business and night of normal living and was in bed getting rest preparing my mind and body to do the routine all over again. There was no knock at midnight, but a phone call at about 11:50 p.m. Tarik's little sister, Shandora, called me to say: "Uncle Wendell! Tarik got shot and we're rushing down [University of Maryland] Shock Trauma! We don't know how bad it is!"

I wasn't offended and all was not lost at that split second. My nephew was in the game. He might be the victim of a flesh wound. Or maybe he was involved in one of those shootings where he would have to wear a colostomy bag for a time. With a little rehab, he would be alright. I decided that this would be my opportunity to school him out of the game. Patience was a concept I would preach. He had a heart and would listen because of his two sons. Deep down inside he wanted more for them because of what he lacked growing up. He promised his boys that things would be different, way different than what he experienced, but he'd been trying the wrong way—following my example. All I could receive was this being an opportunity to scare him into realizing there were other choices.

We buried his ailing grandfather, my father, fourteen months prior. He, too, was still trying to find his way through this thing called life because of the mistakes he made while he was on this earth. Tarik didn't attend for whatever reasons. He was a man and it was his choice.

We placed his grandmother, my mom, in assisted living. She asked for Tarik and wanted to see him all the time. Her requests went unanswered; he didn't see his grandmother.

About three months prior to this Monday when he was shot, we buried his great grandmother in South Carolina. No great-grandchild from up north was able to attend her memorial services. That we understood.

Still in a daze, my first response was to sit on the side of the bed, trying to believe this was a dream. It wasn't. It was a clarion call to respond in support of my nephew's safety. I had to be there to support not only him but also his mother, two sisters, girlfriend and children.

At that moment, all they needed was me there with them, but I had to move cautiously. I had to see my own way through this whole ordeal. My nephew didn't choose me or my new lifestyle. I had to remember I abandoned his dreams for our partnership in crime, but he still needed me.

I was one of the first called that night. As I sat on the side of the bed, my mind started playing tricks on me. In one thought I knew this was a good thing. Something like this never fails to bring our big family together --- if only for a short period of time. Tarik's mother, Marilyn, always tried to bring the family together during the holiday season. The fruits of her labor never bloomed. Tarik, like other members of the family, was a no-show. Maybe, just maybe, Tarik's shooting would bring the family together again. As a tree, we could come together, stand strong and oppose his life and tell him what he needed to hear and also give the help he needed.

This time it was an injury. The only choice left for Tarik and the streets was death. Marilyn needed him to hear this before it was too late. She needed to tell her son that life was giving him another chance. She would tell him how important it was to choose life over the uncertainty and harm guaranteed in the streets. The week prior to Tarik's shooting, Marilyn woke up crying out of her sleep. Tonight, was her opportunity to tell her son about that dream.

His Aunt Bev would tell him how "hardheaded" he and her son, Tremayne had been. Tremayne, now locked away at a Pre-Release facility, would be playing the 'if game' for a long time: "If I was out there, this, that and the other wouldn't have happened."

Aunt Carolyn, Rosailyn and Brenda would tell him how this was a personal call from God asking him to receive his son, Christ, again in his life. He had accepted the light of Christ at least ten years prior.

His uncle Danny would tell him that hustling just ain't worth it. Danny and I had hustled before and failed. He would tell his nephew that saying *yes* to life meant more than saying *no* to selling drugs.

Even I could've told him that saying yes to life meant giving his children their rights to enjoy their father. I would try to make him understand that his mother needed to enjoy her son. That he could get a job, go back to school, own a home and marry the woman he chose to start a family with and so on. Tarik knew the consequences of the game. He had first cousins who had been captured in the war on drugs and were confined.

In all, it was an opportunity for his mother, two sisters, and girlfriend to step back from the forefront and allow him to hear what they had been trying to tell him all along. "You are my only son and our only brother. You have two sons who love and need you and a girlfriend that's in your corner. You have to come out of those streets. Right now you are only hurt. Next, you will be locked up." Knowing my nephew he'd say he wasn't going to jail. He was too sharp for that.

Kayla and Shantierra, his two nieces, would look at him and make bold comments about how ugly he looked wrapped up in gauze, taped up and swollen. His nieces would hold no punches-- telling anybody the truth that comes out of the mouth of babes-- in a minute.

His son, Deshon, and the special woman who gave birth to his son, Theresa Harris, would be there no matter how bad he was paralyzed or how messed up he would become. They simply loved him and he needed to know that. Not fully understanding what was happening around him, Deshon would cry.

I finally responded to my neice, Shandora, in a soft subtle voice: "I'll be there. I got to be there for him."

I was thinking all of those thoughts before I hung up the telephone. I took my time getting myself and frame of mind together. The phone rang again. It was my sister, Brenda, asking me had I heard the news. Shandora, the new phone operator of the family, had called her with the information. Her question to me was, "Are you going into town from all the way out there from where you live?"

I told her I was because Tarik needed me, but still I moved in patience. There was no need to rush because this was our wake up call. I had to allow truth to speak through me that night and make a connection with Tarik. I had to awaken the part of me that died; that part of me that he could still identify with to pull him out. It was his playing field, the game's playing field and I needed to be on the same level if I was going to get him to understand. If we had our way there would be no more *business as usual* for him.

Again my mind was playing tricks on me, so I started moving a little quicker. I accepted the game being *do or die*, a life that I and so many others had chose.

It was somebody he knew that probably shot him. Statistics prove that. One out of every two people that chose this life, one goes to prison and the other to what some would call "a better place." Not many fall in between.

In the game my nephew was a soldier with nothing to prove if he walked away. He had spent years, like I, being a fool … willing to risk life and limb in an effort to win a game that "Robs, kills, steals and destroys." Once this was over, Tarik would admit that it was fool's play and a waste of years. He'd confess that he could've been doing something he was good at-- like creating a new business for himself.

Like an unbroken circle, the cycle continued, Tarik had been shot like his two uncles and cousin. My nephew, who took example from the wrong I once did, was to cool to be a casualty. He admired me like his older sister, Kamila, tried to imitate my younger sister, Brenda. There were things I needed to express to him that finally had gone right from my choices and I really missed him. Besides, he was a Shannon and was too lucky to get caught up permanently.

Before I arrived at the hospital the only information doctors relayed to my sister was, "We are working on him."

Upon arrival, the front desk police was all too familiar with the name because so many others had arrived before me. While following the guard's instructions, a couple more of his friends traveled this lonely road of "I wanna know" with me. With all of us pushing for him...he'd be just fine.

I traveled with them up one floor on the elevator. Those all too familiar sounds greeted us as soon as we stepped off. I was I being greeted with loud and painful screams of "No-o-o-o-o!" That was his mother and sister. I knew the voices. I ran in the direction of the painful screams. Maybe they were complaining about not being told the information they wanted to hear. He had them screaming at the top of their voices because they wanted to see him and were tired of the hospital staff's refusal.

While running I did notice a number of young adults screaming in pain. Right now the room was filled with rumors, each member of his South Baltimore crew had their own to spread. After Tarik got shot, it was said, one of his so-called friends grabbed his money another person, who he called partner, grabbed his stash and personal effects out of his pockets.

That technical info wasn't important. What was important was being there with my family to nurse him back to health. More loud screams could be heard. It was like a chain reaction. Now the name of God was preceded by "Oh! My!" Without mattresses people were falling out on the floor. "He ain't gone." Another young friend said, "I had just talked to him. This shouldn't have happened!" Another unfamiliar voice screamed, "All those *whores* from down South Baltimore is gonna pay! Ain't nobody selling no more dope down there, period." I knew what that meant but wasn't concerned because the street has its own rules. That violence and control in street situations like this one is what brought us to the hospital with my nephew in the first place.

The active red line from the heart machine, the one jumping all over the monitor, had gone flat. My nephew, Tarik Lateef Walker, was dead. A one-eighty-seven occurred that night on South Poppleton Street and Washington Boulevard. His death gave birth to two things: eight million stories about what supposedly happened; and the start of our family's pain. Ended was another soul this life and the Shannon/Walker family could no longer claim.

On the streets of Southwest Baltimore, after another tragic death from the life, it couldn't be *Business As Usual* or maybe it could. Everyday after this gloomy one…his crew that doubled crossed him would have some choices to make without him.

My nephew was "out there" hustling making the corner his choice, but he felt Tupac's pain: "Tired of getting shot at. Tired of getting chased by the police and arrested."

I died on his death day along with him. The only difference between my willful death and his life being taken was my intentional death. My death, the self-inflicted killing of my old life, allowed me to live again. In order for egos to deflate and dreams to come alive … our men have to practice dying.

That's why I believe, instead of being grimly-reaped, like so many of our young who die on the desperate streets of Baltimore, if given another opportunity, he would've transformed his life and gave love a chance to work miracles.

Then again, I guess many think Biggie Smalls was right when he said: "You're nobody until somebody kills you." Ask any mother who has lost a child or any father whose hope was buried six feet deep and they'll tell you in tears and show you photos and trophies…proving that statement is the furthest thing from the truth.

In love, W. Sh.

R.I.P. Westside Ryder:
Tarik Lateef Walker
November 7, 1975 - July 13, 2004

Order Form
Order Form
Go Daddy Productions
P.O. Box 418
Jessup, Maryland 20794

ISBN # 0-9753938-0-4

ISBN # 0-9753938-1-2

Name _____

Info # _____

Address _____

City _____ State _____ Zip _____

Phone _____

	Quantity	Price Per Book	Total
For the Love of Fast Money		$15.00	
Business As Usual		$15.00	
Sales Tax $0.75 (per book) (Maryland Residents Only)			
Shipping & Handling (Via U.S. Priority Mail) $3.50 + 1.50 each additional book			
Total			

Prison orders shipped directly to institutions and/or facilities will receive an automatic 25% discount off the sales price of GDP, Inc. books only. Prices are as follows.

For the Love of Fast Money	$11.25
Business As Usual	$11.25
Sales Tax $0.56 (per book) (Maryland Residents Only)	

Shipping & Handling $3.50 + 1.50 each additional book

*Book club rates are available and autographed copies can be picked up from
Words By Wendell, 512 W. Franklin Street • Baltimore, MD • 21201
410.523.7007 / Out of state orders call 1.877.523.7007
Order on-line: www.go-daddyproductions.com

Go Daddy Productions, Inc. Presents

The Wolf Trap

WARNING!!! THIS BOOK IS NOT FOR THE SHEEPISH OR THE SHY.

The Wolf Trap, written by Dennis Wise, is a gripping story filled with vivid scenes of intense sex, brutal violence, and raw emotions. The tale begins when Bulls Eye gets released after serving five long years in one of America's most dangerous prisons. Soon he meets Alina, a beautiful woman with an ugly past and a dark secret. Together, they set out to build an illegal fortune and to fulfill a slain brother's final wish.

Across their path comes Anna, whose luscious body proves to be both a blessing and a curse. The list of rich hustlers, all pursuing this top-rated stripper, includes a smooth gambler named Eddie and a vicious killer called Wolf. Anna's choice starts a sweet romance and ignites a bitter feud. High level smack dealers line up on one side and a deadly stick-up crew line up on the other.

See what happens when a flock of sexy women get caught between two of the most powerful crime figures in Baltimore trying to destroy each other.

COMING SOON...